GOOD COUNSEL

Also by Tim Junkin

The Waterman: A Novel of the Chesapeake Bay

GOOD COUNSEL

a novel by

TIM JUNKIN

ALGONQUIN BOOKS
OF CHAPEL HILL   2001

A SHANNON RAVENEL BOOK

Published by
Algonquin Books of Chapel Hill
Post Office Box 2225
Chapel Hill, North Carolina 27515-2225

a division of
Workman Publishing
708 Broadway
New York, New York 10003

Printed in the United States of America.
Published simultaneously in Canada by Thomas Allen & Son Limited.
Design by Anne Winslow.

This is a work of fiction. While, as in all fiction, the literary perceptions
and insights are based on experience, all names, characters, places, and
incidents are either products of the author's imagination or are used
fictitiously. No reference to any real person is intended or should be
inferred.

Library of Congress Cataloging-in-Publication Data
Junkin, Tim, 1951–
    Good counsel : a novel / by Tim Junkin.
      p. cm.
"A Shannon Ravenel book"—T.p. verso.
  ISBN 1-56512-284-4
  1. Public defenders—Fiction. 2. Washington (D.C.)—Fiction. I. Title.
  PS3560.U596 G6 2001
  813'.54—dc21   00-045127

10 9 8 7 6 5 4 3 2 1
First Edition

In memory of
Isabel Babson Henry Kirkpatrick

And for William and Isabel Junkin

My nature is subdu'd
To what it works in, like the dyer's hand

Contents

PROLOGUE
Washington, D.C.   1

PART ONE
Boxmoor   11

PART TWO
Dun Cove   109

PART THREE
Allenwood   209

GOOD COUNSEL

Washington, D.C.

I'VE BEEN IN TOUGH SPOTS BEFORE. Mean trials where lives rode the line. And I've always stayed cool. Composed. Clear-headed. But until today I've never testified in a grand jury or played a part in any case where the stakes were right there in my face. Where the stakes were all about me.

I'd thought it all out. Figured I could swing it. That it would play. But there was something about the way the prosecutor postured. Morgan Langrell had always been arrogant and self-righteous, but something else was there this morning. A certain smugness, a visible relish of vengeance. The fact that he spun the questions himself rather than have a deputy do it might have tipped me. But then we have a history, Langrell and I.

When I thought he'd finished, when he should've *been* finished since he'd covered it from ass to elbow, rather than release me he announced a lunch break and ordered me to return at two o'clock. Langrell's arms were crossed imperiously as he watched me leave.

He and his assistant are still in there with the grand jurors. Standing outside the courtroom, seeing the doors close behind me, watching the prosecutors stay inside—all of this—it makes my insides heave.

I'M A TRIAL LAWYER. My career, my success, my prosperity have depended on my ability to size up people, to find the weaknesses in a witness's story, to read demeanor, gestures, to see the truth behind the mask. Or so I've convinced myself. For sure, I've known Morgan Langrell all too well. The way he gloated through his questions, though—I should have sensed it earlier—it all flashes wrong.

I walk quickly through the courthouse, glancing over my shoulder at the federal marshals lounging in the hallway. I begin to imagine the worst, that I really could be found out, that all of it could turn bad. Looking back again, I see that no one seems to be following me. I leave the building and walk past John Marshall Park over to Constitution Avenue where I sit on a bench trying to calm myself. I try to practice my breathing. But I'm beginning to gag over what I've done.

I need to shake this off. To regain my balance. Standing, starting down the sidewalk, I step into the street, moving alongside the cars parked parallel to the curb. Halfway down the block I glance in the bent side mirror of a pickup truck and notice a large black man in a suit about twenty paces behind me.

When I pause, he stops too and looks quickly away. Continuing down the block, I drop my keys, turn to pick them up, and see he's still following. He has that erect, bullish walk of a marshal. I abruptly dart through the lanes of traffic, dodging vehicles, crossing to the other side of the boulevard. He turns to cross as well but is delayed by oncoming cars. I hurry into the entrance of the National Gallery of Art, crowded with tourists. Weaving through the people to the back of the museum, I take the escalator down and hustle through the underground tunnel that connects to the East Building. There, I climb the stairs and pause to catch my breath. No one is following. A massive web-like mobile of fins or blades and tentacles hovers above me.

Outside, I hail a passing cab, give the driver a quick ten so he doesn't complain about the short trip, and have him drop me at my blue Mercedes, three blocks north of the courthouse. My watch reads 1:20. As I steer my car toward home, I notice perspiration on the backs of my hands. Running the string of timed green lights up Connecticut Avenue, I turn onto Woodley, pass by the entrance to our private lot, and park a side street over.

Once inside my townhouse, I punch in Linda's work number. I need reassurance. I'm just overreacting, I tell myself. Projecting the worst. I need to talk to her and then get back to the grand jury by two. The phone rings. I ask for her nursing station. A man answers and tells me she's no longer at the hospital. I call her home. Her voice is groggy as she answers.

"Are you asleep?" I ask. "Are you sick?"

"No," she slurs.

"I called the hospital," I say. "What's going on?"

She asks me if I testified. She sounds half drunk. She then asks me if I mentioned her name.

"No," I say. "Of course not."

There's a pause. Then she blurts out that she lost her job and that I'm about to lose a lot more. She tells me that I've been set up. That I'm about to be arrested. That she had to cut a deal to save herself. That she told them everything. She works herself into a state. She says she's not sorry. She says some other angry things. She blames me for all of it, she says, and finishes by telling me never to call her again.

The line goes dead. The phone in my hand is shaking.

I find myself in the bathroom, sick. After I've lost whatever was in my stomach, I push myself off the floor and begin opening drawers, rummaging through my things to find my passport, only to see that it's expired. I take a duffel from the closet and stuff it with some of the clothes I've heaped on my bed. I grab a bottle of liquor and take a long swallow before throwing it in the bag. From the bathroom I take my pills and shaving kit. A corner shelf is stacked with books. My old journals are there, covered with dust. I grab them to take with me. I'd rather not have Langrell reading my diaries. I find small bills scattered on my dresser. Sirens begin to wail from down Connecticut Avenue. They grow louder and aren't far off. I wipe my slick hands on my trousers, but my fingers still slip as I try to open the bedroom window. It's stuck. I push harder. I'm trapped. I strike violently at the frame with the base of my palms and strike again, heaving upward and cracking the glass. The window gives and grinds open. I push the duffel bag out, duck down, and climb through onto the landing of the fire escape. The iron ladder creaks as I lower myself. The rust from the rails dirties my hands. I have to jump the last three feet and land badly on my ankle. I hear the sirens coming up out front and hobble down the alley and cross a side street to another alley. A neighbor's garage is open, and I crouch inside behind some garbage cans. An hour passes as I wait, rubbing my ankle, trying to think. Finally I limp the one block to my car. Taking the back streets I drive up to the northwest edge of the city to one of the branches of my bank. Acting nonchalant, breathing deeply, summoning up a long-practiced professional composure, I present the teller with a check. She brings up my account on her computer. She's young and gets nervous and apologizes as she buzzes for the branch manager. The manager, older with stiff bluish hair, checks the computer, then makes a telephone call. When she hangs up she apologizes too and tells me that my account has been frozen. All my accounts, she says.

"Christ, I've got nearly a half-million dollars in here," I say. "I just need a little cash . . ."

Her face reddens, and I can see she is embarrassed for me. She offers to try to reach one of the vice presidents at the downtown location, my so-called personal executive banker. Walking away, I realize I've begun to hyperventilate.

I drive back downtown, craning around for cops. There's an underground garage near my office. Parked there, I swap my suit coat for a sweatshirt from my duffel bag, put on my sunglasses, find a wadded up golf hat in my trunk, and make my way to the corner across from my building. From near the metro stop I can see the windows to my office suite and to where my secretaries sit. Both are recent replacements, hired in the past six months. I watch everyone on the block, every pedestrian, study every parked car, looking for evidence of surveillance. Slowly it gets dark. Pretending to wait for the bus, I finally see the lights in my suite go out. A minute later my two secretaries and the paralegal all leave together. Gradually, other lights on the second floor are extinguished. Walking around the block to the back, I use my access key to enter the basement and take the back stairs to the second-floor hall. There are two doors to my office suite, and I wait outside the rear door, listening. There's only the hum of the exit sign above. I enter and in the dim light take the bills from the petty cash box. Maybe three hundred or so. I figure my office checking account is frozen too but that Langrell might not think to lock up my client trust money. I rip a blank check from the trust account checkbook. Then the elevator bell rings. I hurry to the rear. I hear them talking in hushed tones.

"Open the door," one says roughly.

"Yes sir." I recognize the Middle Eastern accent and voice of our building maintenance man, Hamad. His keys jangle as he turns the lock.

"I've seen him in court," another man says. "Before Judge Kellogg. Tore a witness a new asshole. I doubt he'd be so stupid as to come here."

"You never know. He's fucked up bad already, hasn't he," the first one counters.

As the front door opens into the suite, as I hear them enter, I slip through the back exit. I make it to the stairs and am down and out the rear. The nausea returns as I head north up Rhode Island Avenue in heavy traffic watching for signs of police. I hit Georgia Avenue and then the beltway. I drive but cannot think of where to go, what to do. A steel press squeezes my thoughts. I shut down.

Pulling onto the shoulder, I'm sick again on the side of the road. My tongue is swollen and dry. I reach inside the bag and grab the bottle and take a long slug. I put on my car blinker and accelerate back onto the highway. Driving without aim or destination. The rear-view mirror seems key. I check it again and again, fearful of cops. But all the headlights look the same. I'm becoming more disoriented, carried along by the lights, unable to think my way clear, lost in the maze of lights. At some point, too tired to care whether anyone is following, I turn the wheel. The exit I take is east, toward the bay.

PART ONE

Boxmoor

I

I'VE FOUND MYSELF a stopping place, a refuge, at least for now. I spent the night here on a musty couch, with a curtain for a cover.

This morning, the backyard opens to a sky, wide and still. Clouds hang white over the river, like crepe, unmoving as in a seascape painting. Across the water the fields are flat, leveled by the harvest, blending in the distance into a silent brownish haze. The morning is eerily quiet. The only sounds are the breeze and the lapping of the tide. I stand on the back steps of this abandoned house that sits far from the road. With no one around, I should be safe here for a while. I'll take this over the stale air and garish light of motel rooms.

For three days I jumped motels, stayed concealed until check-out, drove to another, asked for early check-in there, sprawled in a paralytic state of sorts, trying to think of what to do. The brain can seize up when overtaxed. Three days chasing sleep, trying to slip free of myself. But the claustrophobic walls closed in. Sleep wouldn't come.

HERE THE LONG sloping yard leads to a wooden bulkhead, a dock, the river—a mile across at this point. The pine needles rustle in the light wind. But I'm not used to such space. Such silence and solitude.

This afternoon I walk out and about the yard. I go into one of the sheds. Spider webs catch the light that spills through the collapsing roof. Three fishing poles hang from the ceiling, draped with the webbing and the ensnared husks of insects. I use the handle of an old broom to clear a path. There are snake skins, brittle, transparent, scattered like dried leaves on the floor. I don't like snakes. Dirt or manual labor either. The smells, the old outbuildings perhaps, bring back memories of my father's farm and then of my father, gripped with illness, trying to keep up. His disease, slow death, the failing farm— reasons why I left this river country.

Atop some rotted burlap I find a rusty handsaw. Outside I use it to cut small limbs and brush from the overgrown box-wood in the front yard to cover my car. I glance down the long oyster-shell lane leading from the front of the property to the road. At the entrance a wooden sign reads BOXMOOR. It dangles askew on one corner chain, its wood warped and splintered. No more decrepit than this unused house that hides me—sway-backed floors, cracked and mud-caked windows.

Earlier today I unpacked my duffel and put things in a drawer. I'm tidy this way. My journals, I left in the bag. I don't need to read them to know how far I've fallen. My career would make an interesting case study. A good seminar topic. My old students could analyze it, debate it, dismiss it. Another lowlife gone over, is all. Another sleaze bag. Christ . . . I've been sick again today. The tedium is stifling. The monotony grates. Memory's all that's left. Something—remorse, regret, my own conscience, maybe, or what remains of it—forces the self-inquiry I have begun.

IT RAINS OVERNIGHT. I lie awake listening to the sound. Later there is thunder. Streaks of lightning flash greenish white, exposing the spectral trees bending to the wind out the window. After the storm passes I walk out on the porch and watch the sky split and divide itself over the river. The can of soup I found and warmed for dinner won't digest. I down another sleeping pill with three fingers of scotch.

Back upstairs I toss and turn. My sweat soaks the curtains I've wrapped myself in. I try to throw them off but get tangled in them. Freeing myself, I cover my face with a sofa pillow. It smells like mildew. I turn it over. My mind won't quit. I keep going over the past few days. The grand jury. Linda's voice on the phone. The Red Roof Inn off Annapolis Road. Jolted by every car horn, every siren. In the morning drizzle I'd found the Annapolis branch of my bank and tendered my office trust account check. While I waited the teller commented on the weather. He thought the sweat running down my face was rainwater. There was only nine thousand in the account, a pittance from a small personal injury settlement. But the bank cashed it.

I bought food at a drive-through and then ate in my car in the parking lot. I started for Baltimore but changed my mind, afraid my car and license plates might give me away. And what would I do there? I felt too tired to go on. I holed up in a Days Inn near the Bay Bridge, the TV droning on hour after hour, and with nightfall the incessant lights of car beams through broken blinds splashing across the walls. Next day the Delmar Motel. More fast food, more of the same.

I'm besieged by thunder again. The lightning casts its wide net. Another storm is overhead. The clammy pillow is suffocating. I throw it off and lurch into the bathroom. Images of my near capture and escape race. My own dread wells up. I kneel before the commode. Driving to escape, to flee the city, the headlights veering by, around the beltway's inner loop, past a maze of exits, trying to keep a lookout . . .

At first light I am still curled up on the porcelain-tiled bathroom floor, reminded by the scratching of the mice in the walls that this is no nightmare, that I am indeed here, hiding out at Boxmoor.

AROUND MIDDAY I pull myself up, throw cold water on my face, and dress. The last of my junk food supply is a half-empty carton of orange juice. I sit with it on the porch steps. The sky over the river is pale, ghostly, like a memory.

In the late afternoon I pull the boxwood branches clear and drive first down Bozman Road, past the dairy farms and woodlands toward the end of the peninsula. I drive up several of the dirt lanes, deliberately hitting the muddy potholes, trying to get the car dirty with red clay slosh. I stop and with my hands slop mud on my license plates. I clean my hands on the grass. The smell from the long, rectangular chicken houses alongside the lane starts me gagging again. I push the button to raise the window and turn on the fresh air fan. Coming back, I'm careful to drive no faster than the speed limit. I pass again through the miles of forest that cover much of this peninsula, all owned, I remember, by the Du Ponts or Rockefellers or some such family foundation.

By the time I enter the Bozman depot, the sky has darkened and the air has begun to mist. I load up on canned foods, beans, sardines, peanut butter, and bread. I buy coffee and beer and a bottle of Johnnie Walker Red. The woman behind the counter is close to my age, plump and with graying hair. She watches me with poorly disguised curiosity. She is talkative, tells me to call her Agnes, and waits for me to offer my name, which, of course, I decline to do. "Got some nice smoked ham meat," she says, pointing to a glass front counter. "Go good with some oysters. Right out of the creek. Got a bushel in the back. Ham and oysters. Yes sir. Take some home to the wife?"

"That's okay. Thanks."

She makes the comment that weekenders usually don't stay around after Labor Day. Her tone suggests it's a question. I don't respond. I ask her about fishing, thinking of the rods I've seen in the shed at the house, trying to provide a reason for my presence. She tells me the rock are running strong, though the perch are sluggish.

"What are you usin' for bait?" she asks.

"Do you have any?" I answer.

"Got alewives froze," she replies.

"Menhaden?" I respond, remembering the word, at least in these parts, that's a synonym for alewives.

She nods, like she knows that I know. "Got 'em in the freezer," she answers. "Hold on. Muddy!" she hollers. Agnes takes a step toward the back room. A rear door must be open to the outside, as I can hear the rain and feel the cooler air from the weather front that is moving through. I hear the outer door close and watch a young woman slowly emerge from the backroom shadow. Her face is impassive, her eyes and affect at first flat. Her hair is wound tight up under a baseball cap and her T-shirt and baggy denim overalls are dappled from raindrops. "Grab me a box of frozen bait, dear," Agnes tells her. The girl wipes her hands on her jeans. She disappears for a moment before walking back into the main store. As she approaches and sees me, she startles, then fixes me with eyes that are strangely probing. She studies me as though I'm familiar. Without averting her stare, she hands Agnes the package, then takes several backward steps before turning away. At the rear door she pivots once more and, leaning against the jamb, continues to watch me.

I buy the frozen bait and toss it out when I get back to the house. The beans and toasted bread, washed down with the scotch, revive me somewhat. I swallow a Seconal with the drink. The clouds have blown through. I linger over the scotch as a blood-red sky tints the river, then eases its way into cooler shades, then into shadow, then into dark.

2

THE LAND HERE IS EMPTY AND BLEAK. An endless flat-
ness. A coastal plain leveled by glacial crush, bordered by the
Chesapeake and Atlantic. There are few windbreaks.

Last night was much like the ones before. I slept little, listening to the wind moan against the eaves, waiting for the
sound of my pursuers, the crackling of tires on the oyster-shell
driveway. I dreamed of being able to bolt out the back door for
the river and to swim free. I wondered if I had the will and the
courage to swim. I was a damn good swimmer at Catholic.

THIS SUMMER HOME BELONGS to an old colleague of mine
from the agency, Everett Wheeler. He and his first wife more or

less stopped using it after their children left for college and moved away. He told me once he lends it out occasionally to clients, but mostly he holds on to it for the land appreciation. It's never used after Labor Day. He keeps the electricity on, I suppose, so the pipes won't freeze. I found the fuse box off the pantry and turned on the hot-water heater. All the comforts of home ...

Stands of hemlock and pine line the sides of the property and shield it from neighbors. The rear of the house faces west, across the river. I visited here a few times, years back, when Everett's children were younger and he still kept it up. That was after I had left the agency and my private practice had mushroomed. I was one of many honored guests. Languorous parties in the afternoon. Women wrapped in beach towels, tanned, flirtatious. Everett was large and red-faced, jovial with his male friends, conspiratorial with the women. One afternoon I inadvertently stumbled in on him and one of his young law clerks in the boat shed. The woman had lost half her bikini. Later he thanked me for my discretion. With a wink he showed me where he hid the house key under the flowerpot on the screen porch and told me to come and use the place anytime. That was then. I'm sure he wouldn't want me here now. Everett is semiretired. He and his third wife have several homes and prefer Florida in the winter, Sun Valley in the summer.

TWO MONTHS AGO I spoke at a luncheon for trial lawyers held at the Army Navy Club in Washington. I was introduced by a federal judge, Asa Cole. He referred to me at the time as a "Brahmin of the bar." Today, here, I am hiding out, shrinking from the glare of my disgrace. How could I have tripped so badly?

EVERETT WHEELER AND I started out together. We were
in the same class at the Public Defender Agency. Asa Cole, the
federal judge who introduced me at the Army Navy Club—he
was the deputy director when Everett and I began. Strange,
how lives intersect. It was Asa, in fact, who probably most in-
fluenced me. Not only did Asa make the decision to hire me,
but he assigned himself to be my first supervisor.

Three other lawyers were hired along with Everett and me,
freshman members of a legal staff of over thirty. Everett and a
woman named Rachel Duboc were coming off federal clerk-
ships. David Hormer, previously *Harvard Law Review,* was back
from the Peace Corps and wore an earring. My office mate was
Harrison Bonifant, from New Orleans. Harry, as he liked to be
called, had spent his first year out of law school working for a
southern prison project. All of us shared an unspoken pride in
our public interest inclinations. All of us were eager to match
our trained intellects against those in the U.S. attorney's office.
Unlike the way states work, in Washington, D.C., the federal
prosecutor's office handles all major crimes committed in the
city.

At the agency I got the training I needed—two months of
classroom trial-practice preparation and then nearly a year in
juvenile court developing my trial skills under Asa's tutelage.
Asa never missed a trick. He'd get the skinny on every judge. If
a judge liked to fish, Asa'd talk fishing. If a judge liked golf,
Asa'd pretend to be putting when the judge came in. One judge
was a Yankees fan. Asa had my client in a Yankees jersey for
sentencing. When the time came, when I was ready, I moved to
felonies. The serious stuff. My first felony case sent me looking
for a potential witness who lived in the projects in Southeast,

the ones across from LeDroit Park. Every lawyer's first jury trial is a milestone.

My client was Manny Owens, a tall, lanky kid with a smile that took up half his face and that was adorned with a gold incisor in the field of white. Manny was charged with possession of cocaine with intent to distribute and was facing at least several years in prison if convicted. Manny had a long juvenile record. Even so, he brimmed with confidence. He would stride into my office unannounced, his face crinkling up around his big grin, his tongue flicking over his shiny tooth. He always wore a Washington Redskins cap slanted sideways. That was in the late 1970s when the Redskins had been coached by George Allen, then Jack Pardee, and were often a playoff contender. Manny would sit on the wooden chair next to my desk and ask me, "We got it beat yet, counselor?"

The cops had gotten a tip and come down on the street corner where he was standing, surrounding it. They found packages of coke near him, not on him. The prosecutor claimed to have a witness named Jerome. Manny told us Jerome would clear him, if anything, but Manny hadn't been able to find him. When I turned up an address for Jerome and told Asa about it, Asa pushed up the octagonal lenses that were always sliding down his long nose and said, "Let's go!"

It was mid-December and late in the afternoon, and I felt tentative, unsure about going into the projects, but Asa was adamant. "Jack, Jack," he ranted, gesturing with his hands and putting on his coat. "We can't ask our investigators to do something we wouldn't do. This guy is key." Asa was whacked back then, half bent. But he'd won many cases and become my mentor, so I went.

I remember the square brick buildings in the LeDroit Park project were all identical: faded, crumbling, spray-painted with graffiti, all with cracked windows, green iron doors with locks jimmied out, trash strewn along the hard-packed grassless dirt out front. The sun had set and it was getting dark and cold as we walked between the buildings. We were stopped twice by groups of young black men who emerged from shadows, curious, aggressive. They blocked our way, fanning out, half surrounding us. Asa would raise himself up and explain we were public defenders trying to keep a client out of prison. Each time they let us pass. Climbing some narrow stairs rank with stale urine, we stepped over a couple nodding against the stairwell wall, the man with dried spittle caked over his lips, a syringe and smoked spoon on the dirty step at his side. We knocked and were let into an apartment, and Asa began talking to the mother of Jerome, the man we were after. The apartment smelled like garbage and it took my eyes a while to get used to the dimness. There were two crying children in the room, a toddler in a grimy T-shirt, otherwise naked, and an infant lying on the floor on a soiled dish towel. There was one sofa covered in plastic and a portable television providing the only light in the room. The woman was vague. She was unhelpful. As Asa finished talking I noticed something moving on the wall above the gas stove. I looked closer. The entire wall was dark, in motion. Roaches, thousands of them, from wall to ceiling, pulsing like one animal, crawling over each other, falling on the stove and floor. Once I saw them, I could hear them, a low, bristling crackle. Asa took my arm and pulled me out. Later that evening we each showered and changed at work, and he took me to a wine-tasting party at the Corcoran Gallery. His girlfriend, Elaine, an assistant to an assistant to the White House counsel for Jimmy Carter had gotten us invited. We were served caviar and Brie on toast points, and everyone talked with an oddly affected inflection. Or so it sounded to me back then.

ASA COLE'S FAMILY was from Houston, southern conservative. His father, we heard, had ties to George Bush. He had an uncle who was a circuit court judge. Even though Asa boasted that he was a fiscal and foreign policy Republican, nobody believed it. He had a ponytail all that long time ago and wore John Lennon spectacles. He preferred black steel-toed work boots to shoes and, like everyone at the agency, was totally intent on winning cases. "These folks," he told me during my first interview, "they've never known a break. Never had a chance. Fettered from the get-go. As public defenders we give them a decent shake for once in their lives." For Asa, law was a natural inheritance, while for me, I suppose, it was a way to gain power in a world where I had known little.

Law school trains and disciplines you to think logically. At the National Law College, typical of most legal institutions, you learn to reason using the Socratic method. You're taught to take a problem and dissect it. Identify and separate out the various issues. Solve them independently. Then reunite the results to reach an overall conclusion. This method blots out extrinsic considerations. It serves the objective purposes of the law. Keeps the eye on the ball, so to speak. As a group our minds were honed sharp. We were anxious to transfer our skills to the courtroom, to employ them on behalf of people in trouble. People far up shit's creek.

When I started our agency's resources were plentiful. We had investigators and a budget for experts. We matched well in talent and resources the higher-paid prosecutors we faced. Over time our class won more trials than we lost, an unheard of record in the defense of criminal indigents. No wonder that by the mid-eighties, after years of backroom grumbling by judges and prosecutors—complaints of too many acquittals, too many criminals getting off—and with the rise of crack cocaine and rampant violence, the agency's budget was cut back, salaries frozen, caseloads increased, resources denied.

MY FATHER HAD TAUGHT me that the way off the farm was through study, good grades. I had listened to him and worked hard to get somewhere else. Coming from rural Maryland, I yearned for the city. Catholic University had offered me a college scholarship. That's where I met Margaret. We were introduced sophomore year, but junior year we fell hard. She liked to get naked and lie down with me. Tease me. I was a late bloomer. She was my first. Watching her strip, touching her skin, learning her body—I couldn't see her enough. Finally, at an off-campus frat party we made love. Senior year, I rented a room in a group house in Adams Morgan. It had a fireplace. Margaret spent most nights with me. We'd get stoned, listen to Springsteen or Jerry Garcia and watch the fire burn. Margaret had gotten on the pill, but something went wrong. She was Roman Catholic. I mean Roman with a capital *R*. She never said it, but I knew she felt trapped. Marriage was all right with me, though. I loved her. The pregnancy and Stephen's birth brought us closer. I had gone to those breathing classes. I had held her hand in the hospital for hours. I'd mopped her brow with a washcloth. When she brought Stephen home I was a very proud father. But law school was a strain financially. We found a day-care nursery near our one-bedroom basement apartment. Margaret worked full time at Sears to help get me through.

I graduated in the top five percent and landed several nice job offers. Margaret fought my going to the agency. She didn't understand my interest in criminal work. Her father was military. She was never comfortable with the idea of representing rapists or killers. I think it was mostly the money, though. She felt she had done her part. She wanted things. A new car. A starter home. Things we'd never afford on a public defender's salary. She wanted to quit work or at least cut back to part time, which I agreed she should do. We talked, argued. I felt strongly about it. I had gotten a law degree to help people. The D.C. agency was the best, and the trial experience would be invaluable. It will lead to even better opportunities, I argued. Asking her to be patient, I took Asa's offer. And so I began my odyssey into the labyrinth of trial work, into the role of advocate, taking on the cause, becoming "my young warrior" as one client called me, and one of "my two champions," as another later called Asa and me. The client in that last case had been charged with murder. Sherman Allen was his name. He was fifteen. The crime polarized the city. But that was later.

ASA AND I NEVER did find the witness, Jerome. And I had to prepare to defend Manny Owens not knowing if Jerome would show in court or, if he did, what he would say. I discussed the case obsessively with Asa, and we both agreed Manny had to testify, to deny any knowledge of the drugs and to explain his innocent presence on the corner. But Manny had a problem, a bad habit. He was always sniffling like his nose was running. Or like his sinus passages were damaged. So I worked on preparing him to testify, and to do so without constantly snorting.

This was necessary witness preparation. I needed to change this habit of his, or at least help him learn to control it, so that the jurors would never see it. What decent lawyer would not have done the same, particularly for a client charged with cocaine abuse? It wasn't easy. As we practiced his responses to the expected cross-examination, under the slightest bit of pressure he'd revert to sniffling. I went to the apartment in Southeast where he lived with his mother, two sisters, their three children, and sometimes a girlfriend. We practiced there. The place had two bedrooms. His mother had an eye missing, which no one ever spoke of. Every time I passed her, she'd say, "Bless you, Mr. Jack Stanton, bless you chile." Grinning, Manny went around pointing out the things he had bought for his family. A television for each room. A window air-conditioner. A microwave oven. I was worried. The assistant U.S. attorney trying the case for the government was Morgan Langrell. He was older than me, experienced, and seldom failed to obtain a conviction. Langrell was a large man who spoke with a preacherlike baritone. Even back then he was known as a bully in the courtroom. The day before the trial I had Manny come to the office early. We rehearsed again. And again. I even videotaped him testifying and showed him his unconscious tendency to sniff. We worked all day. In the end, the witness Jerome never appeared, and Manny's testimony was flawless. Langrell beat at him, but Manny remained controlled and courteous. When he caught himself sniffling, he apologized to the jury, explaining that he had a cold. When the foreman announced the verdict of not guilty, Manny's mother sobbed out, "Bless you jury and judge!" and Manny laughed out loud. Langrell never said a word but neatly and deliberately packed up his books and papers and walked out. In the hallway the jurors came out and hugged Manny. His mother and sisters hugged me. I prided myself on my preparation of my client. I had done what good lawyers do, what the uptown, expensive lawyers do. I had helped Manny become a convincing witness before the jury, convincing as to the truthfulness of his testimony. Preparation of witnesses became a cornerstone of my success.

Back at the office I was slapped on the back. Everett Wheeler, who never missed a chance to party, herded everyone into the conference room for an ad hoc celebration. He sent out for champagne and a bottle of Wild Turkey that he and Asa took turns sipping. Later they all insisted on taking me out to celebrate. I called Margaret and tried to get her to come, but Stephen was feverish so she begged off. "This type of esprit de corps is important for our office," Everett bellowed, overhearing the conversation. I repeated this to Margaret, though she had caught it the first time. Asa rode his Harley, and in several cars we all followed him to the Tune Inn on Capitol Hill. Harry Bonifant rode with me. The early dark had already settled over the city. Asa took us along the Tidal Basin where the cherry trees were draped in blinking Christmas lights that flickered off the water, mingling with the image of the reflected rotunda of the Jefferson Memorial. Asa zigzagged through the traffic and, at a red light, screamed epithets back at us. Harry chuckled. "Cusses like a banshee, don't he?" Harry talked with a disarming New Orleans slang that masked his keen intellect. He rolled a joint that we shared. In front of the Tune Inn was Asa, guarding a parking space that had opened up and directing me into it. Motorcycle goggles were pushed up on his forehead above his spectacles, and I remember kidding him about his four-eyed appearance. Before I had even cut the engine, he had poked his head in the window, fingered the burning roach, and taken a long hit. He handed it to me with a shrug. Elaine was waiting at the door with her cousin, a nursing student with striking red hair, Linda Morrison. She had a strong manner and expressed an interest in my trial. I found her almost desirable. But, of course, I made myself think of Margaret and Stephen. When Everett started buying shots, Linda Morrison toasted me with the others, and I accepted the toasts and congratulations of everyone as my due. Later she asked me to dance to Otis Redding singing, "Dock of the Bay."

"I'd like to see you in court," she said in a breathy voice after we sat back down. "Asa won't let me come watch him." She fingered my hair. It was long at the time and curly, like it's always been. "I'll bet you get the ladies to vote for you," she laughed.

Asa liked the Tune Inn because the jukebox was filled with Motown. It was his regular hang out. He pumped the machine with quarters as we listened to Aretha, Marvin Gaye, Jackie Wilson, and we stayed and drank until closing, talking about the cases in our office, about the quirks of judges, about the rights of our clients, about defending liberty.

3

THE WIND BLOWS HARD TODAY and the river is ripped with waves and white foam. The porch screen door is blown off a hinge and begins banging. I find a hammer and screwdriver in the shed and take the door down. It's good to have a project. Something to do, even for a few minutes.

This is not, I realize, the best choice for a hideout. There's only one way in from the road and no escape out the back except the river. If discovered, I'd be blocked in. Still, I seem unable to summon the will to run farther. Maybe it's the effect of this solitude, all this open, vacant space. This hushing wind. It's turning me inward. My pursuers may eventually close the net. But ennui is setting in. A form of paralysis. The surrender of the rabbit, still alive, but caught in the jaws of the dog.

I'VE BEEN MOPING about here. Sopped with regret. Deprived of the familiar props of my existence—work, deadlines, appointments—there's little left with which to fend off the depression that's taken hold. It's something separate, distinct even from this shitstorm I've brought down on myself. During those first days, I welcomed it, relished it as well deserved. It fit with the desolation of motel room walls and I let it come on unchecked. Now I'm afraid of it. It's welling up like a black tide. I try to numb it with alcohol and pills. Poison replaces poison.

I HIT MY FIRST sinkhole years ago while still at the National Law College. I had landed a fat assignment in the school's trial-practice clinic. The law college, at the time, prided itself as an innovator in clinical programs, offering its students hands-on trial experience under the tutorship of real prosecutors and defense attorneys. I was assigned to work with a public defender in Baltimore, representing indigents accused of crimes.

In Maryland in the 1970s public defenders received an annual salary from the state. They were expected to handle the criminal cases assigned to them but were permitted to take private civil cases for pay as well. The man I worked for, Charlie Sanders, was building a divorce practice on the side. He got a hundred dollars an hour for his civil work, he confided. Charlie was Maryland old boy to the bone. He took me for the same. After supervising me on some minor misdemeanor matters, he handed me a stack of files. "Six cases," he told me. "Two of 'em's felonies. Prepare 'em for me. I might let you try 'em." He winked. "I can see you got a knack ..."

When the first trial neared, he told me to be ready. I was pleased with the responsibility. Full of myself. But I had no business trying those cases alone. During each one Charlie just sat at the counsel table, nodding encouragement. He chewed tobacco and had a supersize soda cup from 7-Eleven at his feet, and periodically he'd spit into the cup. Much of the time he was reading from his divorce files. He knew nothing of the facts. I lost them all, of course. Just before the semester ended he took me with him on what he called "escapee day." I watched him interview eight different inmates, all in the holding cell outside the courtroom. Within an hour he proceeded to convince each one to take a plea of guilty to a prison release violation in return for a one-year sentence. One of the men, doing time for armed robbery, had jumped a medium security fence and been on the lam for nine months. He was arrested while strong-arming a juke joint in Landover for which he faced separate charges. He quickly agreed to the deal. Another, though, a Hispanic kid who hardly spoke English and was serving a six-month work-release sentence for petty larceny, was charged for arriving back at his prison three hours late. He had taken the wrong bus from his job and then had gotten lost trying to hitch-hike back to the pen. He objected at first. Charlie became impatient. "You're guilty," Charlie told him, talking slowly like to a child. "Guilty! You can't win at trial. Understand *compadre?*" Charlie used gestures for emphasis. "Much longer jail time. Much longer." He spread his hands apart. "You go to trial, the judge will punish you worse. Much worse. For wasting court time. For not admitting your guilt. *Comprende?*" Charlie persisted, hammering his fist into his palm until the kid submitted. "The deal is one year. You take it or you'll do a lot more. And be grateful. You're lucky to get it."

Charlie lined all eight of the men up together and had me

plead them out while he read his divorce files. The eight all mumbled in unison when the judge asked them if they understood what they were doing, if they had received adequate counsel, if their pleas were knowingly and voluntarily given, and so on. They were sentenced on the spot.

That afternoon I wrote and posted a letter to the governor and copied the head public defender in Maryland, complaining not about Charlie but about the part-time public defender system. I described my experience and argued that the system encouraged the public defenders to spend as little time as possible on their indigent cases so that they could have more time for their private practices, thereby increasing their incomes. It was an incentive that led to injustice, I argued, such as treating eight different men, with entirely different backgrounds, who committed entirely different acts, the same.

I was almost booted from the program, almost lost the credits I needed to graduate. I had embarrassed the governor, the judge, everyone. The public defender was furious. Charlie never spoke to me or let me see him again. As it turned out, law students were not supposed to try felonies. Nor handle felony pleas. Bar licensing rules forbid it. The judge apparently didn't know this, as student practice was relatively new. I hadn't known it and Charlie either hadn't known or hadn't cared. But the felony convictions would have to be invalidated. The point I'd tried to make was forgotten. The public defender blamed the law college. The clinical director went apeshit. He had me in his office with the door closed. "Just what did you think you were doing?" he asked incredulously. He was an up-and-comer, on his way to becoming dean, a short, bald Irishman with a temper. "Just who do you think you are? Do you know how long it took us to forge these goddamn relationships? To gain the trust of these state agencies? Charlie Sanders stupidly was trying to do you a favor. Give you extra experience. *Nice payback!*" Though he visibly tried to control himself, his voice began increasing in volume. "Our clinics are becoming a banner head for recruitment. They're establishing our law school as one of the most innovative in the country." I started to explain my reasons. "Jesus Christ!" he yelled, cutting me off. "Listen to me, you prima donna! Our clinics are attracting endowments. *Funding!*" Then he stopped. He clenched and unclenched his fists, regaining control. He went to the door. "Change takes time," he growled in a modulated tone. "Maybe we can help improve things once we're in tight. But nobody needs cowboys like you. Go on, get out of here. You're reassigned. You'll do"—he opened the door—"appellate work. Desk work! Go on. Get out. You'll graduate, but stay away from my clinic. And don't you dare say another word about this. You understand?" Leaving, I backed into the crowd of students that had gathered to listen.

Margaret pulled me out that time. She and I'd been married three years then. Although we bickered often during law school, she stepped up for me. I had crumpled. Gone sick inside. I thought my career was over. I hadn't been able to eat or sleep. Margaret spent days with me in our bedroom while I lay mostly inert. She didn't agree with what I had done. It was disloyal, she thought. I should have gone to the law college with my complaints first. Still, she understood that I had meant well. She held my hand. She cooked for me and fed me. She made me get up and take walks with her and Stephen. Finally, she just left Stephen with me. Purposefully, I'm sure. A two-year-old's needs aren't easily ignored. By the end of the day when she re-turned, I'd be up.

I'm not sure why I had let that incident take me down so far. I remember, at one point, even thinking about suicide. More philosophically than practically, but still thinking about it. That was the only other time it ever crossed my mind. Except, of course, later, after Margaret had left . . .

4

PERHAPS THIS SODDEN LOWLAND, washed by the river—
isolated, neglected, empty—had hovered in my subconscious
for a while as a half-remembered sanctuary of sorts. Maybe, in
some recess of memory, this Eastern Shore was still home. I
don't know. When I left the Delmar Motel, I had no conscious
plan. I got here on cruise control.

THE NEIGHBORS ALL SEEM GONE. I've seen no one from
the houses along the river. All the boats are up on lifts on the
docks. Even out on the road, the traffic is sparse. I may have
lucked out. Blindly found my hole-in-the-wall. A place so out
of the way, I'm safe. The only regular activity comes from the

watermen running their trotlines out in the channel, and I'm of no interest to them. Of course, I haven't hit a weekend yet. I'll need to lie especially low come the weekend.

ON THE WALL of the kitchen is a faded nautical chart of the upper Chesapeake with a blue pin marking the location of this house. Built on a bulk-headed sand spit, the house abuts the eastern side of what is called Harris Creek, near the mouth, where the water flares wide into the Choptank River. Visible out the back window and across the way is Tilghman Island, shaped on the chart like a crab claw dangling down, joined to the mainland above by a drawbridge.

I pass the time by studying the chart, the curvature of the shoreline and the names of all the inlets and coves. I have begun, with a mixture of romanticism and self-pity, to envision the course a swim would take. A tide on the ebb would sweep a swimmer south, out beyond the point into the mouth of the Choptank, out further into the wide, open bay, out toward freedom, toward that rift between the water and the sky.

THERE ARE FIVE bedrooms here. Each one is painted a different color, like the rooms in the White House. I tried the blue room last night. Though I've not yet seen them, the mice follow me throughout the house. They scratch within the walls, enclosed in their own mazes. I tried migrating to different bedrooms. Even though I cover my head and ears with the drapes I yanked from the living room the first night, and despite the alcohol and drugs, the mice wake me up in the most forsaken hours of the morning.

Margaret and I had mice once, when we lived in Georgetown.

She didn't tolerate them for long. She pestered me until I went to the hardware store and got glue traps that I set along the carpet molding. We threw dead mice away for many weeks.

I can still see Margaret during those first years of practice, before she left me. She was a fine-looking girl with an angular face and an athletic physique. She liked to jog along the canal. I liked it that other men stared at her, desired her. I recall too that last spring when I would stay home on Sundays to amble down the quay on the Potomac. I can see the two of us on either side of Stephen, swinging him by his hands, the spurs of new leaf, the blossoms of forsythia and dogwood flanking the water—the breeze rippling the current. Sometimes in the evenings we'd get a baby-sitter and walk across the Key Bridge to eat in Rosslyn, in one of the restaurants on the hill overlooking the Potomac and across to the stretch of monuments. We'd sit and watch the receding sun turn the river lemon red and the brightening cast of the city against the dark. I was fascinated with my cases back then, consumed by them, and would rave on about strategy, bouncing ideas off Margaret, entreating her to act as a mock juror. She'd try to stay interested, and her feedback always helped.

Sometimes we'd have a cocktail back in Georgetown at Clyde's on M Street or Chadwick's on the riverfront and just watch the people on the street. There were always black limousines double-parked, chauffeurs awaiting tuxedoed men and tanned women in strapless gowns, people from a different world, attending this or that charity gala. The students hung out together on corners in jeans and long hair, easily distinguished from the Yups, smartly dressed, always on the move, the stockbrokers and uptown lawyers. Immigrants worked the kitchens and were mostly out of sight. Tourists overcrowded the streets, blocking sidewalks at every vendor's stand, stopping to check out every artist, the musicians, the jugglers, falling prey to the street cons offering three-card monte. And by the early eighties, the homeless became visible, their silent numbers swelling, their haggard faces hunched against doorways out of the wind, begging for money on every block, sleeping on grates, using torn burlap refuse for blankets, dirty, vacant-eyed, lost.

I met Mitch Snyder, the homeless advocate, down at the courthouse while I was waiting for a hearing to begin sometime in '79 or '80. I admired his efforts and began helping him pro bono. It didn't require much on my part. When he'd get arrested he didn't want a legal defense. He just wanted a forum. Media coverage. Famous actors came to town to help him protest, and sometimes I represented them as well. A Hollywood studio even made a movie about Mitch's life. During the filming, Mitch staged a sit-in, trying to force the Reagan administration to turn an unused government building into a homeless shelter. Mitch's arrest on that occasion led to my first personal run-in with Morgan Langrell.

Langrell had been promoted by then. He was in charge of the misdemeanor section at the U.S. attorney's office. He wanted real jail time for Mitch. For being a multirepeat offender, he said. For trying to blackmail the government. For repeatedly tying up the court system. Langrell held a press conference. "Snyder is a menace," he declared.

In his office Langrell demanded a plea to more than just trespassing. He threatened to try Mitch for extortion and demanded pleas to the additional counts of resisting arrest and destruction of government property. Mitch, apparently, had refused a police order to leave the building, and a wooden barricade had been found broken. Langrell wanted six months in jail. This was bullshit. I had it out with Morgan that day. We both lost our tempers. It got personal. I accused him of grandstanding, of being a panderer, a press monger, of having lost touch with the times. He called me a farm boy. He said I should take the blood money I made off the victims of crime and go give it to the first homeless drunk I found. We went back and forth. When I called him a damn Nazi, he buzzed for security. Harry, who was with me, pulled me out of his office. "You know better than to let it go that far," Harry admonished me. "It's unprofessional." He chuckled. "Seriously. You'll have to dance with him again, you know."

The next day, through one of Mitch's sympathizers inside the clerk's office, I learned that Morgan was trying to manipulate which judge would hear the case and pass sentence. This was judge shopping. There were some forty judges on the bench, some liberal, some plain mean, a few certifiable. Though we all tried to do it, overt judge shopping was improper. I called Langrell on it and threatened to go to the press myself. To hold a hearing and subpoena the whole goddamn clerk's office if I had to. We met again the next day. He agreed to a trespassing plea. Before we parted, though, he pointed his finger at me. "You're on a list," he hissed. "My personal scumbag list." He tapped his temple. "A permanent list I keep up here."

PEOPLE HAVE FORGOTTEN, but Mitch was the great champion of the homeless. Over a ten-year span he starved himself in more hunger strikes than I can recall, some lasting over fifty days, requiring extended hospitalization. Several times he nearly died. I saw him after he had come home from the hospital following a fifty-one-day fast in 1986. His voice was feeble, hoarse, like that of an old invalid. The skin hung in flaps off his face, off his arms. Strange, after all that sacrifice, that he committed suicide. He was found hanged on July 5, 1990, his note next to him.

Margaret and I argued about Mitch Snyder early on, about his total commitment to his cause. She didn't buy that his work was important enough that it justified the sacrifices he required. Not just his own, but sacrifices from those who cared for him. To Margaret, his martyr's zeal was only proof of his own failings. Of his own inability to relish the normal experiences of life. I suggested that the good he did, his advocacy for others, was near saintly and must have carried with it its own inner reward. "He avoids life," she replied. "The experience of living, loving, marrying, being normal isn't enough for him." Margaret had a stubborn side to her. "Work is only part of life," she liked to emphasize, turning our conversation back to a sore point. "You should learn that time at home, time with your family, time here is what matters most."

"Doesn't a man's profession, his life's work define him?" I would parry. "And in the doing of it? If it's not done well, doesn't that diminish the work itself? And thus diminish the man? What if my colleagues and opponents are working nights and weekends, are more devoted, and prepared than I am?"

She'd cut me off there and accuse me of cross-examining her as if she were one of the hostile witnesses I had become expert at discrediting.

After one of these fights I decided we needed time away. Our fifth anniversary was coming up. I had been at home even less than usual, pressed with work and spending too many evenings at the jail interviewing clients. I knew we needed a break. I called Margaret's supervisor at Sears and secretly convinced him to give her a few days of leave. I surprised her with a trip to a resort hotel in Hilton Head.

The three of us left for South Carolina early in the morning, around five, and drove straight through. We had an early lunch at McDonald's. Stephen mostly played with his Happy Meal. It was late afternoon when we arrived. We were tired and hungry again. The resort offered a ten-dollar afternoon buffet. All we wanted was soup. Soup was part of the buffet. The maître d' insisted, though, that we couldn't order just soup, we each had to order the whole buffet. I became confrontational. "Why can't we order off a menu?" I demanded. "Isn't this supposed to be a high-class resort? Aren't you supposed to be service oriented? Isn't the soup right there, on that table? You can't just get us each a bowl and charge us for the soup? How hard is this?" I became irate and continued after him, forcing him to call the day manager, working everyone up into a state, while Stephen cried and Margaret pulled at my arm to leave, embarrassed, "humiliated," she said later. "You think you're in a courtroom all the time, Jack. That you can just verbally assault people." We broke off the vacation early. We drove home the next day. The trip was grim. I can't remember what we said to each other in the car.

THE NEWSPAPERS GAVE enough information for anyone to guess why Mitch Snyder killed himself. There were, of course, setbacks to his cause. But the note he left referred to lost love. I learned how that can send you down. I learned it from Margaret and from how I felt after she left. Mitch must have kept falling. He just checked himself out of the pain.

While it's true I'm in trouble and struggling, if I were to consider that route here, it'd have to start from a different place. With a grip, goddamn it. With a composure. A rationality and premeditation. If I am to say *sayonara,* it's got to be with a big "fuck you" to the system and "fuck you too, Morgan Langrell, you can't have me." Yes, Christ. From a composed place. A real choice. An act of honor, like in Japan. Yes. I like that. No panic. No frenzy. Just a long swim, maybe. A final release. Just a dignified and private good-bye.

5

A PECULIAR URGE TO WALK overtakes me this morning. I fix coffee and sweep a covering of dust off the radio in the kitchen, turn it on, and listen to the news for the first time in days. The newscaster gives the date—September 30, 1999— and then launches into coverage on the early presidential primary campaigns, still led by Al Gore and George W. Bush. Reports follow about the increasing concern over the Y2K computer problem, then something about a Central American trade conference to be held in Wye Mills, just up the road where the Wye River Middle East Peace Conference had occurred. Bored, I turn off the noise and push open the screen door. The rising sun is hot, and the sun's heat banks off the gray wooden porch landing. I walk down the lane to the road and sit on the far culvert that runs alongside it. A yellowing field of soybeans extends to a pasture, dotted with cattle, and running to the river. I take off my shoes and socks and start across the field. I don't know why. My feet sink into the dark compost between the rows. The beans droop under the fluttering leaves of the plants. Using a stick as an aid, and squeezing carefully between the wires of the electric fence, I step into the pasture, breathing in the manure-scented air, and move up close to the nearest cow. My father raised a few Holsteins when I was a boy. He also grew feed corn and winter wheat. As a little boy I'd often ridden with him on his tractor, plowing the fields, laying the seed, carting the straw bales in the fall. We had nearly a hundred acres skirting a creek off the Chester River, though the farm was mostly mortgaged. I never knew how tight things were until he got sick. Until the bank started taking his machinery away.

As I approach the large animal, it turns its head toward me, its dull gray eyes like opaque marbles, and snorts. I reach out to touch its taut leathery hide. It shudders, its skin sending flies swarming, and then lumbers off.

I walk back toward Boxmoor, through the field, down the lane. I drop my shoes and socks at the porch, and then continue down the sloping yard to the dock and river. The water is clear, and I can see the green eelgrass fanning toward the channel in the tide, and the silty, mottled bottom. A ladder on the dock allows me to climb down to wet my feet, though I almost slip on the first submerged step, slimy from the accumulation of sea moss. Something about the sensation of the green sea grass, slick and cool under my feet, takes me back. A kid on the river.

I sit back down and let my feet bob in the water, trying to savor the feeling, but it's gone as quickly as it came. I watch the river as it makes its way into the wider Choptank. The temperature of the water is still mild from the summer but beginning to cool. I'd want a wet suit, I realize. I wouldn't want to lose courage and turn back from the cold. No. Resolve requires preparation. A plan. And a sign to those left behind that this is more than a mere desperate act. With a wet suit I could swim a long way before exhaustion took me. Far from this bank, out into the current of the bay, and toward the distance, that rift between the water and the sky.

RUNNING LOW ON FOOD, I drive up to the depot in Bozman. As I enter, no one appears at the register. I load more canned goods up on the counter, looking around for Agnes. I go for another bottle of scotch. After waiting awhile longer, I call out. "Hello? Is anyone here? Anyone in the back?" I hear a chair scraping against the floor and watch as the same young woman—I guess she's in her early twenties—slips into the frame of the doorway. She sets on a stack of boxes the sketch pad in her hand. I say hello, motioning at the groceries on the counter, and try to smile. When she sees me she hesitates at first. She tilts her head, considering me, uncertain. Then, lowering her gaze slightly, she strides forward. "Sorry," she answers. "I tune out sometimes when I'm drawing." She wears blue jeans and an olive pullover. Her hair's tucked under a red cap and strands drift over her temple. Her only jewelry is a small hard shell, skin colored—a carapace or scarab—on a leather thong around her neck. Behind the register she begins adding up my groceries without speaking further. As she finishes and rings up the total, she points to it, the sum showing in the register's window. "There you are," she says. I pay her. She gives me my change.

"I'm looking to buy a wet suit," I say, trying to force a normal tone into my voice. She turns then, raising her eyes to mine, direct but doubtful. "A wet suit," I repeat. "For scuba diving? Skin diving?"

She blinks. She makes no effort to hide her skepticism. She takes her lower lip between her teeth. Ignoring the question, she begins to bag up the groceries.

"Do you know where I could get one?" I persist.

She sets a can down in the bag and pauses. She begins to study my face. She does so with an unabashed directness, defying good manners. She canvasses it piecemeal, feature by feature.

"Why?" she finally asks in a whisper. Her voice is earnest, and I think I catch a tremor in it.

A simple but genuine question for which I should have been prepared. I stumble out something about needing to fix a propeller underwater.

She frowns at the explanation. "How old are you?" she asks.

Drawn in by her straightforward manner, I answer. "Forty-eight. How come you ask?"

"Where do you come from? Originally?"

"I grew up around here." I look out the window, across the road to the tiny chapel and the fields beyond. "On a farm up off the Chester. My parents are both buried there. I went to Easton High School but left the area after my father died. I was just a kid. I've come back only recently. But it's been a long time away. Thirty-some years. Can you help me with the wet suit?"

47

She doesn't reply but continues to study my face, my hair, my mouth. Then she reaches under the counter and takes out a small white pad of paper and a pencil. As she writes, I read the words upside down. "Cambridge Dive Shop." Her handwriting is clean and firm. "Dorchester Street. Take a right off High Street. On the left-hand corner." When she hands me the paper, I notice her palm is rough with calluses.

"It's about a half-hour drive," she says. This time she holds my eyes with her own. I step back. Her eyes are no longer flat, but have somehow unshielded themselves, and are like none I remember seeing. They are kind but look as though they've been stamped hard and dark by some cruelty retained in their core. Then she moves, quickly, gracefully, sliding out from behind the counter and, retaking her sketch pad, vanishes through the rear door into the back room.

IN THE SILENCES HERE, surrounded by this immaculate space, I have taken to my scotch to try to hush the voices inside, to try to slide away. The liquid I pour is the color of dying leaves, amber, reflecting the failing light of the equinox. Its taste is that of compost and peat. The days grow shorter. With a certain juvenile fervor, I set out to get drunk in the afternoon.

I'M DOZING ON THE DOCK, my back set against a piling, when I hear Canada geese calling. Opening my eyes, I find them in the distance against the northern sky, a spreading cloud of black smoke, their bleating reverberating off the river land. The first flocks come in formation from over the bay. I recall running beneath them through the fields as a child, trying to keep up. I wait until the last honk recedes into silence, until the last shadowy line is swallowed by the dusk. My bottle empty, I retreat to my shelter inside.

In the bathroom the vanity mirror is cracked. I brace my hands on the sink. The liquor may have gone to my head, but the broken image before me seems unfamiliar. I see a stranger's face, one that seems to change in texture as I stare at it. Studying the skin, the pores around the nose, the tired eyes, trying to see what is truly there, I observe a face barely recognizable. Every morning, for twenty-five years in Washington, I showered, shaved, dressed, knotted my tie with a double Windsor, and used the mirror to check my appearance. But it's as if, over this two-decade span, I'd stopped seeing it. The face before me is older than I recall. There are some small moles or warts, some liver spots. The skin is thickened, dry. There's fatigue and dull resignation in the eyes. I pretend to be an actor. Robert DeNiro in the mirror. No matter how I concentrate my features, how I try to infuse my eyes with emotion, with vitality, there's the absence of both. The best description I can give would be to call them an observer's eyes, mostly blank. Only my teeth look good. They're white still. Sturdy. Good teeth are important. I've always had good teeth.

6

I SLEPT BETTER LAST NIGHT and today feel almost human. I found some flour in a cabinet and tried an old recipe of my father's—Maryland beaten biscuits. I use the bottom of a skillet to beat the dough, and the biscuits come out half decent. I fix some eggs and coffee and eat a regular meal.

Rocking on the porch, I start, for some reason, thinking about the Code of Professional Responsibility. There was a time, years ago, when I knew it well. I had even memorized its twelve precepts . . .

THE CODE WAS OUR GUIDEBOOK. We studied it in law school. We analyzed it at the agency. Its set of rules has been adopted in one form or another by every jurisdiction as the ethical standard for lawyers. It was during my second year at the agency that it provided me with the comfort I needed to justify a course of action that I had questioned briefly but then concluded was one any committed attorney would pursue. The code became the book I leaned on. I took pride in being able to quote it by citation.

The case has stayed with me, though I had forgotten the name of the client until this morning when I looked it up in my journals. Rupert Johnson. He had been charged with boosting a liquor store at the corner of Sixteenth and Chapin Streets at 10:00 P.M. on a chilly Saturday night late in April. A Korean clerk, threatened at knifepoint, had handed over the cash in the register and watched while the assailant carried out a carton of Courvoisier. Johnson was black, had a record, lived in the neighborhood, and met the general description given by the clerk. Of course, so did dozens of other black men who lived in the area. The day following the crime, a robbery squad detective showed Johnson's photograph to the clerk, who said the person in the picture looked similar to the robber. Johnson was picked up and put in a police lineup, eight men behind a glass window. The clerk picked Johnson and told the detective that this time he was certain. A search warrant turned up two bottles of Courvoisier from his apartment.

Rupert Johnson was in a sad state. He was past middle age, effeminate, crying foul over every aspect of his life, and acting bewildered at this new charge against him. He had lost his job because of his gout. His feet would swell up and hurt so that he couldn't stand for long, and his supervisor at the Safeway where he worked as a bagman had warned him once too often not to be sitting. He had recently lost his mother to cancer, claimed that he himself was ill much of the time, and was barely staving off eviction from his apartment, where he lived with his sister and male friend, Maurice. He was cold in the jail, sick from the food, and couldn't raise the money to get out on bond. The only thing he proclaimed affirmatively was his innocence, insisting that on the Saturday night in question he was home with his sister and Maurice all night watching television. Both would testify, he assured me.

The problem surfaced when I met with his witnesses. His sister remembered coming home from work, a beauty shop where she washed hair, at about 8:00 P.M. She told me that the three of them spent the evening watching television. I asked her what shows they had seen. "*Loveboat* and *Dallas*," she recalled. She told me that Maurice made popcorn and Rupert and Maurice never left the living room until after eleven when they retired. She was avid and insistent, and I believed she'd make a decent witness. Two days before trial Maurice came to the office for his preparation. He also told me they sat together all night and watched television. When I asked him what shows, he seemed bewildered. Then he smiled, pointed his finger at me like I'd caught him, and said, "Yeah," and named off the programs he remembered: *M*A*S*H, The Jeffersons,* and *Sanford and Son,* and afterward, he claimed, they watched *Saturday Night Live.* I asked him about *Dallas,* and his face drew a blank. He never mentioned the popcorn.

At that time I shared an office with Harry, who had been assigned to appeals, was eager to move to trial work, and liked to hear about my cases. He shuffled in as Maurice left, and could see that I was, well, disconcerted. Harry always wore gray, lizard-skin cowboy boots whether with jeans or a three-piece suit. I remember him propping his boots up on his metal desk as he listened to me describe the discrepancy.

"Which of them is right?" he asked after I had finished.

I shook my head. "I don't know."

"Folks do get flummoxed about things like this. You need to find out."

"Of course."

An hour later at the library I had the back issue of the *Washington Post* in my hand from the date in question, and I turned to the television guide. No *Dallas*. No *M*A*S*H*. No *Jeffersons* or *Sanford and Son*. They all aired on different nights. *Loveboat* had been on from nine to ten, but followed by *Fantasy Island*. *Saturday Night Live* also had been on but hadn't started until eleven-thirty. Neither witness had the programs right. I ran off a Xerox copy of the newspaper and went down to the jail to show it to Rupert. He studied it for a while and then pointed to *Loveboat* and *Fantasy Island*. "That's what we watched," he said emphatically. "We watch a lot of TV, but that's what was on Saturday night."

"Your witnesses appear to be confused," I said. "No one even mentioned *Fantasy Island*."

"They sometimes don't remember so good," he said. "Maurice drinks a lot of cognac. My sister is absentminded herself. But they'll remember, if you show it to them."

"You better talk to them," I answered.

"You know I won't get to see them before trial. Not here. They can't get in here. And I got noways to show them nothin' in here." He furrowed his brow and stared me in the face. "It *was Fantasy Island*. We *was* all there together I tell you. You got to help unconfuse 'em. That's all. Jesus. You're my lawyer. Just tell 'em what I remember and show 'em the paper there. You got an innocent man here. This here jail'll kill me. I can't not have my witnesses. You know that. You're my lawyer, Mr. Jack. You know what'll happen to me at Lorton Prison. Please now. I'm counting on you to help me."

When Harry and I visited Asa in his office late that afternoon, to go over our cases, Asa admonished me. "What do you think witness preparation is about anyway? And who's going to help these people recall accurately if you don't?" His office was one of the largest because he had been at the agency longer than anyone, a corner room on the ground level with broken tile flooring stained a grimy brown. Double doors led from the street into the hallway adjacent to his office, so Asa had the habit of parking his Harley inside it, an oil-leaking centerpiece sculpture, and liked to climb on and pretend he was riding while he talked, which he did then. Like a kid he gunned the handlebar throttle, going "varoom" as he moved his torso from side to side rounding first one curve, then another. "Speaking of *Saturday Night Live*," he went on, "did you see the one a couple of weeks ago? Richard Pryor in a police lineup? It wasn't so different from some of the ones I've seen the cops run across the street." He nodded toward the city's main police station visible through his office window. "Pryor with white refrigerators on either side of him. The cops kept prodding the victim, saying, 'Come on, you can identify him; come on, we know you can.'" Asa tilted his head back smiling, then imitated the sound of a whining engine. "Pryor was hilarious," he continued, "looking at the refrigerators. Like side to side and then trying to look like one. It took a while, but the victim finally picked him out." Asa climbed off his bike, snickering to himself. He took off his spectacles and wiped them with the triangular end of his tie. "Our job has never been to determine the truth," he said flatly. "That's for the judge and jury. Even if it were, how do you know that this time they aren't honestly confused?" He motioned to the door. "I've got work to do. Go on and do your job for these people. They're entitled to it."

On the way back to our office I asked Harry what he thought. "I reckon he knows" was what he answered. "You need to handle it the proper way is all. Point out the problem and give *them* a chance to fix it. At this here dance we're in, there's a right way to curtsy and a wrong way. Just do it the right way and don't get your skirt dirty."

When Rupert Johnson's sister came in the next morning, I showed her the television guide in the paper and told her that her brother remembered that it was *Fantasy Island* they had watched, not *Dallas,* and asked whether she might have been mistaken. By then I had also called the station to confirm that, in fact, *Loveboat,* followed by *Fantasy Island,* had aired between nine and eleven that night. Additionally, my investigator had found the copy of *TV Guide* for that week, which described the episodes, and I showed this to her as well. Maurice came in about fifteen minutes later and I basically repeated the conversation with him, adding the reminder about the popcorn. I left them alone for a few minutes. When I returned they both remembered that it really was *Loveboat* and *Fantasy Island,* and that the popcorn was buttered and salted. I also told them about the Courvoisier that was taken and the two bottles found in the apartment. Maurice thought for a minute. "What does Rupert say about them?" he asked.

"He said you bought the two bottles as a present for him a month before."

"Oh," Maurice answered. "Yeah. Sure. That's right in fact."

I spent the next day at the jail with Rupert in one of the lawyer conference rooms. He didn't seem well and was coughing frequently, raspylike and breathing heavily. I offered to request a jail infirmary visit but he looked at me like I was foolish, and we both knew no help would come of that. I repeated to him my conversation with his sister and Maurice and his eyes grew hopeful, and he thanked me, over and over. I worked with him getting him through his testimony as best I could. He took my hand toward the end and began thanking me more and wouldn't let go. His palm was moist, fleshy. He told me he had made some mistakes, but if I'd help him get free, just this one time, he would be right, would be a man to his community. He started to weep, and I told him the battle was about to start and that I needed him strong, and this seemed to bolster him.

That evening, like most, I stayed late at the office. While preparing my cross-examination of the Korean clerk, I had a stab of—I don't know—nostalgia for something I sensed was slipping away, for some purpose that was true and was in and of itself mine and not on behalf of someone else. Fighting a wave of fatigue, I found myself flipping through the Code of Professional Responsibility. I kept a copy on the corner of my desk. I was thinking of Maurice and of the thin line between preparing a witness and coaching one to give fabricated testimony. There was nothing in the code specifically addressing this point. But close enough was Rule 2. I can still recite it:

> A lawyer shall serve a client with skill and care commensurate with that generally afforded to clients by other

lawyers in similar matters, and where the bounds of law are uncertain, an advocate should resolve in favor of the client doubts as to the bounds of the law.

Other lawyers? Certainly Asa, with all his experience, condoned what I was doing. He served his clients in similar fashion and taught bar members at all the local seminars. And I remember thinking of Edward Bennett Williams, uptown, who at that time was defending a wealthy city developer charged with corruption and bribery charges. Previously Williams had successfully defended Jimmy Hoffa and John Connally. He had bought the Washington Redskins and was trying to buy the Baltimore Orioles, and I figured he probably wouldn't even think there was an issue here. And then I thought of Rupert Johnson and figured he deserved as much.

IN THE EARLY HOURS before the day of trial I dreamed about Rupert. Like a shadow witness peering in from another dimension, I saw him in his own world, trying not to fall too fast, an aging impoverished gay man, plagued by an undefined chronic illness, uneducated, clinging desperately to what little dignity he could muster, afraid, hoping not to lose Maurice. I wanted to help him. I got up while it was still dark and went back to the office to rewrite my planned opening statement to the jury and reanalyze my strategy. And once in the courtroom, once the jury had been selected, once I had begun speaking for Rupert Johnson, in some way I was him, feeling for him, conveying the despair of his life, the bleakness of his future, the sympathy he now needed, the mercy he and all of us deserved. And too, as his spokesman, I rooted out the weaknesses in the government's evidence against him. After all, the victim had been less than positive about the photographic identification. Naturally, having been earlier shown the photo of Rupert, he chose Rupert from the others in the lineup. Who else would he choose? There was, I pointed out to the jury, and then repeatedly emphasized, no one else in the police lineup who was first shown to the victim in a photograph. It was like Richard Pryor and the refrigerators, just subtler. Moreover, the alibi, as planned, was convincing, even up to a rendition of the story line of the *Fantasy Island* episode by Maurice, with gestures and emphasis. Finally, I had told my two alibi witnesses that I would not ask them about the popcorn during their direct testimony and that they should only mention it if asked the appropriate question on cross-examination by the prosecutor, Morgan Langrell, who was back trying felonies. Langrell fell for the bait. The final coup de grace came after he got Rupert's sister, who testified first, to recall the popcorn on cross-examination. Because there is what is called a rule on witnesses, Maurice was outside the courtroom during her testimony and would have no way of knowing what she said on the witness stand. Langrell figured he had elicited from her a made-up detail—one that I had overlooked and that would show the alibi to be false. When Langrell went after Maurice on cross-examination, he thought he had me. While I can't be sure, there was a moment when Langrell seemed to second-guess himself. He paused, as though for just an instant wondering whether I could actually have prepared my witnesses for this. But if the suspicion ever did cross his mind, it must have been no more than the flit of recognition, like a fast-moving cloud, for he bullied ahead, demanding from Maurice whether any food had been consumed during the evening. Then, turning away from the witness and looking knowingly at the jury, he awaited the answer. Of course, when Maurice took a moment to reflect, and then slowly seemed to dredge from his memory the recollection of the popcorn he had made and that it was buttered and salted, I knew the case was over. As the jury was polled I shut my eyes and listened to the sweet sound of "not guilty" repeated over and over. When I opened them, I caught Langrell glaring at me. But the victory was empowering. Rupert Johnson was free. Even Asa was impressed.

Filled with exhilaration, I stayed out late again with my colleagues. We all got to laughing over Morgan Langrell's expression when Maurice described the popcorn.

"Looked like he ate something bad for lunch," Asa said.

"Yeah. Some rancid popcorn." Harry chuckled. "He stepped right into that briar patch and found himself stuck."

I can't remember anymore why Margaret didn't come or wouldn't even try to get a baby-sitter, but I can still see myself going back to the office afterward, not ready to surrender the elation of victory, opening files of other cases, until finally exhausted I found the couch in Asa's office and fell asleep.

That next night brought a major fight with Margaret. I was reeling from the night before, still wasted, but I called her in the morning, apologizing for having failed to come home. I pleaded with her to understand and then offered to get a baby-sitter for the evening, promising to take her out for a special dinner. Her voice told me how upset she was. I probably should have left work then, but I had three new case pickups scheduled for that afternoon and needed to meet the clients in the cellblock and represent them at their initial bail hearings. I talked one of our investigators into coming over that evening to sit for Stephen.

I don't recall exactly how it started. These things between couples have a way of simmering until any little thing triggers the boil. I had taken Margaret to eat at the Iron Gate Inn on N Street, and because the night was mild, we were strolling through Dupont Circle, planning to catch a cab back to Georgetown. She wanted to stop for coffee at the Afterwords Café. We sat outside to enjoy the night air. I remember an unshaven old man shuffling up the sidewalk in a dirty trench coat, hunched over, holding something close to his chest, cupped in his gnarled hands. He stopped before us, making small, intermittent throaty sounds, like the low hiss of an animal sending out a warning. We saw striding toward him a stylishly dressed woman, attractive, aristocratic, restraining a black and tan Doberman pinscher on a leash. The dog was large and tugged ahead. When the woman approached the old man, the dog started to growl and bare its teeth. That was when the man suddenly thrust out in front of him a live mouse or rat, a rodent of some kind gripped in his fingers, and took several quick, aggressive steps toward the dog, spitting out unintelligible sounds in a threatening tone. The dog turned, whimpering and whining, and began dragging its owner back where they had come. The woman, barely able to hold on to the leash, was yanked back up the block and lost a shoe in the process.

Margaret and I were both jolted by the old man as well, though he soon wandered off. But the incident impressed me and I began remarking on the old man's unexpected show of aggression, on his surprise attack, and how potent it was. "How can I use that at work?" I wondered aloud. "How can I take that lesson into the courtroom?"

This set Margaret off. I know there were underlying tensions and that my reference to work was just the detonator for what was smoldering, but she wouldn't quit. She resented my work, my hours, my commitment to my clients, my failure to be the husband and father she and Stephen needed. She wanted to quit as a salesclerk, to be home with Stephen, but felt impoverished. We took a cab back home, hardly speaking and then spent hours at the kitchen table trying to talk things through. I'd made a three-year commitment to the agency, I reminded her, and had only been there for two. I couldn't break that commitment, not in my first job as a professional. But she was angry, unyielding. As the discussion ensued, she just became quieter and finally completely unresponsive. Around midnight, when I was past tired, she told me maybe she just needed a break. She would take Stephen for a month to her parents, she said. They had recently moved to Jacksonville, Florida, where the navy had posted her father. The warm climate will be restful, she said.

"What about Sears?" I said.

"I hate that place," she answered.

I started to protest again when she held up her hand. "I've made up my mind," she finished. When I returned to our apartment from work the next evening, she was gone. I called that night, but her parents said she was worn out from the long drive and sleeping. When I finally talked to her, she seemed distant, unresponsive. We spoke a few times over the following three weeks, but she didn't improve. Then her letter arrived. She was not coming home.

7

EASTON, MARYLAND, IS NO LONGER the small town I remember. When I was in high school, we'd spend our afternoons at Trader's Drug Store on Washington Street across from the County Seat. The long soda counter could accommodate twelve, and Trader's mixed its own Cokes at the soda fountain and made its own lemonade. Next to Trader's stood Shannahan and Wrightsons, the town's hardware and marine center. Its brick facade was always freshly scrubbed, clean and red. Through its display windows new boats on shiny aluminum trailers glistened white. Mr. Farnsworth's men's clothing store, Blazers, was next on the block. Farnsworth often sat outside his entrance on a wicker chair, greeting us as we passed. Rowens, the stationery store and bookstore was adjacent to Farnsworth's building. The barbershop and a specialty gift shop completed the block. Around the corner was the pool hall and bank, and down Dover Street was Reed's Diner and beyond that the Tidewater Inn. Many of the girls from school worked in these shops in the afternoon and on weekends. After school the sidewalks were packed. You pretty much knew that you would run into anyone you wanted to in town. At night, once we had our driver's licenses, we would hang out at the Tastee-Freez on the highway. The girls would come by, cruising, in and out of the parking lot. It was like a dance without the dance hall. The ones already out of school would go to the Dover Street Tavern. We'd hang around outside the tavern and older friends would bring us out six-packs. There were some good times then, at least until my father turned sick.

Trying to stem a growing despair, I decide to drive toward town, recklessly searching for this Easton in my mind. I take the bypass and try to cut through a sprawling mall. The first mall leads into a second. There's a Wal-Mart and a Rite Aid. Increasingly panicked, I have trouble finding the exit to the parking lot. Malls encircle every road.

It's thinking about Margaret, and then about Linda Morrison, I'm sure, that has sent me spiraling down. After Margaret, another lifetime after, I fell for Linda Morrison—a companion, a friend, and then lover. We had some fine years together. It was those last words of Linda, though, that cut through. After she'd told me she'd turned and testified against me in the grand jury, after she had told me that I'd lost it all. "They're coming for you, Jack," she'd said. "They want you bad. And, God, why did I listen to you . . . Trust you to advise me . . . My attorney is preparing suit papers. You better have insurance. Plenty of it. You better find a good lawyer too. A better lawyer than you were to me. One who's not always trying to fuck his client . . ."

Escaping the malls, I finally reach the town center. I realize first that the drugstore is gone, then that most of the other stores are gone as well, even the tavern. Several buildings are empty with FOR RENT signs nailed to their facades. I drive into the lot adjacent to the Tidewater Inn and enter, seeking the bar. There's a solitary customer in its large, dim enclosure. I sit a few stools over from him, but he never speaks or acknowledges my presence. The bartender takes my order and pours out a drink while whispering on a cell phone. I gulp down a Dewar's and take a sedative, then return to the car and drive back toward Boxmoor.

I SEEM BENT ON thinking back. Flashing through the past. Robberies, burglaries, domestic assaults, rape. Things I learned, took from lectures, watching other lawyers in court, hard-earned experiences from trials gone awry.

As an eager initiate, I believed that by honing my faculties, my intuition, I could come to read a person, to discern the hidden bias, to even tell the truth from the lie, the dissembler from the honest witness. I cultivated my ability to study a face, to listen, to hear the tremor in an answer, to detect the unnatural hesitation, the nervous blink, the eyes seeking avoidance. I was on fire with ambition and confidence. But the lessons filtered down.

During jury selection in a robbery case, a frail, elderly black woman, dressed for church, was called to the bench for questioning. She walked slowly, stiff with arthritis. Nearing the bench she tripped on the court reporter's wire and would have fallen if I hadn't lunged to catch her. She thanked me over and over, patting my hand. She was genuinely grateful. For some reason the prosecutor left her on the panel. During the trial, each time I looked her way, she smiled. I presented a strong alibi defense. As I argued my summation she kept nodding her head at me. When I'd emphasize a point I could read her lips whispering the word *amen.* I knew, at least, I had one vote secured. The jurors, though, deliberated for three days without reaching a unanimous verdict. The marshal reported hearing shouting from the jury room, but they remained dead-locked. The judge polled them before ordering a retrial. The split was eleven to one for acquittal. Only the old lady held out against me.

It was harsh schooling, but not without its compensation. As Asa drummed into me, I didn't need to be a mind reader. And I was not there to discern the truth, but to defend. To root out the frailty, the flaw, the blemish in the prosecutor's case. To zealously champion my client. I refocused, working to master the law of evidence, criminal procedure, cross-examination, strategies on how to discredit a prosecution witness, the pros-ecutor's case. We were taught and I learned well to turn every rule to our advantage—to make the most of every fact, every event. And as I progressed, I showed all the instincts. Everyone acknowledged this. I had the gift.

We learned to file pretrial motions and ask the court for ev-identiary hearings on the motions. Often the motions were near frivolous and had no chance of being granted. But through the evidentiary hearings, held before the jurors were selected, we might gain insight into the government's case, see how the witnesses looked, reacted. We filed motions to suppress evidence as the fruit of illegal searches and the police officers involved would have to testify. We filed motions to suppress identifications, claiming the police techniques were unduly suggestive and violated constitutional rights. This would give us a pretrial run at examining the prosecution witness. We did this looking for inconsistencies, traces of uncertainty, anything in which to drive a wedge of misgiving, of doubt.

Rape is one of the most serious felonies. People were once hanged for rape. Now rapists, if convicted, are given long prison sentences. In my first rape case, T-Bone admitted from the beginning, to me at least, that he had enjoyed intercourse with the complaining witness in his car under the Roosevelt Bridge. But, he claimed, she was a prostitute who had agreed to the sex and then gotten angry in a disagreement over how much money he was supposed to pay her. This was her way of getting back. The woman, on the other hand, swore out a warrant that he had offered her a ride home from a bar and then taken her under the bridge and forced her at gunpoint to have sex. That he had raped her.

Even though T-Bone admitted to me that the sex had occurred, I filed a motion to suppress the identification of him, trying once again to turn every rule to my advantage.

T-Bone had been picked up the same night as the alleged offense, and the complainant had identified him while he was seated in a patrol car. I knew the judge wouldn't suppress the ID, but I was entitled to contest it, and I hoped to learn something, to see and gauge the victim on the witness stand. The hearing was held the day before the actual trial started. I called the victim to the stand and made her go over the crime: how well she'd seen the face of her assailant, the lighting conditions, the amount of time she was with her assailant, and so forth. Responding to my questions, she described the entire incident, calmly, quietly, quite composed, and with convincing certainty. She worried me. The case really came down to which witness the jury would believe, and she was very credible.

At trial, however, with twelve jurors seated in the box and with a courtroom full of people and with the atmosphere charged and thick with drama, her testimony was different. This time a female prosecutor directed her testimony. She asked the witness questions that were of a more personal nature, questions designed to elicit emotional responses, questions about how it felt to be subjected to sodomy at gunpoint, about her fear, about what was going through her mind, and gradually the young woman on the stand began to break down and sob as she testified. The judge had to find a box of Kleenex, and there were long pauses while the witness tried to compose herself. When she finished her direct testimony, there was a silence in the room.

I stood up to cross-examine her. My job was to step into T-Bone's shoes. To fight for his freedom, to fight for his life.

"Miss," I said. My voice was soft, at first, controlled. "You testified yesterday, did you not, in this very courtroom, in a pretrial hearing, before this same judge?"

She wiped her eyes and nodded her assent.

"I need you to answer yes or no for the jury and for the record, please." I tried to remain gentle in my tone.

"Yes." Her voice was still thick and breaking, her eyes glistening.

"This same judge was on the bench, and the prosecutor,

Ms. Fentress, was here in the courtroom, and my client was here next to me, and I was here, as well, in this courtroom. Is that correct?"

She nodded her head again, and answered, "Yes."

"And this was just yesterday afternoon?"

"True."

"In fact"—I pointed into the gallery where numerous spectators sat, including her mother and brother, who had watched the day before—"there were people seated in the well of the courtroom yesterday as well?"

"Yes."

"The only real difference between yesterday and today is that the jurors were not here yesterday but are here today?"

At this point the prosecutor objected, on relevancy grounds, though still not sure where I was leading, but the judge overruled the objection, permitting me to continue.

"And yesterday, in this courtroom, before this same judge, you testified, just as today, about what happened to you under the Roosevelt Bridge and how you were able to see and identify my client, is that correct?" I spoke more firmly.

"Yes," she answered, and her tone now seemed to lose some of its certainty.

I took a breath and slowly, deliberately delivered the next question. "But yesterday, when the jury wasn't here to watch you perform, you testified during a two-hour hearing about everything that you claim happened to you that fateful day, everything you have testified to here today, but with the jury not here, you did not shed one tear, you did not need one Kleenex, you did not cry, you did not weep, you did not sob, not once, not one time, is that not true?"

The witness froze. She swallowed, looking toward the prosecutor for help, who waited too long but finally objected. The judge paused and grimaced but overruled the objection and instructed the witness to answer. I repeated my question again for emphasis. "Not one tear? Not one Kleenex? Not until the jury was here to watch you?"

She couldn't answer. I asked her then how much time she had spent with the prosecutor in preparing her performance for today, and the prosecutor objected to the word *performance*. So I repeated the question substituting the word *testimony* for *performance* and emphasizing it. I finished by asking her a rhetorical question about acting school. I sensed we'd won. I silently thanked that frivolous pretrial motion for saving my client.

I would, of course, take more pride in that victory if it weren't for what happened two years later, after I'd left the agency. I ran into T-Bone. He was down at the courthouse on another charge —another sex offense. When he saw me he rushed over, thanking me again for saving him before, complimenting me, and inquiring whether I could take over this new case he had. I told him, no, that it was out of the question. I explained to him that I had left the public defender's office and gave him the excuse that I was doing very little criminal work. He started to argue, but when he saw I wouldn't change my mind, he made the comment over his shoulder as he walked off. I don't recall his words exactly. Something about enjoying that girl under the Roosevelt Bridge. And how the gun wasn't even loaded, which of course, she didn't know. He winked at me, as if I'd been in on it all along.

Sure, this throttled me back some. But over the next several days I worked the argument through in my head, employing, of course, the Socratic method. Wasn't our system a good one? Doesn't it require lawyers with equal training, equal skill, to level the playing field, to enable the system to work? And mustn't those lawyers discipline themselves to suspend their own judgments? To zealously represent their clients?

For the system to work, I reminded myself, the lawyers are duty bound to play their part, to suppress their individual consciences. This is required. But can we do this without consequence to ourselves?

8

HERE AT BOXMOOR I TRY to nap when I can. This afternoon I nod off briefly but wake up to sirens on the road. I jump from the sofa and hurry out the back, down to the bushes along the riverbank, and hide there, watching. The screech of the sirens gets louder, then recedes. A boy, maybe ten, is fishing two docks down and sees me. I wave to him, like everything is normal. He hesitates but waves in return. I convince myself I'm still okay.

AGITATED, UNCERTAIN OF my next move, wishing for a key, a way out, thinking of the wet suit, hoping that distance, a change of scenery, anything might bolster me, I drive down

Route 50, bypassing the town of Easton, on past Trappe, and over the Choptank River Bridge into Cambridge. I can't out-race the tightening inside. I walk around in the old part of town. Many of the buildings are boarded up. Cambridge always was worse off than Easton. Less affluent, with little economy, a smattering of struggling poultry and factory workers, water-men, and unemployed, remembered, if at all, for starting the '68 summer race riots, leading to Watts and Detroit. Not much has changed here since.

On Dorchester Street, I find the dive shop. A second-story room with hardly any inventory. All it has is a wet-suit vest, but I purchase it, figuring it might have to suffice. On the way back I stop off at the depot. Muddy isn't there, but Agnes rings up my groceries and alcohol. She's as talkative as ever. I ask her af-ter a while about the girl and mention that on my last visit she'd seemed curious about my appearance in some way. That she'd surprised me by asking my age. A strange question, I suggest.

Agnes turns thoughtful for a moment.

"Well, how old *are* you?" she asks.

"Near fifty," I say.

"Uh huh," Agnes answers, studying me herself. "Figures." She shakes her head back and forth. "Well, I suppose there's no harm in anyone knowing, really. See, she's a troubled girl, mister. Not that you can blame her. Her father, he was her only parent. Her mother passed when she was a baby. Her fa-ther, well, he was killed down there in Central America. Was where he shouldn't a been, is all. Stickin' his nose where it don't belong. I think he'd a been about fifty, now. You favor him some." Agnes pauses, giving off a deep sigh. "A car blew up," she goes on. "He was in it. Worse part is, she was there. Saw it all happen."

"When was this?" I ask.

"Been ten years or so," she responds.

"I'm sorry."

"Yeah." Agnes clucks her tongue.

"Did you raise her?" I ask.

"My cousin, Ruth, may she rest in peace. Looked after her for a few years, or tried to, until Muddy turned eighteen. The Good Lord took Ruth soon after. Sudden, you know, her heart it was. But Ruth tried to help that child. In every way. Early on Muddy just withdrew. Never would speak about it, far as I know. Hardly even to the counselors Ruthy got. Just closed up." Agnes lowers her head and confides. "They put her on medication. She's supposed to take it still, though I doubt she does."

I nod, which Agnes seems to take as encouragement.

"Yes," she says. "Poor dear."

"Must've been hard," I say.

Agnes bobs her head, agreeing. "Yes, and course after Ruthy passed, Muddy started in where her father left off. Got herself arrested. Mixed up with them union people. Scoffing at the law. Twice. Don't know how all that began. It did seem to bring her round some. That and the river." Agnes takes a handkerchief out of the cash register drawer, turns away and blows her nose. "Thank the Lord for the river," she says, sniffling. She turns back. "Muddy's a tomboy of sorts, if you haven't noticed. She's strong-willed. Like her daddy. She's never really been a normal child, but she does seem to manage."

"She live with you?"

"She lives just outside Tilghman, in a cottage on the point off Dun Cove. It was her father's. Works here three days a week. She got some money from her father's in-surance. Fends for herself, mostly."

Dun Cove, I recall from the chart on the wall, is across and just out the river from Boxmoor. I wonder if I can see her house from my dock. "Funny name for a young woman," I remark.

"Her father gave her the nickname. 'Cause as a child she was always in the river. Always comin' home covered in river muck. Her real name's Susannah. Susannah Blair. But she won't answer to it."

After wiping her nose again, and dabbing at her face, Agnes returns the rag to where the twenties are stacked in the cash drawer. "I do go on," she whispers. "Sorry."

"I sympathize," I say. I have the urge to tell Agnes about my own father, about how I lost him in high school from a series of strokes, how he raised me, after my mother died from breast cancer when I was still a little boy. Whenever I think of him, I always see him from that one photograph I have, taken in his prime—unshaven, grinning astride a farm horse, a trophy buck across the pommel of his saddle, holding a snow goose with an arrow through the breast in his hand, his bow strung across his shoulder. Several of his burly friends stand at his horse's side with bottles of Schlitz beer in their hands. People said he was the best bow man in the county. I start to speak, to tell her, but she's turned away and I stop myself and hold back.

Agnes pulls two paper bags out from an underneath shelf. She puts my scotch in one and the groceries into another, carefully, taking her time. I pay her and she gives me my change.

"You don't say much, do you?" she quips, eyeing me. "I mean about yourself."

"Just taking a little break," I answer. "Taking some quiet time."

"How's the fishing been?" she then asks. "Them alewives work all right?"

"Oh sure," I answer her. "Thanks. I caught a mess of rock using those alewives."

Agnes's face begins to cloud. "How many?" she asks.

"How many what?"

"Rock did you catch?"

I'm suddenly unsure how to respond. "Half dozen or so," I answer.

"How big?"

"All over a pound," I make up, trying to cover. "Nice ones." I'm trying to smile.

"I mean, how long were they?"

"Twelve, fifteen inches. Good size."

Agnes crosses her arms, frowning. "State's been working for years to bring the rock back. It's been a hardship all around here. Two's the limit, you know. And a keeper's got to be over eighteen inches."

I begin nervously apologizing, indicating that I hadn't realized there were such regulations.

Agnes places her hands on the countertop. "I bet you just didn't know, did you? Bet you don't have no permit, neither."

"No," I admit.

She shakes her head. "Fishing without a permit. Over the limit. Keeping small fry. That's about five hundred dollars a fish in fines, mister. If you got caught." She pushes my grocery bags aside. "But you seem a decent sort. So what I'll do, this one time, is forget you told me this and sell you a permit. You get a book of rules with it so you'll know better." She opens a drawer from under the counter and pulls out an application form. "I see you got D.C. plates on that car," she says, squinting through the glass doors. "Needs a wash too, it does. Bet that's an expensive car, ain't it?" She taps on the paper. "Here's an out-of-state permit application. It's only fourteen dollars. Nothin' for a man with a car like that."

"Hold on," I stammer.

"What? Now mister, you need a permit. I don't plan to report you or nothin' long as you get one. Like I said, with the permit you'll get a booklet so you'll know better as to size and limits and such. Now what's your name? And I'll need to see your driver's license."

"I hadn't thought about a fishing permit," I say hesitantly. "I'm not sure I want . . ."

"Apparently not. But it is the law, mister." Her tone is turning slightly suspicious. "Now you gonna give me your driver's license?"

I try to stay calm. Even with my license and knowing my identity, Agnes would have no reason to be aware of a lawyer's crimes in Washington. I take the license from my wallet and hand it to her. She looks at it and reads my name. "Nice to meet you, Jack Stanton," she says. She holds out her hand and we shake. Then she takes the application and starts walking toward the back with both it and my license in hand.

"Where are you going?" I quickly ask.

"I've got a scanner in the back. It's all new and computerized now. Hooked up to the state system. I just run your license through and it goes right into the state computer and then spits out your permit."

"I've changed my mind," I blurt out. "I'll get it later. I'm too busy now." I approach and reach to take the license from her, but she pulls it back. "What are you so busy about?" She waits for me to reply. "We take our fishing regulations serious." She looks past me. "You best decide quick there, mister. Here comes Billy Solomon."

I turn to see a state trooper cruiser pull into the parking lot. I mumble something about having given up fishing. That I was leaving soon. I snatch my driver's license from her hand. She startles, like I've slapped her. I leave hurriedly, passing the trooper as I exit out the store. As I pull away, I see Agnes at the door with him, talking rapidly, pointing at my car. In my rear-view mirror I watch as the trooper steps to his vehicle and reaches through his open window for his radio microphone.

No one knows where I live. Even so, my mouth has gone bone dry. If the trooper calls in my name, the information about my warrant will come up. Not only my identity, but my general location will be known. I quickly pull off Bozman Road onto a side lane that winds around out of sight, park, and walk back to where I can look through some bushes. A few minutes later my worst fears come true. The cruiser speeds by, its emergency lights on, heading down the peninsula in the direction I've come. The sun has begun to set, so I decide to wait until the cruiser returns or at least until dark. Two more cruisers come after. I stay there, huddled in the bushes for a good half hour, but they don't come back. Afraid to risk driving, I leave the car and groceries, slip on the vest, grab the scotch, and start along the riverbank toward Boxmoor. It's a mile-plus walk, I'm guessing. I'll retrieve the car in the morning if it isn't discovered. My heart is still beating fast as I reach the river. The going is more rugged than I expected. I climb several fences and squeeze through hedges and try to be very quiet when I cut through some yards. I can see families in their warm houses, a mother fixing supper, some children laughing and running on a back porch. I sit for a while on a grass bank, catching my breath. Out on the water the channel buoys pulse their timed beacons, the reds just offshore and the greens across the expanse, as though harbingers of my future, soft and beckoning. The river night is loose around me like a comforter, and on the water swans float in the current, luminous under the moon, stately. I wonder at their poise and at my own calm, there breathing in the river's mist, and I seem far away and almost separate from the swirling thoughts that again begin to pulse through my mind.

Safely back, I pour a full glass of whiskey and rock on the dark porch, resting and wondering at myself. I admit it's strange, for example, that after so many years of lawyering, of learning to turn any ambiguity to advantage, when faced with my own indictment I find the prospect of participating in the charade that would be my trial sickening. There's something in me that revolts. I've developed a psychic allergy. I'd prefer almost any course to the shame of standing trial, of having to participate again, but this time as the central actor, in all the dissembling and manipulation. And then there's Linda Morrison. Just the thought of her now undermines me. The specter of her testifying against me is too much.

I used to remind my private practice clients that the trial of a matter is an entirely different phenomenon from the underlying event itself. The trial and its outcome have no bearing on what actually occurred. If the light was green, a jury saying it was red doesn't change the fact that it was green. I note this now for myself. What's done is done. A trial can't help me.

Rather, it's this remembering that seems to matter. Maybe

by remembering I can find some peace. I mean where, really, did I start to slide? Wouldn't any lawyer have camouflaged his client's habit of sniffling? Assisted his client's alibi witnesses to remember accurately, consistently? Turned the strategy to emotionally inflame the jury in a rape case against the prosecutor? These are not actions that are indictable or even suspect. And there were so many good outcomes, so much that we accomplished that anyone would agree was right.

MY FIRST YEAR at the agency I mostly worked with juveniles accused of crimes. This, truly, was God's work. When they were clearly guilty, when their chances of beating a rap were slim, we worked to find them alternative programs, inpatient drug centers, foster homes, social workers, psychiatric treatment, anything to avoid losing them to the youth detention centers, the kid jails, Maple Glen, the Receiving Home, Cedar Knoll. Harry was obsessed with the kids and had a way with them. He used to give them nicknames that sometimes they'd take on as their own. Pepperpot. Bluecat. Lifeboat. He even arranged for one boy, twelve years old, to go to a camp in the mountains near Cumberland Gap. Harry used that southern twang of his to talk a local Baptist church into funding it. The boy called Harry after a week. The child was amazed. It seemed like a wonderland to him. He had never seen a mountain before, or a rabbit.

On the whole, though, resources for juveniles were scarce. Of all the constituents of the city, the lost children moving toward crime were the most neglected. Adult inmates had programs, rehabilitation classes, counselors, even at Lorton. There was a carpenter's shop and an electric plant to work in. They manufactured the city's license plates and could earn pay. There was a library and classes, even work-release programs. But at the child prisons, where the twelve- and fourteen-year-olds were housed at ages when they were still susceptible to positive influence, there was nothing. Early on, we all were discouraged at the horrors the kid jails presented. A twelve-year-old sent to one for any length of time was almost certain to come out more set on crime, more vicious, than when he went in. This fact was confirmed again and again as we learned the histories of our adult clients. Story after story bore out this sad truth.

I remember an interview I had with Ernie Booth, one of the more notorious prisoners in the federal system, who had lived in Washington, D.C., before his lockdown. I saw him at the pen in Marion, Illinois. I was writing a research paper on recidivism for a national bar organization. He had been transferred out of Lorton because he had been considered responsible for the worst riot in the prison's history, though the inside truth was that he didn't start the riot, he ended it. With one word. Nearly eighty maximum-security inmates had taken five prison guards hostage. The guards were blindfolded and forced to kneel on the edge of the third tier balcony, ready to be pushed to their deaths three stories below, when after nearly twenty hours of negotiations Booth asked for his lawyer, Asa Cole. Asa, of course, ignoring the warnings of the authorities on the scene, agreed to walk into that snake pit. Booth asked Asa to obtain a guarantee from the police surrounding the prison that there would be no physical reprisals if the inmates surrendered. When Asa returned with a verbal promise to that effect, Booth shouted to the other inmates that it was over. He ordered the inmates to get back to their cells. Some grumbled. But eventually all went. He was feared that much, even by the strongest of the prisoners. Booth was serving consecutive life sentences for three murder convictions. Asa provided me with a letter of introduction to take to Marion. I had taped the interview and later pasted some of the transcription into my journal to keep some of what Booth told me. I drag the journals out and look for it:

Entry—Marion Federal Correctional Institution—
March 27, 1981

I was ten years old the first time I was ever arrested . . . And I was sent to the Receiving Home for Children on Mount Olivett Road in Washington, D.C., and then to Maple Glen where I stayed nearly two years . . . You know, I've marched right up the line since then. From Maple Glen to Cedar Knoll to Oak Hill to the Youth Center to Lorton, and now I'm in the federal system. I ain't missed nowhere. Like grammar school to high school to college. I went the only way I could go. Least once I started at age ten at Maple Glen . . .

What you are taught in juvenile institutions is that the weaker always got crushed. It was a known fact. Over at the Receiving Home you couldn't eat. I mean you wouldn't even be left with toast, if you couldn't fight. They'd take all your food, even your toast in the morning. We used to have buttered toast, and we used to call them slabs. And you had to rumble to eat. You had to be violent to survive. That is what I learned from age ten on . . .

I remember, in Washington at that time, after about seven or eight at night, white people that came into our neighborhood was considered as prey. They would come up to buy drugs or solicit prostitutions, and they would come and park their cars, and we would break into their cars and steal from them. As far as we were concerned, we wasn't doing anything wrong because they came to us, to our neighborhood. We weren't in their neighborhood or nothing like that. If we'd see a white man go into a tourist home with a black woman and with his car there, we'd take his tires or his battery, and we could make money off this. There was a garage and the guy used to give us ten dollars for every battery that we'd bring him. That's how I got started. But I got busted. And my old man was gone and never came for me, so I went to the Receiving Home, and from there to Maple Glen, and that's when my trouble really began . . .

My first day at Maple Glen, in a little joint known as Post Orientation, which was supposed to be more protected, I had just gotten a plate of supper when two dudes came across the floor and one of them just walked up to me and he just punched me in the face and then took my food. No "Hi" or "Can I share your supper?" or anything. As soon as he got close he just cracked me in the face. I was ten years old, and I was new there. I was on the ground just bleeding all over. He kicked me twice, in the groin and belly, before walking away. I just lay there, but I was waiting until supper was finished. And when they started to walk back toward their cottages the two dudes split up and I had gotten up and followed the one that had punched me. And so there was some big rocks around the blacktop, big like baseballs, and I just picked one up and ran after him. I caught him in the vestibule and I just started hitting him with the rock, all over, as hard as I could. And I was really cracking him good with that rock, until a counselor dragged me off him. And the next morning, nobody bothered my breakfast. But for two years, this is what I learned, and this is what I did. To make sure that everyone thought I was crazy. That I was more violent than the next guy. And so when I got out, finally I was ready. Ready to go on to the next level. That was when I found my father's sawed-off ... I ended up shooting a lot of people with it ...

9

I'VE PUT THE JOURNALS BACK. I am sitting on the wooden bench out on the dock thinking about Booth and how good the work to keep juveniles out of prison used to feel. The moon is up. I'm remembering how for the juveniles especially I was willing to go to the brink of the crevice, to that dull, unsharpened edge where the ethical and the unethical meet.

All at once I realize that circling red emergency lights are reflecting in the treetops from around the front of the house. Then I see the beams of flashlights through the screened side porch. There are three of them hunting for clues. I figure they are state troopers, though I know they are just as likely Morgan Langrell's feds.

They circle the house, shining their lights through the windows as I lower myself down the dock steps and into the water. I can see their lights and feet through the wharf planking as they come halfway out the dock. Their beams illuminate nothing but wooden piles and water. They turn and retrace their steps.

Afterward, I shower in the dark, shivering from both fear and cold, and dry myself with a slipcover stripped from one of the couches. Wrapping myself in the drape I use for a blanket, I gather myself on the wicker rocker off the porch landing, my hand shaking as I pour out my first glass. I down the pills that bring the rise and rush of dulling relief. I wake several times, starting up, hearing noises, cowering in the dark, afraid. Finally I move inside to the couch. My dreams are disjointed, disquieting, a parade of faces, a steady stream from my past—clients mostly, young and old—clients for whom I had taken up the gauntlet, whose worlds I'd entered, trying to alter what the fates and base poverty had decreed. In many of those cases I failed. Though, as Asa always argued, just having a competent, passionate lawyer, even one time, maybe meant something.

I heat my last can of beans for breakfast. The food tastes stale, of paper and tin. I eat for the nourishment, washing down each bite with sips of black coffee. My time, I know, is running short. I'm tired, when what I need is strength. While last night I seem to have escaped detection, I know they won't quit. They'll close the net. I have to go back for my car. It's my only way out. I'll go this evening, after dusk, when it's near dark and safer. As I lie on the bed, though, I am haunted by a face from long past. A face from my last trial that last year at the agency. Another one I've never exorcised from my consciousness. The ghostly face isn't that of a client but of a victim, an accuser. The accuser in the Sherman Allen case. The accuser's name was Wilson Stark. Sherman Allen, the accused, was a juvenile, a kid just fifteen years old.

IN THE EARLY 1980s there were areas in D.C. that had been zones of neglect for years but that were starting to revive. Tax incentives were offered to those who would buy in these neighborhoods and renovate. This process of gentrification was encouraged by the local government and mayor. It was therefore not only a tragedy but a public relations setback for the city when the wife of a young white engineer, who with her husband had bought and begun to refurbish a townhouse in a poor black area off Sheridan Circle, was shot and killed in her own living room on New Year's Day 1982 during a burglary attempt by three young men.

Citywide the newspapers headlined the crime, and the media went haywire. Reporters followed around the grief-stricken widower. Residents of the neighborhood were interviewed. Fingers were pointed at the cops for providing inadequate protection to the citizenry. The chief of police deployed the city's entire homicide unit to solve the crime. Shakedowns occurred on every street corner. Informants were collared and threatened, but evidence was scarce. There was little to go on, even as the outcry for retribution, at least from the affluent side of town, continued.

The doorbell of Wilson Stark's home had rung around dusk while he and his wife were in the back of their townhouse, in their kitchen, celebrating a New Year's Day dinner together. Wilson Stark had gotten up and gone to the door. He had opened it just a crack, glimpsing three black faces on his stoop, when he simultaneously felt pressure pushing the door toward him. He was a large man, though, strong, with a hockey player's legs and quick reflexes, and he reacted by pushing back and leveraging his weight behind the door and yelling for his wife to call the police. The door was open just enough for one of the assailants to fit his hand through. As Stark's wife came from the back room to help her husband, one hand did slide through. It held a small caliber pistol. Stark saw the gun and pushed harder jamming the door against the man's arm. The gun blindly went off. The assailants fled. The one bullet tore into Mrs. Stark's liver. By the time the medics arrived she was dead.

For three weeks, despite their efforts, the police hadn't made an arrest. Stark had worked with police sketch artists, and composite drawings had been distributed of the faces Stark remembered seeing, but they were unfamiliar to both the detectives and the hood boys the police had browbeaten for information. Another week passed. There were no clues. Not until Stark, on a cold Saturday in January, around three in the afternoon, while staring out his front window saw a familiar black boy walk down the sidewalk and go into a house across the street. He claimed to recognize the youth as one of the assailants on his front porch and called the police. Sherman Allen, age fifteen, who lived directly across the street with his mother and siblings, was arrested. He was charged with first-degree felony murder. Under the law, juveniles arrested for crimes were supposed to have their identities kept private, but the media got a tip and the news was everywhere. Asa called me at home. He wanted me to lead the defense. He'd back me up, he said.

When we first met Sherman we began by talking to him about ourselves, trying to assure him that we could be trusted. He was visibly frightened, and his limp hand shook when I took it. Acne blistered around his chin and perspiration oozed from his face. He was innocent, he murmured, his soft voice trembling. He just couldn't remember where he was that day. He'd told the police the same thing. It was nearly a month before. He was probably home, he said. We tried to help him take his memory back in time, remembering first Christmas Day, then New Year's Day. He was confused, uncertain. We spent all afternoon with him. Toward the end of our interview he wanted to know if he could ask one question. If we would keep it private. I assured him we would. "Just what if," he began. "I ain't sayin' it's true, cause it ain't, but just what if them guys axed me to go with 'em and never told me there was no gun, an' I was jess standin' there? Would that be a crime?" Asa explained to him the law. That anyone who participated, no matter how minimally, was legally guilty of the murder. I also told him that if he was involved and was willing to cooperate with the police and testify against the others involved we could probably get him a light sentence, maybe even get him a juvenile disposition. He shuddered the length of his body when I said this, and he turned his eyes away. "I un'erstan' what you're sayin'," he mumbled. "No one'd live who tried to do that. Not in our neighborhood. Anyway, I'd heard that was the story some boy over Fulton Street was sayin'. As for me I was home with my mother." He raised his head up and his eyes were squeezed shut, and then he opened them. "It's comin' back. I'm sure of it. I was home with her. Will you tell her to come and see me quick?"

We said we would. That was when he told us that he trusted us. He spoke tentatively, with an inward gaze, almost vacant. He fumbled for the words to say that he felt we would do right by him. "You two is my champions," he finished in a whisper. "My two champions."

Did this exchange give me pause? I don't recall that it did. Certainly not at that time. I knew my job by then. And I knew what would happen to Sherman Allen if he ratted out other stick-up boys in the neighborhood, and I knew where he would go if convicted. He'd end up as bad as they could make him, like Booth. And I didn't look on what he said as even close to a confession. It was just a question. One he was entitled to ask. He was no more than a scared kid.

That night, at home, I suddenly missed Margaret and Stephen. Even though Margaret was divorcing me, I ached for them both. My home seemed sterile, unfriendly. Dirty dishes were piled up. The refrigerator was empty. I called down to Florida. Margaret and I usually talked every month or so, but it had been several since I'd spoken to her last. I tried to tell her about the case. She wasn't interested. She kept interrupting me. She had news, she told me. But then she grew vague. Stephen was asleep and I shouldn't call so late, she scolded. She had a boyfriend, she finally blurted out. Someone serious. She said she'd write me about him. Then she hung up.

IMPORTANT TO ASA and me, none of the descriptions Wilson Stark had given to the police, nor the composite drawings that had been painstakingly sketched at his direction as similar to the assailants, resembled Sherman. And Sherman's mother, after she had visited him in the detention center, backed him up. He was home all New Year's Day. His sisters would swear to it as well. Given all the information before us, it seemed likely that Stark had perhaps recognized him from the street or from the neighborhood, but not from being on his front porch the night of the murder.

All of this, however, was counterbalanced by Wilson Stark's certitude. He had identified Sherman with no prompting from anyone. After Sherman was arrested Stark identified him again from a police lineup. He told the media in a press conference that he would never forget that face as long as he lived. It was the same face he saw on his front stoop that terrible day. Sherman Allen was the one, he swore. There was no doubt.

Morgan Langrell was assigned the case. He was a deputy U.S. attorney by then and he was out for blood. The case was political. It impacted city policy. He had been given the limelight. And he relished, I knew, the prospect of taking me down.

The first thing he did was to file a motion to have Sherman tried as an adult, which meant he would receive a life sentence if convicted. We fought the motion, but the seriousness of the charge justified such a ruling, and the judge, a former prosecutor and colleague of Langrell, granted it. If Sherman was found guilty he would start at Maple Glen, but he would never get out. He'd be transferred up the ladder and would work his way to Lorton. He, like Booth, would have to learn how to be cruel to survive.

Not only was Wilson Stark's certainty about his identification unwavering, but his grief, from the few times I had seen him, was wrenching. He was a large, masculine figure, yet on the several occasions I'd been in his presence, at the hearing on Langrell's motion to try Sherman as an adult and, later, at the bond review hearing we requested, he was visibly in pain, often sobbing uncontrollably. I wasn't sure how I could discredit such a witness. I spent days in the library researching identification cases, pouring over transcribed cross-examinations, reading about memory and perception. By luck as much as anything, I came across an article in the magazine *Psychology Today* that put me on track. It led me to my first real expert witness. The kind civil lawyers are always using in medical cases, the kind who in reality become advocates for the cause.

This one's name was Cyrus Reiser, a psychologist from Florida State University. For several years he had been conducting research on the accuracy of memory and perception under various circumstances. One aspect he had written about was the difficulty inherent in cross-racial identifications. An Irishman, for example, not used to living around Vietnamese, not used to differentiating the subtleties of their features, would have a much more difficult time in identifying a Vietnamese person after a brief encounter than would another Vietnamese. To the Irishman, the oriental eyes, the shape of the nose, the black silky hair, and the short stature would all stand out as remarkable to him, though these very features are common to most Vietnamese and would not provide the basis of distinguishing one Vietnamese person from another. The same was true for white people with limited experience among blacks.

Even more interesting was Reiser's research on a phenomenon known as unconscious transference. This frequently occurs, Reiser explained, when a witness recognizes someone from a previous encounter, but transfers that recognition to a slightly different setting, albeit one close in space and time, thereby mistakenly connecting someone he had actually seen with the wrong situation, confusing the actor and the act. He gave the example of a cashier selling tickets at a race track who is robbed at gunpoint, but who then later identifies not the robber but the customer who bought a ticket just prior to the robbery, convinced that the customer was the robber. The cashier, he explained, unconsciously transferred the face he had recognized, confusing it with that of the person who robbed him moments later. When I described the facts of the Sherman Allen matter to Reiser and explained that both before and after the crime Sherman had lived in the neighborhood, had used the sidewalk in front of Wilson Stark's house, had crossed the street daily, and that Wilson Stark must have seen him there before, Reiser felt confident that this theory might apply. When I informed him that Mr. Stark had grown up in an affluent white Richmond suburb, had attended private school and played hockey throughout college at Amherst, had then attended graduate school at the University of Virginia, and had little experience with black people until moving into the neighborhood two months before, Reiser agreed to come testify as an expert witness. We were beginning to raise the flag of reasonable doubt.

BY THE TIME Sherman Allen turned fifteen, he had pretty much stopped going to school. He was a product of his block, of his world. The only people he knew who owned cars, who got women, and who got respect were the dealers and the strong-arm boys. For Sherman there weren't a lot of roads open to the promised land. His circumstances weren't so different than mine are now, I suppose. Being trapped, I mean. Caught, or nearly so. Just waiting to be taken by the tide. Still, I have been given chances. He never had. And Asa and I didn't want to lose him. Not at fifteen.

Sherman, as the trial neared, claimed to be more and more positive that he was with his family all New Year's Day, and they all were clear and consistent on the details of what they all had done at home. But the alibi was just too perfect. Asa and I were concerned as to how Sherman would look to the jury if he so testified and was then confronted with the repeated statements he made to the police on the day of his arrest that he could not remember where he had been. Reiser gave us the ammunition to challenge the identification. I didn't want to lose the case because Sherman was pretending to remember something that he actually didn't.

In our bond hearing before Judge McCallister, I was not able to get Sherman released altogether from the Children's Center, but the judge did agree to allow me to bring Sherman to our offices, in the custody of a marshal, for preparation each day during the last week before the trial. We set up in our office what we called mock juries. We hired people from the community to serve as jurors, three different panels, and Asa pretended to be the prosecutor. The three mock juries together heard Harry, playing the role of Wilson Stark, testify, and all three heard the family testify to the alibi. We then separated them into three different rooms. With one of the mock juries Sherman did not testify at all. Before the second he testified to the alibi and was essentially destroyed on cross-examination by Asa using Sherman's prior statements given to the police. We asked Sherman to testify before the third mock jury, just as an experiment, that he was innocent of the crime but could not honestly recall where he was at dusk on New Year's Day. We observed

silently as each mock jury deliberated. Only the last one acquitted Sherman of the crime.

Asa and I used this experiment to try to convince Sherman
that his defense would be stronger if he would admit on the
witness stand, just as he had to the police, that he could not
honestly remember where he was when Mrs. Stark was shot. At
first he refused. He was adamant that he was home with his
family. We continued to discuss with him our concerns. We
feared the defense would fail once Langrell Morgan attacked
him with his prior statements. It seemed so clear to us that he
really did not remember, that he was jumping on the alibi
bandwagon, thinking to help himself but doing just the opposite. "But I was home, with my mother," he insisted. Asa explained again how it all would play out. How Langrell would
use his statements, make him out as a liar, make the whole alibi
look concocted. I interrogated him further, made him answer
my questions just as though he were a witness and using the police statements hammered at him just as Langrell would do.
During all this, naturally, I reiterated to him the cautionary
phrase that we had woven throughout our discussion, that we
only wanted him to tell the truth. "It was the truth," I asked,
"wasn't it? The real truth? That you just don't know for sure
where you were when that shot was fired? Isn't that the truth?"

A WEEK BEFORE THE TRIAL was to start I got the letter
from Margaret. She was going to remarry, she wrote, as soon as
the divorce papers came through, to a stockbroker she had
been dating for nearly a year. His name was Traywick. He was
well off, she said. I was sitting on the storage boxes that lined
the broken marble hallway where our offices had been relo-

cated when I opened her letter. I recall the cracked and peeling plaster walls that loomed in an arch and ran down the dirty institutional corridor. Florescent lights beat on my head as I tried to assimilate the words on the page. She was demanding that her husband-to-be be granted the right to adopt Stephen. She wrote that she was certain this was in Stephen's best interests and that if I loved him I would agree. She didn't want to file the papers in court for a contested adoption but would do so if I refused to consent.

When Margaret had first left me, after the Rupert Johnson trial, I'd tried to get her back. I'd called repeatedly and tried to reason with her. She'd say little, but refused to come home. I arranged to leave for a weekend and flew to Jacksonville, booking a room in a nearby motel. Her parents took Stephen for a drive and left us alone. Margaret sat in a window well. The light streaming through the blinds layered her profile in shadowed strips. She wouldn't turn her face toward me, but offered only her silhouette, her manner distant, detached. The room was cool from the air-conditioning. "We made a mistake," she said firmly. "It happens to people. Better to recognize it early, move on." A radio from the kitchen droned on about Reaganomics.

I'd planned a strategic approach on the plane. To lead her where I wanted, to find the threads of affection that I knew remained. To stroke them, breathe new life into them. I began with the day she first felt Stephen kick in her belly. Halfway through she rose from the window without a word and walked into the bathroom, shutting the door. On her return she sat on the couch, her face impassive, a mask of self-control. I asked if she ever thought of our days together. Our honeymoon cruise to the Bahamas. Taking turns feeding Stephen at night and making love in between. Teaching Stephen to walk. "I'm not asking anything from you, Jack," she interrupted. "Not that you have anything. I'll be reasonable about child support. I'm only asking that you leave me be."

I became frustrated, anxious. I went off on a different tack. "Where did this coolness, this . . . disinterest in me start?" I demanded to know. "When? What was so wrong that couldn't be changed?" I implored her to answer my questions. I began to wade into the problem, dissecting our relationship with the blade of logic. She complied, quietly for a while, then lost her patience and grew angry, accusing me again of treating our marriage like a courtroom controversy and her like a witness on the stand. After she had closed the door I remember sitting on her lawn in the Florida swelter, feeling lost, hoping only to say good-bye to Stephen before I left, thinking that Margaret might see us and soften in her attitude toward me. I held Stephen there outside their home while her father stood like a guard. I can see the child to this day. He was sleepy and unaware of much. His curls were blond and fine like eiderdown. I picked him up and he laid his head on my shoulder and shut his eyes. He purred through his dreaming like a kitten. All through the flight back to Washington I tried to stifle my feelings. To hide my face from the passengers next to me and from the flight attendants.

Following that trip I dove ever deeper into my work, trying to drown myself in it. Gradually, I lost interest in anything outside of work at all. I lost my appetite. Eventually, even the idea of getting up and going to the agency seemed pointless, too much. I missed three successive days at the office, curled up and unable to get out of the bed. On one of these a court hearing had been scheduled and the judge called our office to complain. It was Harry who received the call. He saw that something was amiss and came to get me. Harry took one look at me, then used the phone. When he was finished he physically picked me up, under the armpits, and walked me to his car and took me to a psychiatrist friend. I went just four times, but that started me back. Later Harry took me out to a country-and-western store and bought me a pair of leather cowboy boots. "They'll protect you," he told me. "'Cause all good people got to wade through shit sometimes."

I visited Stephen several times more during that first year of separation culminating in Margaret's filing for divorce. The visits seemed awkward, contrived. Each time, Margaret acted put out, as if I were unnecessarily interfering in her life, naively prolonging the pain. Each time, Stephen was surrounded by doting grandparents, by friends of the family, well cared for, oblivious. When I got Margaret's letter, just before the Sherman Allen trial, it had been five months since I had seen him. I should have gone more often. It was just hard with my schedule, my clients, their pressing cases, hearings, trials. There was also the cost of the airfare, the rental car. Public defenders are not paid well, though now that seems a trivial concern. And seeing Margaret was always like picking a scab.

The letter requesting my consent for Stephen's adoption came at a bad time. In addition to being jammed by Sherman's case, there were some thirty other felony cases I was juggling, and Asa and I were leading and losing the agency's battle against the budget cuts and caseload increases that were being imposed on us by the city government. That was the reason for the change in our office space. To conserve funds we had moved to the basement of an abandoned city-owned building. By that time we didn't even have money for file cabinets. Our cases were in cardboard boxes stacked in our offices, covered with the raw plaster dust that drifted off the ceilings. Across the street Morgan Langrell and the rest of the U.S. attorney's office had just moved as well. They were on the fifth floor of a new glass impaneled monolith, new carpet, state-of-the-art equipment. Their secretaries were even furnished with word processors instead of typewriters.

DURING THE COUNTDOWN to Sherman's trial, the newspapers rode the grief of Wilson Stark hard. Pictures of his wife were plastered in every rag, a portion from his funeral oration was published, pictures from their wedding album appeared. As though all of this weren't enough—the fate of Sherman Allen, the budget crisis we were having with the city council, and Margaret's letter—Asa, riding his Harley home from work one Tuesday evening was broadsided by a drunk driver. I learned of the accident while at the office and called Harry. We met at Suburban Hospital. Asa's right leg had been hit directly and mostly severed at the knee. He also had suffered a severe concussion. His parents were en route from Texas. The doctors told us he'd be in surgery and then intensive care all night. Harry and I had been joined by our director and other colleagues. We all stayed, huddling together, until Asa's parents arrived, and then went back to the office. As grieved as we were, we knew we couldn't lose focus on the upcoming trial. The consensus was that since I was lead counsel, there was little chance the judge would grant a continuance. And all the scheduling of experts and witnesses was in place. Harry, to his credit, waded into the breach, agreeing to second chair the case with me.

Between vigils at the hospital we continued to prepare, though Asa, once he was stable, demanded we cease visiting until after the trial. Harry and I made an effort to approach Morgan Langrell to see if he would offer any type of deal worth considering. He made us sit in the waiting room for an hour but eventually saw us. Given my history with Langrell, Harry made the pitch. With a poker face Langrell stopped him before he had finished. He told us he'd allow Sherman to plead to second degree, with a recommended twelve-year sentence, but only if he identified the other perpetrators. Harry asked him to be more compassionate. To remember that Sherman was only fifteen. "Cooperation would mean a death sentence," he added.

Morgan was of Slavic or German ancestry, with striking blue eyes. His shock of hair was turning from ash to a distinguished silver. He used different voices for different audiences. When Harry said this, Morgan rose out of his chair. He coldly regarded me rather than Harry. "How compassionate was your client to Mrs. Stark?" he answered. "She was only twenty-seven herself. She *got* the death sentence. Now she's cold as clay." Ten days later when we met to begin the trial and I held out my hand to him to shake, he looked at it distastefully and walked away.

This time around, Langrell held little back. He had an engineer design a scale model of Wilson Stark's front stoop, front door, and vestibule, and he had two carpenters nail it together inside the courtroom before the jury was selected. The voir dire, or jury selection process, took three days, as many of the prospective panel members knew about the crime and had already formed opinions. Late in the afternoon of the third day, after both sides exercised their allotted peremptory challenges, a jury of seven women and five men were sworn. Nine of the twelve were black, and most had listed on their jury questionnaire their religion as Baptist or Lutheran. When Langrell stood the next morning to present his opening statement to the jurors and began strutting back and forth, glowering and pointing at Sherman Allen, he held in his hand and often pressed to his chest a large white Bible. Toward the end of his presentation, he opened the Bible to Deuteronomy and began in his preacherlike voice to read selected passages about how Moses came down from the mountain with his tablet of the Ten Commandments, about how, at God's direction, he summoned all his people, about how he reiterated to his people the sacred laws of the Lord, and how of all these laws, perhaps the most fundamental one of all, the one indelibly etched on that tablet and ingrained in the conscience of every person no matter what age, the one law essential to life itself, to community, to civilization was, of course, *thou shalt not kill.*

On the fifth day of trial, at the height of the government's case, Wilson Stark took the witness stand in a black suit, dressed for a funeral. He dragged his feet slowly when he walked, like an old man, his face gaunt, drawn. He described with cracking voice his upbringing, the foundations and growth of his love for his wife, which began in high school, their marriage, and their desire to move into, contribute to, build a home in the neighborhood that, in the end, treated them so savagely. He was a compelling witness. He used the constructed doorway to act out what happened that evening. They had built into the porch ceiling a bright light and Stark verified that the wattage was the same as the light that had shone down on the perpetrators that night. The courtroom was without windows. Langrell turned off the courtroom illumination and demonstrated how bright the porch became under that light, surrounded by the dark of the courtroom. It was like watching a play under a spotlight in a theater. Stark eventually became so upset in acting out the events that Langrell had to assist him back to his chair. When asked to identify the defendant, Stark pointed at Sherman Allen and in a cold, certain voice marked him as one of the men. He explained how he had seen him that night, momentarily but clearly under the porch light, and how the face was ingrained in his memory, and he explained his sighting of Sherman several weeks later as providential. When I began to question him he was ready, staring me down like I was the evil one. He ignored my questions but answered to his own agenda.

"It was dusk outside?" I asked him. "Not dark like the prosecutor made this courtroom?"

"The porch light was bright," he answered.

"Did cars on the street have their headlights on?"

"I don't recall," he answered.

"You only saw through the door for a split second, and that was only through a crack in the door?"

"I saw his face clearly."

"And in only a split second, through a crack in the door, on a murky evening, with only an overhead light and the distorting shadows it cast, you saw so well?"

"I'd know the face anywhere. I'll see it forever."

"And while fearful for your life, in the pandemonium of

fighting for your life, there were three different faces to try to look at—or should I say the split-second blur of three faces to look at—and you saw all three clearly through that sliver of an opening and could not possibly be wrong?"

He glared at me but did not answer.

"You admit you were scared?"

"That's why I'll never forget what I saw."

"And afterward, when you tried to recall what you had seen, you were traumatized? Wracked with grief?"

"*I was and I am still, sir,* and that is why I will never forget." He almost spit when he said the word *sir* like it was a curse. "It was *that boy,*" he bayed out, pointing at Sherman. "It was *him.*" I paused, then walked into the well of the courtroom. Wherever I went his eyes followed mine, boring in from his pallid face, severe, accusing, like I was somehow responsible. I continued. I asked him about his experience with black people and he called me a racist. I mentioned the discrepancies in the descriptions and the composites, and he said the police made those mistakes. The artists were inept. I kept on. "Do you think," I finally asked, almost in a whisper, "that when you squeezed that young man's wrist in the vise between the door and the door frame it caused the gun to go off?"

He didn't reply. His face clenched and then drooped, settling into his hands. I pushed further. "We are all sorry for your loss but it *is* true that you have a great need to see someone blamed and convicted here, don't you, Mr. Stark?" I did whisper this last question. I did it for Sherman's sake, to save him, but it was difficult. No one watching could fail to feel the pain in Mr. Stark's heart. I kept telling myself that he was mistaken. He certainly believed he was correct, but he was mistaken. It was my job to uncover this error, to reveal to the jury that despite his protestations of certitude, despite his obsession with bringing the culprit to justice, he was wrong that it was Sherman Allen. He was driven by his own need, by his own grief, but he was wrong.

Langrell had gotten wind of my plan to call Dr. Reiser, and on the morning I was to begin the defense case he handed the judge a ten-page brief on why Reiser should be prevented from testifying, that his so-called expert opinions were not accepted by the scientific community. He presented to the court psychology articles that questioned some of the theories. The jury was excused as we argued these issues. In the end the judge compromised. He allowed Reiser to explain his research into these areas, to explain the potential difficulties of cross-racial identification that his and others' research had confirmed, and also to explain the concept of unconscious transference. But he refused to let Reiser give any opinions. Still, Reiser knew why he was there, and he made known through insinuation, through emphasis, through expression and gesture his suspicions.

I called Sherman's mother and sisters and they elaborated on the alibi and were unshakable. Naturally, Harry and I had spent hours preparing them, making sure they were able to consistently answer any question about the details of the goings-on in the house that evening, details such as what people were wearing, doing, eating, saying. We called Sherman to the witness stand last. He testified humbly, quietly, telling the jury he was innocent, denying any involvement in the crime. He even asked the jury to forgive him for his own poor memory. He couldn't be certain where he was that evening, just as he had told the police. At the time he had no reason to remember it. To him it was just another holiday over the Christmas break. And then nearly a month went by. He only knew and was positive that he was nowhere near Mr. Stark's house when the crime occurred. Listening to his mother he was pretty sure he was home, but he honestly hadn't been able to remember back in his mind. I thought he did well, and on cross-examination, Langrell couldn't shake him.

Langrell used the white Bible again in his closing, remonstrating again about the laws of God and man, about the sacred duty each juror knew was theirs to fulfill. But by the end of the trial, by the time I rose to deliver my closing argument, I had in my hand my own Bible, and mine was black. I feigned a reading from Proverbs 28. I say *feigned,* because it was an interpretive reading, really. I took what I would call a lawyer's license with the verse. The text itself reads, "The wicked flee when no man pursueth: but the righteous are bold as a lion." I held the good book high, quoted the chapter and verse, and recited my interpretation. *"The wicked flee-eth,"*—I quietly quoted, pausing for emphasis as the jury leaned forward to hear—*"but the just remain."* It suited so well the facts. I repeated it, the second time in a strong voice. "If Sherman Allen had been on that doorstep and had been seen by Wilson Stark that fateful night," I then argued, "would he just have stayed around the neighborhood waiting to be seen again by Mr. Stark? Would he just be casually lounging on the sidewalk in front of Mr. Stark's house, knowing the man inside could identify him as a murderer and send him to prison forever? Of course not. He did not flee because he was not wicked. He did not flee because he was not guilty. He remained because he had nothing to be afraid of. He had done nothing wrong. The just remain. He had remained."

There were many reasons to doubt whether Wilson Stark was accurate, I went on. He was certainly sincere. But was he accurate? Or had not his own terrible need for vengeance and retribution driven him to unconsciously transfer young Sherman's face onto the body of one of the villains on his porch that tragic night? "Unconscious transference." "The alibi." "Mr. Stark's lack of familiarity with black people." "Reasonable doubt."

The trial had lasted two weeks. The jury deliberated for three days more. When they finally reached a verdict, they agreed with me. Sherman Allen went free. As the words "not guilty" echoed out, a howl of pain welled up from inside Wilson Stark, almost inhuman, it caromed off the circular walls of the courtroom, clawing through my consciousness. Stark was pointing at me as Langrell's junior counsel assisted him out of the courtroom. His face was ashen, that of a ghost. An accusatory ghost. I watched him as Harry pumped my hand in congratulations, as Sherman's mother rushed into the well of the courtroom and took me to her bosom.

WAS THAT A TURNING POINT in my journey through the moral morass of the law? Was it suspect to alter the words of the Bible to illustrate a point? Is there a distinction to be made between helping a client to remember properly and convincing him that one type of testimony will work better than another? Wouldn't any able lawyer have seen through the subterfuge of this fifteen-year-old's attempt to spin an alibi he didn't really remember? We had done our survey with our mock juries and learned the better strategy. And so we disabused the client of his inclination to fabricate, all for his own good. It was brilliant, really. I mean there's no way for us to really *know* the truth. Our advice to Sherman was certainly sound, ethical, required. We only convinced him to abandon a tack that we sensed was not only ill conceived but untrue. We gave him fine legal representation. An impoverished teenager, with little opportunity, for once got something in his life that was first class. And my cross-examination of Wilson Stark? I had learned to use the fine scalpel. It was regrettable but necessary. "Such artistry," Rachel Duboc, our new acting deputy, complimented me afterward, "marks the true trial lawyer."

It was about a month later that Sherman Allen was found murdered. Shot twice in the temple in an alley off of Benning Road. There were no suspects and to my knowledge no one was ever arrested. It happened the same week the city council voted to slash the agency's budget. Soon after, I received the court papers from Margaret. She had grown impatient waiting for me to reply and had filed them in Florida. A process server placed them in my hand with a smirk. I was tired and felt emptied out. Like there was nothing left inside. My years as a public defender, I realized, were ending. I was tired of the hopeless cases. The eyes, dull from endless poverty. I was tired of having an empty wallet. Of going home to an unkempt basement apartment every night. Harry had a similar sense. He had just been assigned to represent a heroin addict accused of killing his two children. The man went on a binge, leaving his two-year-old son and a five-month-old baby girl alone in a locked apartment for three weeks. They died from dehydration and starvation. In Harry's file were the photos of how they looked when they were found. That was when he asked me to start into private practice with him. I didn't give it much thought. Asa, we had learned, was not returning. He would be in therapy for months, working with his prosthesis. I needed some kind of change. If I recall correctly, I simply shrugged and told Harry sure. I was so drained, the idea of fighting Margaret in court also seemed impossible, seemed wrong. What was I to Stephen? How could I be the father he needed from so far away? I tried to imagine him at just six years old, to put myself in his shoes. I wanted to love him but he needed love from someone with him, someone in his life. I wanted to do the right thing. To do the best thing for him. I sent her back my signed consent to have my son adopted by another man.

PART TWO

Dun Cove

10

IT WAS AROUND DUSK that I had gone on my mission, back to get my car, over near the Bozman depot, dressed like a commando. Wearing dark jeans and zipping my black wet-suit vest over my cardigan, just in case, I skulked along the river's shore. When I got to where I had left my Mercedes, it was gone. I had locked it and still had the keys, so I looked for broken glass or other evidence of criminal entry. There wasn't any. The cops, I figured, must have taken it. I knew I was cut off.

Back at Boxmoor, I finished the last of my pills with whiskey, chased with beer. Around 2 A.M. I woke in a sweat. Bad memories sheered my sleep—scenes of my lost son, of my work dishonored, and of Linda, the one last person I had clung to as family, the one I never expected would so coldly turn away.

In the morning I lay inert. I could hardly find a reason to dress. Trying to replace the harpylike visitations of the night, oddly enough I had thought of the strange girl at the depot, Muddy, in her jeans and red cap.

In the kitchen, there was nothing left to eat. To stave off the tide of despair, I started to the depot for food. It was the girl I hoped I would find. I had hit bottom and was trying to come up with a plan. I thought that maybe Muddy, with her quirky interest in me, with her apparent disinterest in authority, might help. Might, at least, sell me some food without calling the police. I didn't even know whether she'd be working that day. But she drew me—I'm not sure why—like a last spark of light in a caving tunnel.

Heading for the depot, I pushed my heavy limbs through the back yards of the houses just off Bozman Road. When I had gone less than half a mile from the oyster-shell lane of Boxmoor, I saw through the trees ahead a roadblock. I crept closer, hiding myself well. There were several police cars with their lights circling. A tow truck had my Mercedes attached, raised up onto two wheels. There was a police van with barking dogs inside. A handler took one out on a leash—it was a bloodhound. He led it to the Mercedes and opened the door for it to sniff. As I stumbled backward, I saw an unmarked car pull up. From the passenger side emerged Morgan Langrell— the new U.S. attorney for the District of Columbia, appointed by President Clinton just months before. He wore army fatigue pants, a flannel hunting shirt, and sunglasses. He stretched his arms toward the sunlight like he owned it.

My throat closed around my breath. I moved back the way I'd come, the bloodhounds baying behind me. Stumbling through yards I made my way back to Boxmoor. In the kitchen I found my cash and journals and took them out to the bulkhead and hid them. I lurched toward the end of the dock and lay on the boards in a fetal position until I heard the dogs nearing the driveway. I sat up and took off my shoes and socks and then took my wallet out of my pocket. My wet-suit vest was already zipped tight.

I REMEMBER SWIMMING. I have a long reach, and the crawl was my stroke in college.

I pulled steadily, confidently at first, sobered some by the shock of cold water, trying to pace myself, trying to maintain a cadence with mind and body, counting each stroke in a measured beat, focusing on the beat as a mantra of sorts, seeking its mindless asylum, using it as a shield to ward off the trickling fear, the fear that accompanied any thought of what I was doing. I would have turned back, but the idea of Morgan Langrell swaggering on the shore, waiting to bask in my pathetic arrest, drove me forward.

The water was chilly only in the beginning. With the wet-suit vest and my exertion, it grew tepid, almost hospitable. Its brackishness filled my nose and mouth. As I turned my face under I tried to stare through the olive murk but the visibility was poor.

I have always been a good swimmer. After all these years I still felt the power in my limbs. But I was soon overcome with the sense of the immensity of the water around me. I swam toward the black spar to flee my own rising panic. I swam and never looked back.

It wasn't until I was well out past the channel marker and felt the strong current sweeping me south that I began to tire and to worry. And with this sense of vulnerability crystallized my growing realization that I wanted to live. It was then that the tentacles of the first sea nettles swept across my face, lashing my cheeks, mouth, eyes. It was late in the season for jellyfish, and I hadn't expected them. I panicked for a moment, swiping at the waves around me, trying to tread water, but I must have swum into a thick nest as my feet and then hands began stinging as well. I scraped at my eyes, but the slime from the tentacles clung to my hands and fingers. The tentacles spread themselves across the vest and adhered there in a gelatinous film, and neither it nor my sleeves were any use in wiping my face. I kicked my feet and swam through the nest, wincing from the poison, squeezing my lids shut, then opening them under water in an effort to wash out the sting. But even after several minutes, I could see little through the tears pouring over my burning eyes. I tried to calm myself, working my arms to regain a rhythm in my stroke. I was beginning to breathe hard. When the second group of nettles washed into me, I reacted with more discipline. I knew better this time. My eyes were already clamped shut. I swam on with a breaststroke, pushing the jellyfish away the best I could with my palms. But wherever I swam, taken by the current, they seemed to find me. And the waves took them up across my face again and again.

I began hallucinating. At least I remember conjuring up the image of my father. Versions of his face passed before me, both healthy and sick. My father had only made me promise one thing: never to allow him to languish in a hospital or nursing home. Once he lost his vigor, he told me, I needed to let him go. To help him, even, if necessary. It was his only fear. Yet when the time came, after the strokes had deprived him of speech, of his ability to walk, even of his continence, I could see in his eyes that he still clung to life. He wasn't ready. I kept him at home with me. A lady came every day while I was in school. He wasted away for a year. His organs shut down. He was in pain. Yet he wanted to live. Seeing his face there, out in the channel, I felt the same.

Striking out harder against the waves, I knew that I needed a direction. I needed to find a point of land—one ahead of me that the current would push me near, one I had a chance of reaching. Raising up with the crest of a roller, I tried to find the shore. Tears and salt clouded my scalded eyes. Hoisting myself up as high as I could, I saw nothing but a blur of foam cascading from the next wave. I tried again in a different direction. I was blind. I could hear more than I could see. Swept by the current I turned crosswise to it. I guessed where the land might be. I tried to swim while feeling the current. If I stayed crosswise to it, at least I wouldn't be going in circles.

Other faces replaced that of my father. I saw Margaret's and then Stephen's. It was there before me in the water, a boy's face, growing into a young man's face, one I had never seen. I reached out for it. Water came down my throat. I came up choking and struggled again to swim. I was getting cold. Less buoyant. I pulled hard to stop myself from shivering and kicked my feet and pulled again, and again, the face of my son, there in my mind. I pulled for what seemed a long while until my arms were heavy. Just lifting them clear of the water took all I had. I caught another draft of the brackish water in my lungs and spewed it up, coughing and flailing my arms. Rolling on my back I tried to float, to rest, but the waves broke over my mouth and nose, and I took more of the salty river choking down my throat. I struck at the water again but felt myself sinking. I was very tired, very heavy in the current. I rolled around and around and then struggled back to the surface. It would be good to rest. Perhaps it was time to rest. The sensation of floating was nice. My mouth and nose began to sink again. I pulled up to breathe one more time. A distant sound, from far off, barely registered. A motor whirring in the waves. Even the hardness of a bobbing fiberglass hull, bumping cold against my cheek, seemed to come from a distant world. There was a tugging from the top of my vest. I fell back into the water. The tugging started again. I was limp. Willing to sink. Ready to sleep. And then the muted yell, close to my ear but still fuzzy, seemingly a ways off. Sounds close but as though filtered through something thick and sticky. "Damn you!" I remember hearing. "You help me! Hold your arms up here! Grab on!" I remember hearing it. Then again. A woman's voice. "Pull, damn it! Pull yourself, mister! Pull!"

II

DURING THESE FIRST DAYS—my eyes covered by white gauze—I take comfort in sounds. A drawer opening. A faucet turned on, then off. The bleating of engines far out on the water. The wakes slapping the shore. Her footsteps in the cottage around me.

It's like being in rehab. Like a patient in a hospital. I've survived my own train wreck. At least physically. I feel as if I've emerged from a long illness. Weak, barely mobile, but strangely serene, I lie on the canvas cot, listening.

I've read that in blind people the sense of hearing is very keen. Lying in this cottage, I actually hear through the window screens the squirrels grinding nuts in the trees. The rustle of leaves is constant. The birds. The changing wind against the landscape, over the cove — all this has its own texture in sound.

THE FIRST TIME she changes the bandages on my eyes and face, I make out through the sliding glass doors the blur of red lights rotating on the river, and across as well, to what I guess are the grounds of Boxmoor. My eyes are just slits in swollen skin, and they sting and run wet as I try to focus. The images, though smeared, suggest boats dragging the channel. Curiously, I feel detached from it all, stone cold. "They're feds. They'll give up soon," she says. "They posted notices along the road. To call if you were spotted. You sure got 'em all in a wad." She half smiles. "They're sure you drowned. *Morons* . . ." She reattaches the gauze. "Don't know why the river sent you this way," she adds in a whisper. "But you'll be safe here. Least for a while."

It's the girl from the store. Muddy.

SOMETIMES SHE PLAYS MUSIC from a stereo. I recognize an old Joan Baez collection. And then a jazz guitar and saxophone. "Charlie Byrd and Stan Getz," she utters, walking by. Once, like from another world, the passionate voice of an Italian tenor. I'm not sure . . . Pavarotti, maybe. At times she hums to herself as she cooks. This evening, after I have drifted off, I wake to the sound of her sketching on her pad. The sound of charcoal on paper.

At night the tree frogs and cicadas tune up. Their song, overlaid by the wind, fills the dark. Moths beat against the glass pane. Mosquitoes whine. Gulls wake me up in the morning, crying over the beach. She's always ready to help me to sit up and to walk to the bathroom and then back to my cot.

At first she was just a shadow here, through the gauze. She uses some kind of salve on my face and on the backs of my hands and on my ankles and feet. She spreads it with her fingertips. It smells like camphor. Sometimes she cusses at me, while she dabs the stuff on. "You damn fool," she calls me. "Look at your face. Look at what you did to yourself. You look butt-ugly, you know that? All I need now are *your* problems . . ." Under her breath she'll sometimes sigh. "Of all the friggin' luck," she murmurs. "I'd get stuck with a lawyer. Shit. Figures."

I'VE BEEN SLEEPING MORE than I've been awake. Even during the daylight, I drift in and out. The hours blend together. I've lost track of time. I've been here four or five days, maybe. I'm not sure, exactly.

While Muddy is out, I take my bandages off. My face stings still, but the white fire has gone. I stand up and move away from the makeshift cot she has set up for me in the main room, which faces out back toward the water. I hobble to the telescope that looks through the sliding glass doors out to the cove, and the mouth of the river beyond. Dabbing my blurry eyes with the sweatshirt she has lent me, I focus the lens. The search boats have gone. Across the way I find the dock at Boxmoor. A white egret with a fish speared in its bill stands on a dock piling. I can see the changing shape of its throat as it swallows its prey. I refocus, scanning the cove out front. A line of swans drifts near the shore. I count fourteen, all in single file.

THE ROOM WITH MY COT is stark. There's a tuner and an old phonograph in a plywood cabinet. Record albums are piled up alongside. A door laid flat on stacked cinderblocks serves as a desk on which sits a fax machine, computer, and printer with wires running into the baseboard. But no pictures, photos, posters, anything like that, decorate the walls. Propped in one corner is a double-barrel shotgun with an open box of shells on the floor. Several fishing rods rest on hooks over the fireplace. Kindling and small logs are stacked on one side of the hearth. I know the kindling is cedar from its smell that fills the room.

The telescope faces out the glass doors. Next to it is a writing table with a sketch pad and pencils and, protruding from a drawer, a pair of binoculars. A large bookshelf stands against the opposite wall, filled with, from what I can tell, a hodge-podge of titles, paperbacks and hardcovers all mixed. On the floor is a stack of old newspapers. In the open closet sits a chain saw and a pile of netting. The netting gives off a faint scent of the sea. Rubber hip boots are pushed to the side. On a hook hangs a holstered snub-nose pistol. On the bottom shelf of the bookcase is a pile of drawings. The top sketch looks like a man's face scratched over. A short hallway leads to a step-down kitchen. Off the hallway, on the left, is the bathroom. Opposite is where she sleeps. She keeps her bedroom door shut and locked, even when she is gone.

TODAY MUDDY IS WEARING a blue cap with UFCW stitched above the brim. She sits on the edge of the cot studying the scabbing where the burns were worse. "I don't even know you," she says. "You remind me of someone, though." She pushes hair away from my forehead and dabs at a raw spot with the camphor salve. "You have his build. You're his age. And you have something in your face. Hard to explain. Like a question's there you can't answer. Like you're hard-shelled but maybe not so much so inside." She tapes a clean gauze pad over a spot that's still blistered. "You'll have to leave soon. Soon as you're well." She sets the tape on the side table. "I'd been watching you through my telescope, across the river. That story about the wet suit was so lame. And I saw your hands. I doubt they've ever cleaned a propeller. Not in this life anyway. So it was luck, I guess. If you call it that. Through the telescope I caught you swimming . . ."

I haven't talked since she pulled me from the river. Just nodded now and then to answer her. I'd like to thank her. With my face bandaged and half raw, I must be a sight. My throat is still swollen from the salt, my vocal chords inflamed, and my words come out so hoarse, they're useless. She leans away, quizzically, and says, "You might wait till you can speak clear."

THIS AFTERNOON SHE GOES out in her boat, which is about twenty feet long. An old Mako that she keeps tied to the small buckled dock off her cottage. I shuffle over to the telescope and watch her through the lens. She drives the bow across the glassy surface of the cove, rousing the coots from the river. The engine glints in the sun. Cutting inside the green buoy, she disappears around the southern point, marked with a stand of pine.

Though the skin over my ankles and feet is still tender and tight, I decide to make the effort to walk around the cottage, testing myself, wanting to get my blood moving. I put a hand on the wall for support as I move. I reach the bookshelf. The stack of newspapers against the wall is next to me. A yellowed issue of the *Baltimore Sun* is on top. One of the headlines describes the February 1990 election of Violetta Chamorro as president of Nicaragua. I pick it up to look closer and see that the paper beneath, an old copy of the *Washington Post,* features an article on a kidnapping in El Salvador. The next paper down carries a piece on the disappearance of two nuns in Honduras. I go through the whole stack. Each paper headlines a story on Central America. The bombing of a government building in Guatemala. The murder of a union activist in Panama. I mean to read some of the articles but a wave of vertigo overtakes me, from the exertion of walking and standing I suppose, and I go back to the cot and sleep.

Muddy's return wakes me. She has two rockfish on a string and holds them up for me to see. She starts a record of Bob Marley singing "Buffalo Soldier." I limp into the kitchen and watch as she scales and fillets the fish. She has poured herself a gin over ice, dumps in some olives, and sips it as she works. She motions, offering me some, but I pass. On the back wall, by the door, she has hung about a dozen baseball caps. There's an Orvis cap, a Duck's Unlimited cap, and one that advertises Red Eye Dock Bar. There's one that says Cocks on it, which I know from school days stands for the South Carolina Gamecocks.

I point to the one she's wearing.

"Poultry workers union," she answers. "What little there is of it. I like hats. Certain ones. I sort of collect them."

She dusts the fillets with flour and browns them in a heavy pot. She adds vegetables and water and a bottle of Budweiser before covering the pot to simmer. "You should go in a poultry house sometime," she says. "Real sweet. The company carts in the immigrants, from Mexico and Central America. Treats 'em *so* nice. Dumps the chicken shit, guts, blood, all of it in the river.

Does whatever the hell it wants. It's all good business. You know that I suppose ... being a lawyer ..."

She grabs the hat from the wall that says Cocks on it. "Here," she says, tossing it to me. "You might go outside tomorrow. It's gonna be warm. Best keep your face out of the sun. That hat, there, probably fits you."

In the living room she starts another record. "Old Satchmo," she says. "Your generation." She drops the needle on the first cut and turns up the volume. From a lacquered box on the mantel she takes out a bag of reefer. She rolls and lights a thin joint, takes some in, and then offers it to me. I shake my head no. "Not good for your throat anyway," she says, inhaling again deeply as if to spite me. My eyes water from the smoke. I lean back. I watch her glaze up. She takes her cap off and shakes her hair loose. It's full and falls to her shoulders. Around her neck she wears her scarab on the leather thong. She shuts her eyes and sways her shoulders while Louis Armstrong sings, "What did I do to be so black and blue ..."

Back in the kitchen, she fixes herself another gin to drink while she finishes the fish chowder. She wobbles some as she brings the bowls to the table and then has to clean up with a sponge where she's spilled. She eats, then sips her gin and watches me as I spoon in a second helping of the rich fish soup broth. For my portion she has strained the broth clear and cooled it in the refrigerator so I can swallow it without pain.

MUDDY'S MUSICAL TASTES seem oddly old-fashioned. Even to see a record player these days is strange enough. I pick through some of her collection. There's early Dylan, Judy Collins, Janis Joplin. She's strong on blues—John Lee Hooker,

Billie Holliday, B. B. King. And old country and folk—Hank
Williams, Patsy Cline, Woody Guthrie. Some jazz too. And a
smattering of opera. Verdi and Puccini mostly. She places several albums on the turnstile rod at once, as it has an automatic
drop. She listens as she works on the computer. "My father
knew music," she tells me. "He loved opera. He sang when he
was young. Most of this"—she motions to her albums—"was
his."

"I don't care much for pop," she goes on. "This stuff's from
deeper places. You should listen . . ." She speaks to me as a peer,
with little deference to my age. In some of her pronounce-
ments, though, I hear a pretty thin layer of self-assurance, a
false certainty.

IN THE MORNING, Muddy drops the town paper in my lap.
It features the manhunt by local and federal authorities, tells
how my identification and still sweaty socks and shoes were
found on the end of the dock, and how I'm assumed drowned.
The article mentions my career, the charges, my flight, though
it provides a confused account. Muddy doesn't come right out
and ask me anything, but it's obvious she wants to know more.

"We'd heard from Trooper Solomon," she says, "that you'd
rigged some big case. I suppose you had your reasons. For
whatever you did. Not that you have to tell me. I hope you did
anyway. Have reasons, that is. Seeing as the river handed you
over. As you're here in my house. As I've near had to adopt
you."

I'm afraid to answer her. It isn't my throat, which feels better. It's something else. I don't want my explanation to fall
short. I don't want to disappoint her.

"This is all temporary, you know," she adds. "You're getting better. You're going to be okay, I think. I mean your sight and all. You should be making a plan. About what you're going to do." Her face is serious, but her eyes aren't judgmental. For whatever reason, she has already gone so far with me. She's reserved a space there, I believe, in which the possibility of understanding remains.

12

I'M HEALING. THE SWELLING around my face has gone down and my eyes are no longer teary. Even the fog from weeks of downers and booze is starting to clear. While Muddy's at work, I mix my beaten biscuit dough and arrange the makings of an omelet. I find onions and tomatoes and cheddar cheese in the refrigerator, along with large brown country eggs. I set the table. Out by the patio, in her garden, I find some thyme and rosemary. Along the riverbank is a patch of wild burning bush, with leaves turned scarlet. I break some stems and put them in a vase. I set an old Tom Waits album on the turnstile.

Muddy's surprised when she gets home. She mixes herself a

martini. I ask her if it's okay for me to cook. While she doesn't say much, she sticks around the kitchen watching me. When I try to flip the omelet, a piece of it catches on the edge of the pan. I swipe at it, but send it splattering across the floor. She covers her mouth. This is the first time I hear her laugh.

WE EAT AT THE SMALL table under the window in the kitchen. Muddy fills her plate with the broken omelet, and hot biscuits. Over dinner, she tells me that Agnes has been bragging that she was the one who found me out. Over a fishing license. "Sorry about that," Muddy says.

"Yeah. Pretty stupid," I say.

"The way Agnes tells it, she outsmarted a big city lawyer." Muddy giggles as she finishes a bite. "She is sorry you drowned, though."

"Yeah. Well, I guess she did get the best of me." I clean my plate and lean back. "Agnes told me about your father," I say. "Earlier that same day. I was sorry to hear about that."

Muddy glances up, then back to her food. She sets her fork down. "Yeah. So everybody dies sometime." She wipes her mouth, then finishes eating. When she's done, she asks whether I have any family, any money, anywhere to go.

"I'm divorced," I say. "I have a son somewhere, but he's been adopted by my wife's second husband."

"Huh?" She considers this. "How old is he?"

"He's twenty-three."

"Funny. So am I," she says. She shrugs. "What's his name?"

"Stephen," I say.

"Stephen . . ." she repeats.

I tell her about the cash and journals I hid in the bulkhead at

Boxmoor behind a stone marked with a rust-yellow stain the shape of a fox's tail. I hadn't wanted Morgan Langrell, the U.S. attorney, to get them, I explain. The cash, if it's still there, just under nine thousand, will be a help when I leave. With the money I could buy a used car, go south, rent a room somewhere, find a job. I tell her that I'd like to pay her, for all the food and everything. She frowns and says no. She won't take any money. She isn't interested in money.

She asks me about Morgan Langrell. How I know his name. Why he, personally, is after me. I begin to tell her about all the face-offs we've had, starting back with Mitch Snyder and the grudge Morgan developed then.

At the mention of Mitch Snyder, her face lights up. "You knew Mitch Snyder?" she exclaims. "You did work for him?" She goes to a side drawer and takes out a scrapbook.

"My father worked some to help the shore migrants. There he is," she points. "The man next to him is Cesar Chavez. Daddy was proud of that meeting. Cesar Chavez came east, I think, in '87. He had made a movie he was promoting, *The Wrath of Grapes* or something." She hands me the scrapbook. The picture shows two men, each with a hand on the other's shoulder. Muddy's father is the taller and leaner of the two. He resembles his daughter. His carriage and features are stately. Only his hair is different from hers. His is curly.

She turns the pages for me, and points to another photograph. It's her father again, but standing in a group. "And," she says, "see?" In the center of the group is Mitch Snyder, wearing his customary army jacket. "Small world, huh? Daddy went to the city a couple times to march for the homeless. He got to know Mitch Snyder. I can't believe you knew him too. You might've even met my father . . ."

I start to turn another page, but Muddy takes the book back.

"When did you know Mitch Snyder?" she asks. "Did you see him around the time he died?"

"No. I sort of lost track. I worked with him more in my early days of law practice. Up through the mid-eighties or so. I just got too busy later."

"Shame." She moves to the counter and tops off her drink with gin. She signals to me, whether I want one, but I shake my head.

Muddy takes a jar of olives from the refrigerator and dumps several into her glass. She sees me watching her and furrows her brow. Abruptly she heads out the doorway and through the hall to the living room. I follow her and sit with her as she rolls herself a joint and lights it. She takes a long, deep pull on the pot.

"Live fast, die young, and have a good-looking corpse," she says. The smoke swirls around her. "You don't have any vices? They're saying a drink or two is good for the heart, you know." With the joint between her lips she gets up and sways toward her bedroom. "That's right, you like scotch," she says through her teeth. "Anyway," she adds, "you're my guest, and maybe becoming my friend, but you're definitely not my keeper . . ."

A VIBRATION AGAINST the glass wakes me up. A fluttered drumming. I walk to the sliding doors. The new moon is high overhead and shines through onto the wooden floor. Outside, in the upper corner of the door frame, is a giant cicada, bigger than my thumb, with an iridescent green belly, caught in a spider's web. The web drapes from the gutter down to the top of the door and reflects the moonlight. The bug looks too large and powerful for the slight almost invisible strands that restrain it. Its one free wing quivers, beating against the glass. The spider, in the opposite corner, is motionless, patient. I watch the cicada drum its wing and then stop. Drum and then stop. And then it quits moving altogether. Stays still. The spider doesn't move either. The cicada, perhaps, has the instinctual sense not to enmesh itself further. There's a standoff. I get tired of waiting and go back to bed. In the morning I look. The web is gone. Perhaps the cicada broke free or maybe a bird got it. I could have dreamed the whole thing.

MUDDY'S RETRIEVED MY JOURNALS and the cash, which is a relief, but she's insisted on reading the diaries. I hope she'll begin to understand the path I took and how it may have led here. I hope for a dispensation, a judgment that my character, though perhaps lacking in grace, is not past salvage.

After a couple of hours of reading, she comes out of her bedroom. She carries two of the three journals in her hand—the earlier ones, written while I was at the agency. Muddy holds out the two journals for me to take. "What an ugly business," she says.

"Yes," I answer, rising from the cot. "I suppose it was."

"I see about Morgan Langrell. You burned him pretty good."

"He's getting the last laugh, though."

She purses her lips. "I don't know. He thinks you drowned. You look pretty alive to me."

"Thanks to you."

"Thanks to the river. It handed you over."

"That's an interesting way to look at it."

"Once I saw you swimming, it wasn't like I had a choice." She sits on the corner of her desk. "It's all timing anyway," she says.

"How's that?"

"My timing. It's usually not been very good."

"You got to me in the nick of it."

"That's what I mean. It seems to have worked for once. So I don't know whether to trust it."

"Well, I'm sure thankful for it."

"I mean so far it's been okay." She kicks her desk chair out with her foot, then sits on it, crossing her legs. "I liked reading your journals," she says. "I see your aim was to help. And you did help some."

"Yeah. Maybe."

"But the law's its own world, isn't it? I guess I just don't much like how it works. I guess I've never been much for rules."

"The rules make it reliable. Make it fair for everyone."

"Rules that regular people can't figure out? I don't think so. And they don't exactly apply even, do they? It seems you needed to be there for those clients. Otherwise what chance did they have? Rules or no rules. And there are folks maybe more deserving, you know. And just as much in need as those clients. That is, if your aim was to do good, which I can see it was—" She stops herself. She fiddles with a paper on her desk. "I'm sorry . . ."

"It's okay," I answer. "But that's the job I was offered. It was there before me. It seemed the right choice. You choose from what's there on your plate."

She's slow to respond. She runs her finger along the edge of the desk. "I suppose that's right," she says. "I mean everybody's got their lump of coal. So Agnes always says." There's a slight tightening in her voice.

"You don't like lawyers?"

She stands. "Will you have some tea?" she asks. "Come on in the kitchen. I'd like some too. I'll make us each a cup." I follow her down the hall. "I mean maybe I'm learning," she says over her shoulder. "You're a lawyer." She swipes at me gently, brushing my shirt. "Though I still don't even know what you really did." She puts water on the stove, opens a kitchen cabinet, and takes down cups and a can of tea bags. "Are you going to tell me?"

"What do you have against lawyers?" I ask back.

"It's just that I've been through it."

"Through what?"

"You know. It's all there in your books. Even though you were trying to help. I mean, isn't it just cover ups and lies? Politics? Bullshit?"

"Politics is just how the world works."

"Well, you should know. You've lived it."

"What legal stuff have you been through? To give you such strong opinions?"

"I have a friend from Nicaragua. She worked in a chicken factory over near Preston. Her brother was killed there. Electrocuted. We went to lawyers and got nothing but sorry excuses and pity-crap."

"How'd it happen?"

"They used him for a handyman. He was told to fix an ice-maker. He shut the fuse off. Nobody told him they'd hot-wired the machine to the main power cable some months before, a jerry-rig to save money, a code violation. When he grabbed the wire it was hot. He was caught between the machine and the wall. Trapped. Nowhere to get thrown clear. People watching said he looked like he was havin' a seizure, bouncing back and forth. Didn't have a green card. Since he wasn't legal, no one cared. I went with my friend to the state's attorney's office. It wasn't a crime, they said. It was his fault, they said. It all made me want to puke."

The water starts to hiss, and Muddy turns off the stove and pours the water into the cups with the tea bags.

"I went inside after. Once was all I needed. The stink is bad enough. The floor's covered with chicken gore. People're always slipping and falling. They use sharp blades and hooks. They all had scars. They get a half hour for lunch and it takes that long to undress, wash, and dress again. They never get overtime. Used to get locked in, till that fire down south burnt up those women workers. I got involved with the union some. For a while. But every time the big poultry companies get pushed, they threaten to leave the state. To move. Then everyone starts to grovel. From the governor on down they just bend over."

Muddy takes a jar of honey from the cabinet. "Want some? It's local. Wild honey. There's a Jamaican named Raptite works with Chula, my friend. He's a Rasta man. He showed me how to smoke the hives. Get the bees all nappy and take the honey." She spoons some into each cup. It's thick and dark.

"Agnes told me you got arrested?"

"Twice. Once at a sit-in. Just trying to get some overtime paid. That wasn't too bad. The union bailed everybody out, paid the fine. The second time was more on my own. It was after Chula's brother died. I made a big sign about how they were hurting the workers and polluting the river. I showed up on a Monday. They just ignored me. Tuesday the same. I got madder. I went over to the crab docks in Claiborne and bought myself a barrel of chicken necks from Barker Cull. He sells them to the crabbers for bait. I poured out the brine and left 'em in the sun just setting there until they were ripe. That Friday, I drove over to the county courthouse in Easton. From a pay phone I called the newspaper, told 'em they should get down to the court-house 'cause something wasn't smellin' right. I rolled those chicken necks up on the lawn with a handcart and dumped 'em all over the courthouse steps. I had my sign there. They made me sit in the jail until Monday before a judge would set bond. He was pretty pissed. There was some press showed up, but nothing came of it. I knew nothing would . . ."

We sit at the table sipping our tea. "Sorry," I say.

"Oh, don't be. Not for me. Sometimes people just need to stand up. Those rotten chicken necks smelled pretty rank, though." She laughs. "They cleaned 'em up fast enough, but people said you could smell 'em all summer. I had to fumigate the car, I know that."

"What happened? After your arrest?"

"Agnes got me a lawyer. He told the judge it was an accident. That I didn't mean to spill 'em. That the barrel tipped over. That I was just taking them there to make a point. I tried to in-terrupt the fuck and he hissed at me to shush. I was too afraid not to. He got me so pissed, changing what I did like that. Turn-ing it into something it wasn't."

"You've got a crazy streak," I say.

She tilts her head in that way she has, pondering this. "Yeah, I suppose I do," she answers. "Good. I like it."

"I could give you some names of some lawyers in D.C. who aren't afraid to fight. There's a clinic there that handles cases for poor people. An old friend of mine runs it. They might come down here."

"I've had my fill of lawyers," she replies. "The system's broke."

"You had a bad experience, Muddy. One bad experience ..."

"More'n one."

"Well, a couple maybe ..."

"More'n a couple. I've had all I need."

"What else?" I ask. "What other experience?"

She had started to rise but stops halfway up, then sits back down. She looks at me, undecided for a moment. Gradually her face undergoes a change. She begins to look more like she did that first time I saw her in the store. She bites her lip. "I learned enough before, is all."

"Before what?"

"Just having my daddy blown apart by a goddamn terrorist right in front of me, is all. And no one giving two shits. How's that? Though it's ancient history now. Over. Done with."

Muddy's stare has gone vacant. She looks around. She wipes her face with her sleeve. "Forget it. I don't want to talk about it, Jack. I'd just rather not."

I shrug. "You can if you want to," I say quietly.

She changes the subject. "What happened to you, though? After you quit being a defender?"

"I'm not quite sure," I answer. "I went into private practice. Some of it's there in that last journal. The one you left in your bedroom. That's when I got so busy. Lost track of Mitch. The rest I'm still trying to work out ... Trying to make sense of ..."

Muddy nods, and excuses herself. "I'm off to work," she says. "For a few hours. And to finish my reading. I'm going to take your last journal with me. To find out what you did next."

"Don't let Agnes see it," I remind her. "Or lose it, please."

"Jack, come on. Have some faith. Really ..."

13

THE LAST JOURNAL DESCRIBED the early days of private practice, after Harry and I left the agency, after we went out on our own. At first we were both broke. We borrowed to rent space, to hire a secretary. In those days I used to walk two blocks back to the agency to use its long-distance line for telephone calls. Every fifty cents counted.

When Harry and I made the decision, several colleagues called our venture foolish. To this day I can see the smirking face of Everett Wheeler, who had six months earlier landed a partnership in one of the uptown firms. We had taken Everett to lunch for advice. "This is Washington, D.C.," he told us. "Not some podunk backwater. You two have talent, of course. But the firms here are established, connected. No client worth having'll hire you. I mean, I'll help you if I can. I predict, though, you'll be representing local drug addicts if you're lucky. Drunk drivers. Hoods."

Before he left the agency, Everett had wanted to take on a notorious client, a doctor charged with two counts of manslaughter for the deaths of the two women who'd died in his abortion clinic on South Capitol Street. The doctor was Korean. All his patients were black. His medical office was reportedly filthy, his instruments unsterilized. Everett was looking for favorable exposure to improve his employment prospects uptown, but the office was divided over whether we should even be representing Dr. Kim. The doctor had a large house in the Maryland suburbs but had transferred all of his assets to his wife's name and filed for bankruptcy protection to try to avoid his civil liabilities and to qualify for a free lawyer. Everett was persuasive and convinced our director and then the judge that his client met the statutory requirements of indigency. He mapped out his strategy, first working the abortion issue in the press, suggesting that Kim provided an affordable and necessary service to a poor neighborhood. Over time, and through careful manipulation, Everett leaked the substance-abuse problem. The doctor had a habit—Percodan and alcohol. Everett hired three different polygraph examiners, in-house, their results shrouded by the attorney-client privilege, before one declared that Kim was truthful on the Percodan gambit. Then he interviewed the psychiatrists and had them interview his client, eventually finding two willing to testify that Kim lacked *scienter*, the criminal intent necessary to be convicted of manslaughter. He had been dysfunctional, in a narcotic daze, unable to intend the acts of wanton recklessness with which he was charged. The prosecutor got nervous and a plea deal was arranged. The doctor agreed to a suspension of his license and six months of rehabilitative detention served in a private drug treatment facility. It was good lawyering, and Everett got hired uptown.

Despite his pessimism about our prospects, after Harry and I got started Everett did try to help us and, in fact, sent us one important case. Later he went on to represent a number of Capitol Hill types, forging the connections he wanted before opening up his own specialized lobbying firm. That's when Everett struck gold. After I became successful myself, he included me in his social circle and invited me to Boxmoor. He went on to build a powerful lobbying firm, representing primarily tobacco, and international agricultural, coffee, and mineral interests. He plays golf now with congressional leaders and enjoys power lunches at The Palm, where his framed caricature hangs on the wall along with hundreds of other lampoon portraits of Washington insiders. He only works about half time. I saw him just before I ran, before the news about my problems broke. He was getting his shoes shined on Pennsylvania Avenue, sitting in the elevated chair, a cigar in his mouth. His waist has expanded with his success. He boasted that his work for big tobacco is a natural successor to being a public defender. "I stand for freedom," Everett wheezed from his jowly face. "For the freedom of people to smoke what they want, to live the way they want. If we lose tobacco"—he winked— "liquor will be next." He chuckled as he called himself a libertarian.

Everett was not the only one who discounted our chances

for success. Asa shook his head when I told him of our plans. "You won't like working for fees," he said. "Practicing law for money, you become a lackey for the client, a mercenary. You'll lose your passion. You'll lose your edge." He was at his home at the time, a Victorian townhouse bought with family money, and still recuperating from his accident. He still wore his kaleidoscope glasses, but his hair was cut short and there was a change in his tone and manner. "The profession is turning. You'll have to compete with lawyers advertising on television. It's demeaning. Lawyers used to be honored. Not anymore. We're seen as money chasers. People have started to hate lawyers. Until they really need one, of course. Then they want you hammer and tong." Unstrapping his prosthetic half leg, he placed the plastic assemblage on the table before him, glaring. "Take a look, Jack. The bionic man ... The drunk didn't even have insurance. God damn it. Damn him. People need to take responsibility in this world—" The doorbell interrupted us. His home health aide had arrived and urged him to get ready to exercise. Before I left I asked him about the future. "My juvenile delinquency is over," he announced, reattaching his leg and foot. "My family's working on trying to get me appointed to a D.C. judgeship. My father's got some pull. There are several slots opening up. Now that my body is wrecked I'll migrate to a universe of the mind. I'll learn discipline. Control. Perhaps find nuggets of wisdom to disseminate. I mean, I've learned all the tricks. Maybe it's a good thing. Who knows?"

HARRY AND I WENT FORWARD with our plan anyway. We gave notice to the agency and, after various briefings and introductory meetings between clients and other staff attorneys, transferred our cases. We rented space in an old building on Fifth Street, near the courthouse, where the street lawyers mostly hung out. We opened the office of Stanton & Bonifant, P.C., and scraped together the money to send out announcements to everyone we knew. Our noon hours were spent taking lawyers in firms out to lunch, asking them to think of us when they got cases too small for them to handle or out of their practice areas. If all else failed, if no private clients came through our doors, we knew at least the judges would appoint us in cases the agency couldn't take. We wouldn't starve. But that never became necessary. The phone started ringing that first week. It turned out there was a niche for small, unconnected firms, and we were one of the first to fill it.

One of the early cases we considered that first year in private practice, the one referred to us by Everett, concerned a woman in her late twenties named Sarah Simmons who worked in the cafeteria in the building Everett's firm occupied. She was a high school dropout from West Virginia. She had been married, and during her first year of marriage, seeking birth control, had been given an intrauterine device called the Spartan Guard. Six months later she had developed severe pelvic inflammatory disease, which put her in the hospital for three weeks, required two surgeries, almost killed her, and left her sterile. Afterward her husband divorced her. Hearing about cases against the Spartan Guard's manufacturer, Starcore Pharmaceuticals, Inc., she had sought legal advice at one of the larger and most prestigious firms in town, Barings & Huckleby, Chartered, and from one of its senior partners, Reynolds Newcombe. Newcombe had listened to her story but told her that too much time had passed to file a case, that she was barred by the statute of limitations.

She had believed him. Two years later she saw him on the local news and realized that he was defending a case against Starcore Pharmaceuticals, working on behalf of the company. She brought to our office a copy of a letter she had sent to Newcombe seeking his advice about suing. She also had his old bill, for an hour's consultation. When she came to us, too much time had passed to sue the manufacturer, but that had not been the case when she'd been given the fraudulent legal advice by Newcombe. She had been to four firms in town, she told us, and no one would touch the case. When Everett called and told me about her, he asked that I keep his name out of it. His firm didn't want the association. No local firm was willing to turn the powerful Barings & Huckleby into an enemy. The connections between the large firms were too intertwined, too binding. Everett said he figured a couple of young bucks like us, with nothing to lose, might be foolish enough to take them on. We signed her up.

Because it was a legal malpractice case, we had to prove both that the lawyer gave her negligent advice and that had he not done so she would have prevailed in her original claim and been awarded damages. On the first prong, we had strong evidence. She had the letter to Newcombe and his bill for the consult. She had also kept her original notes from her meeting with him, taken in his office, which clearly reflected his deceit in telling her the claim was time-barred. Moreover, he had never disclosed his relationship with Starcore, one we learned had gone on for six years. When we made Newcombe come to our offices to have his deposition taken, he called us "crackpot lawyers, bringing a crackpot lawsuit," but he was clearly shaken by the questions we posed and the evidence we had amassed.

The second prong of proof was more difficult and more complicated. At that time, Starcore Pharmaceuticals was still defending the Spartan Guard as a safe product, though the company had removed it from the market and arguably knew otherwise. The Guard looked like a tiny plastic spider, with a string extending down from its lower end. One of its flaws was that the string was a multifilament fiber, encased in a plastic sheath but unsealed at its end. It acted like a wick, allowing bacteria to travel easily up through the string into a woman's uterus and cause infection.

In our case, the defendant hired three firms to fight us. They set depositions across the country trying to bankrupt us. They hired a panoply of experts to denounce us. But we held on. As we learned more about the case, about the science, as we spoke to attorneys experienced in this litigation, we discovered one of the defense tactics would be to probe into our client's sexual past. The defense would contact every lover our client had ever had, seeking to embarrass her and them, hounding them for intimate details of their sex lives, all under the guise of trying to develop medical evidence that Sarah had prior contact with a sexually transmitted disease, and thereby establish another potential cause of her infection.

Harry and I knew that Reynolds Newcombe had defrauded our client. We knew that the Spartan Guard had crippled her. Medical records from her local ob-gyn clinic vouched that she was disease free and otherwise healthy when the IUD was inserted. We had exhausted our credit to hire experts and keep up with the case. Everything for us was at risk. Sarah, also, had become dangerously dependent on the case. She had a deep need to prove this wasn't her fault. She called regularly on the phone, confessing her daily sadness, her grief over losing her husband, over the prospect of a barren, childless life, her fears about the case. She was nervous as we prepared her the day before her deposition, and she wanted to convey her pain, her misgivings. We both empathized with her and tried to understand her loss. In the office that day Harry encouraged her to talk, to let it all out. Apparently, when I was in the next room taking a telephone call, she blurted out to him something about having had a bad time when she had first moved to Washington, when she was nineteen. Before she had met her husband. About having trouble at first finding a job. About how a man had offered her money for sex and how she had agreed and then found herself working for him for a while. Three months was all, and then she had stopped, gotten decent work, and straightened out her life. Should she mention this in the deposition, she asked Harry, as I came into the room?

Harry sat in stunned silence. Slowly he raised his legs, taking his lizard-skin boots off his desk where he had been resting them. He bent down and dusted them with his hands. After a few moments he excused himself, and I heard him running water in the bathroom. I knocked and entered. He was drying a face that looked ill, that was downcast and defeated. "We're going to lose the whole plantation here," he stated. "They'll kill her in court."

"She asked a question," I responded. "She deserves a full answer. One that any client at Barings & Huckleby would have the benefit of."

Back in the office I began by explaining to her how such a revelation made in deposition would end our chances to settle the case and, made before a jury, might cause her to lose the case as well. I told her that if I had learned anything over the years as a trial lawyer, it was the uncertainty of memory, how unreliable it could be. I then went on to explain that her duty in the deposition was only to testify to things she could clearly remember. That the defendants had no way of knowing who she had ever slept with or how many boyfriends she had or their names, unless she told them. And that if her memory was poor, the response, "I don't remember," was a good one. I explained to her the history of the Spartan Guard litigation and how in case after case the defense lawyers had dug into the private lives of the victims, trying to humiliate them, embarrass them, deter them from going forward, contacting past sexual partners with embarrassing questions, innuendoes, and how women across the country were just no longer remembering their past sexual contacts in these cases. I spoke for twenty minutes or so without either Sarah or Harry saying a word.

As I finished, I asked her if she understood what it was I was trying to tell her. She nodded that she did. I then asked her how she intended to answer when they asked her about prior sexual history.

"Not much to remember," she mumbled.

"Sarah," I interrupted, covering my tracks once again. "It wouldn't be proper for me to put words in your mouth. This is your case. It's your obligation to answer their questions."

"I understand," she answered.

"They will try to contact your ex-husband," I told her.

"Let them. He won't know any different."

"Are you comfortable in answering their questions that way?" I asked.

"Are you comfortable with the answers?" she asked me back.

"If you think of something after the deposition, after it's over, that you overlooked or were too embarrassed to mention, that you think should be included, we can always supplement your answers in writing. Do you understand?" I asked.

She indicated yes.

"And do you understand that, naturally, it is our duty to urge you to tell the truth?" I added, looking at Harry.

"Yes," she replied.

"Are you ready for tomorrow now?"

"Yes. I think so," she answered

Through all of this, Harry watched me. He never said a word.

Sarah completed her deposition the next day. Her mention of prior sexual history, prior to her marriage, that is, was limited to a man named Smith whom she had lost track of. He took advantage of her, she told them, when she first moved to Washington. She thought she loved him and then he left her. But he left her healthy. She offered no more details than that. She had also dated some boyfriends back in Berkeley Springs, she ventured, but never slept with them. When they asked for the names of those boyfriends, I instructed her not to answer.

"You're just trying now to embarrass and harass her," I objected. "You'll need a court order before she'll answer that question." They hesitated. "This line of questioning is over for today," I finished.

A month later, with the trial weeks away, the defendants offered us a confidential settlement of six hundred thousand dollars. Sarah cried when we told her about it and accepted. The court documents were placed under seal and Reynolds Newcombe's reputation remained intact. From our fee, one-third, Harry and I each bought our first new cars. He joked that

I should order my license plate to read BARINGS, and his to read HUCKLEBY. Less than two months later they started referring business to us. Either they were impressed with the job we'd done or they wanted us part of their network, to be won over by the steady stream of referrals coming our way, financially bound and loyal to them like many of the city's other firms.

Perhaps I was wrong in my response to Sarah Simmons's question about what she should reveal of her past. In my eagerness to allow her to make an informed decision, or, put more bluntly, in my eagerness to win, perhaps I went too far. I knew it had disturbed Harry. Even in his delight over the outcome, he remained bothered. Over lunch at Jaybird's Cafeteria one day I raised the subject for discussion. Not that I had concluded it was wrong, because I hadn't. But I hoped for Harry's concurrence that my actions were okay. Harry could wrangle with questions on ethics with the best of them, but in the end his judgment was solid. I trusted it.

He pondered the issue and answered tactfully and only after considerable reflection. "You never lost sight of the big picture," he responded. "I credit you for that. That bastard Newcombe defrauded Sarah. Hell, he is probably the one who designed the defense strategy to attack the victims in these cases. To humiliate them. To delve into every personal detail. You heard the questions his goons asked Sarah. 'Have you ever had herpes? Genital warts? Lice? Oral sex? Anal sex?' They even asked her about urinary tract infections. All this after they had maimed her for life. Their tactics are plain mean. You know and I know what caused her illness."

I can see Harry now in my mind, sitting there, taking a sip of coffee and watching me over the lip of his cup. "So she made some mistakes in her past," he added. "Who hasn't? They had nothing to do with what Newcombe or his clients did to her or why she became infected."

He put his cup down, staring into the grains at the bottom. "The object of the law, I suppose, is twofold," he continued. "First, to provide folks with a way of settling fights. Second, on a higher level, a tougher one, to be just. We lawyers, simply by doing our jobs, contribute to the first goal. I could argue that you, by doing the curtsy you did, that you gave a helping hand to see that the second had a chance in this case." But then he shook his head. He had begun rubbing his chin and his expression had turned fretful. "I don't know, though, Jack." He paused. "Looking at the big picture is one thing. But having to do what we did . . . And I was certainly your accomplice, don't misunderstand me there. But I wasn't that keen on it at the agency. And I'm not here. Back home they say the devil is in the details. They know devils in New Orleans. What with all the voodoo. The gris-gris man." He briefly smiled before turning serious again. "It worries me where this will all lead. It takes a stronger stomach, maybe, than the one I have."

14

MUDDY COMES IN OUT of the rain this morning, shotgun in tow, with two mallard ducks. "I have hunting rights over on the Wye River," she says. "Billy Granger's farm. He was friends with my father. He's got two river blinds and some field pits." I watch as she plucks and cleans the birds on the patio. She works methodically, without a trace of squeamishness. She has a natural self-sufficiency I cannot help but admire. She's in sync with the world she inhabits. Intuitively aware of its order, its balance, her place.

THOUGH MUDDY WAS DISTANT at first, and is still at times reclusive, she seems to have begun to take some pleasure in my presence, in my witnessing her life. Yesterday, when she came home, she pulled me to the front door to watch a large bird circling the cornfield. "It's an eagle," she said. "A baldy. I've seen it several times. Its nest is somewhere up the marsh." It glided our way and its shadow passed out front, covering Muddy's Jeep. Wing to wing it spanned a man's height. I watched her watching it. She put her hand on my shoulder. Her skin is tanned from the sun but smooth, and lightly freckled on her shoulders, neck, and around her cheekbones.

MUDDY DOESN'T OWN a television. Although there are radiators in the cottage, she seems to prefer heat from the fire in the grate. She tends two crab pots in the river that are tied off her dock. There are still late-growing squash and turnips in her garden. One evening I watched her sketch. She sat in the corner chair, her legs drawn up in the lotus position with the pad in her lap. She held her sketch pad close, like a poker player, and clearly didn't want me to see what she was drawing.

She doesn't seem at home with anything modern except her fax and computer. Yesterday she mentioned a three-way conversation in one of the chatrooms she visits—herself, a student in Guatemala City, and another in Baltimore. I've looked over her shoulder to catch snatches of text. A bulletin from the State Department on a proposed trade treaty. References to a National Security Archive database. A Freedom of Information Act index. She's private about these electronic exchanges, though. I have seen her shield the computer with her body as I come near. Or she just pushes a button and the Yahoo! homepage covers the screen.

• • •

WE HAVE AN UNEXPECTED VISITOR. Muddy is in the shower. The knock on the front door scares me and I burst in on Muddy to tell her. She pulls the shower curtain partially back. Enough to lean her head out and understand me. I see for the first time the tattoo of a blue seabird above her left breast. She turns off the water and motions for a towel, which she wraps around herself. She whispers for me to stay in the bathroom and closes the door behind her. I hear her walking toward the door. There's a greeting in Spanish, some conversation, and then Muddy calls for me to come out. A short, stocky woman with Indian features stands in the room. In her hand is a folded fabric.

"This is my friend, Chula Perez," Muddy says.

"Chula, this is Jack, the lawyer who drowned. Give me a minute while I get dressed." Muddy leaves wet footprints on the floor.

Chula speaks broken English. "How do you do?" she says. "Sorry you drowned. Or maybe. I don't know."

"It's okay," I say.

"Don't worry," she adds. "Muddy and me are friends. For a long time." She nods, nervously. Her skin is weathered, tawny, and her forehead and cheeks etched with broken creases. Her eyes are small and black.

"Are you from Nicaragua?"

"Yes."

"You lost your brother here?"

"Yes."

"Muddy told me. I am sorry."

"Yes. It was very bad."

I wonder what Chula knows about me. I feel awkward, like I'm the intruder. I ask a question about how often she visits Muddy.

"Sometimes," she replies. "Muddy's young but is a good fisherwoman." She looks out the back toward the river. "Brings me nice crabs. Fresh. Eel too. Very strong. I help her with Spanish. But she needs nice man." Her face crinkles up even more as she smiles.

When Muddy returns, Chula presents her with what she is carrying—a woven shawl. Spreading it open reveals the rough design of a mother cradling an infant.

"This is what I wish for you," Chula says.

Muddy embraces and thanks her. She tells me not to worry, that Chula is rock solid. Those are her words. She offers to make tea for Chula, who accepts, and Muddy walks her into the kitchen. I overhear them talking about some meeting coming up later in the month. I grab my cap and go out on the patio to give them privacy. The sun is warm over the river. The swans preen themselves along the shore. A single sailboat lazily runs the channel out toward the bay. I lie on the lawn chair and doze off. When I go back inside the cottage a little later, Chula is pointing to the charcoal drawings on the shelf. She's mixing phrases in English and Spanish. "Very much rich," I hear. *Muy peligroso. Tiene poder...*" Muddy sees me and seems uneasy. *"Hija, evita este señor."* Muddy takes Chula's arm and moves her toward the front door, where she says something in a rapid tone. They go outside. After I hear Chula drive off, I go out onto the front landing. Muddy's in her Jeep, just sitting there in the driveway. I walk down the front steps. When she sees me coming, she turns on the ignition and starts to back it up to turn out. I see her eyes are red and wet.

"What is it?" I ask her through the window.

"Nothing. I'm late." She waves me away and drives out into the road.

Toward the middle of the afternoon Muddy returns.
She acts like nothing has happened but tells me she takes a
class once a week at Chesapeake College in marine science.
With Chula there, she lost track of the time. She's brought me
magazines to read—*Chesapeake Magazine, Esquire,* and *Men's
Journal.*

"Why were you so upset?" I ask. "In the driveway?"

"I get upset sometimes over things. It just comes on. Like
thinking about Chula and her brother. Over the way things
have to be."

"What were you all talking about? About some man?"

"Nothing important. Nothing involving you, Jack." She shifts.
"But now that you have money, and you're getting better, you
should make some plans. About leaving here."

"I know. I am."

"It's been a week and a half. They've given up and think
you're drowned. You can start again. You've got some money
now, and if you need more, I'll lend you some." She points at my
face. "Let your beard grow. Change your appearance. It'll give
you a fresh start. But you have to leave. You need to plan your
next move."

I nod.

She hesitates. "You like it here?" she asks. "With me?"

"I do," I answer. "But I know it's time to go. I need to get to
the city to buy a car."

She sighs. "Yes. A few more days of rest and you should be
ready. Early next week, if you want, I can take you." She steps
close and fingers my hair. "You should probably dye this too.
It's a shame. Your hair is so nice . . ."

• • •

MUDDY HAS GONE for some scotch for me. I told her it wasn't necessary, but she insisted. I take the opportunity to look at the sketches on the shelf. The top one is scratched over, a discard. Underneath is another drawing of the same face but finely done, detailed. And there are more. A dozen or so portraits, all of the same man. All of them are in charcoal or pencil. In one he's clean-shaven; in another he has a beard. In another, a mustache. Several seem to show him successively aging. Like *Dorian Gray.* Underneath the portraits are other drawings—unsettling, jarring. One is of an adult and child inside a car, but both are skeletons. Under that one is a sketch of a different sort—it's of a city street after an explosion, with shards of metal and debris and people lying wounded. Apart from the subject matter, what is striking is the artistry. The pictures are skillful and compelling. There's a depiction of a prison cell, empty, and finally a graveyard on a hill beside a tiny chapel, a moon overhead.

IN THE GARDEN I squat, helping dig up daylily and iris bulbs. It's near dusk. Muddy has given me the hand spade and she's dividing the bulbs with a kitchen knife. She wears a gray gardening glove only on her left hand. She's sawing at a root ball when I mention first the sketches and then the stack of newspapers with stories on Central America.

Muddy glances my way as she finishes separating the bulb. She takes the spade from me and digs two holes, and places each severed section in a hole. Then she covers them, filling the holes with soil. The sun is low but still warm. The river is a deep powder blue behind her.

"I was obsessed with it. For a while," she says softly. "I'm better now." With the back of her right hand she wipes some sweat off her cheek, leaving a smear of dirt just under her eye.

"Those pictures are something."

"They were an outlet. A way to breathe."

"You have a real talent."

"Thanks."

"Who's the man in the pictures?"

"I'd rather not talk about it," she replies.

"Do you ever draw in color?"

"No."

"This would be lovely to paint."

She looks out to the river. A waterman tongs for oysters against the far shore, his form small in the distance. "Maybe one day. I'm working on other stuff right now."

I lean toward her, and with my thumb, rub off the smear on her cheek. "You have a gift," I add. "Really."

She seems to appreciate this. "When I'm ready, maybe," she says. "If I'm allowed."

"Allowed by who?"

"By myself. I don't know."

I take the knife and a turn at dividing another bulb. I hand it to her to plant.

"It's hardly enough for me to just thank you," I venture. "This is just all so . . . so unexpected."

"What?"

"You. To find such a generous person. From out of the blue, so to speak. I'd like to help you back."

"Having you here's been kinda nice. That's been a help," she says.

"The newspapers? The pictures?"

"Thanks, but there's nothing you can do to help with that. That's the past. We can't change it."

"Your father . . ." I try to speak gently. "You were how old when he died?"

She buries a severed bulb in the ground.

I try again. "Where were you when the accident happened?"

"It wasn't an accident. It was a murder."

"Yes," I say. "I didn't mean—"

"Forget it. I was thirteen."

"Well, will you tell me about him? Something? I mean I've seen his picture. He *is* the person I supposedly resemble?"

Muddy pats firm the soil around the roots. She examines her work, then turns toward me.

I wait.

"In some ways," she says. "He had hair like yours." She smiles furtively. "And he was handsome. You're near his age and size." She looks up quickly. "But don't worry. I know you're not him. He never had to run from the police, that's for sure. Even though he was an old-fashioned lefty. That's where I get it, you know. He was a big McCarthy man. Remember Eugene McCarthy? Daddy was into helping the migrant folks, mostly. Back then they had it really bad. Like the chicken workers but worse." She moves her head and again stares out over the cove. "There's a likeness you have. It struck me the first time I saw you. But there're differences. He was totally at home here. At ease. He was a marine biologist. An expert on places like this. On estuaries. Couldn't stay off the water. Didn't like being inside. Even in winter. He'd go crazy if he got cooped up."

"How come you were in . . . where was it, Central America?"

"Honduras."

"What were you doing there?"

Taking her glove off, she brushes off her palms. She picks up the knife and spade and puts them on the table. She reaches for my hand, pulling me to my feet. She starts back inside. I open the sliding screen door for her. "I'd like to hear about him, Muddy..."

"This is why you're such a good lawyer. You don't give up, do you?" Muddy shuts the screen. She stands there at the door.

I move the magazines I've been reading off the cot and sit down.

"Nice breeze this evening," she says. "It'll be a nice night. These warm days, one after another. La Niña, I guess. How does anybody know, really? It's what they tell us, though."

She stays at the door, continuing to look out toward the water.

"Daddy was doing research on fish farming," she says. "He was early on into building fish ponds and breeding and raising fish. He got asked down to Honduras to help set up a program there for some farm collectives. He was sympathetic to some of the political factions trying to make things better. It was a three-month deal. We'd never been apart that long. He brought me down for a visit over the Christmas holiday."

"Honduras is close to El Salvador? Nicaragua?"

"We were near Nicaragua. In Choluteca, Honduras, by the coast, not far from the border. I didn't know much of this then. The contras were still fighting the Sandinistas and crossing back and forth to Honduras at will. We thought there was supposed to be a cease-fire in place when I was there." Muddy stops and turns toward me. Her face has begun to contract.

"Where were you? When it happened?" I ask gently.

She squeezes her eyes closed. She shakes her head. She steps toward me, and for a moment she looks as though she's going to strike at me. Her fists are clenched. Then she seems to fold. She sits down on the edge of my cot.

"I'm sorry," I whisper. "I'd like to know, is all."

"Oh hell," she quietly sighs.

She rests her hand on my arm. She seems to be trying to measure her breathing.

"I was outside," she starts. "At the top of the front steps. On the step landing. It was like . . . a townhouse . . . on a side street of the city where we were staying. A man had come over for lunch. He was a trade union person, involved in organizing farm collectives. After lunch he was going to take Daddy to tour some sites for new ponds . . ."

Her voice drifts off.

"Was he a friend of your father? Did you know him?"

"Daddy had met him once before, I think. He must have been the target. Must have been involved with the Sandinistas. I've never been able to find that out. His name was Gutierrez. It was just bad luck. Bad timing."

Muddy looks at me. "I was playing with a cat just before," she whispers. "The lady who owned the place had three cats. I was playing with the calico. It had only one eye. I was petting it and looking out the window. I saw a man raise up from behind the car on the curb. He wore a brown army coat. He backed away across the street. I saw his face through the window as he backed away. Daddy kissed me good-bye. He was happy. Daddy and his friend were out the door. I had a sense then of something not right. It was that man's face, his expression. I set the cat down and started out after my father. Daddy

157

turned and looked at me from inside the car. Through the glass window. I stood on the landing. The strange man I'd seen was gone. I saw Daddy wave from inside the car window. I wanted to shout . . ." She halts and tries to swallow. She takes several deeper breaths. With her fingers she begins massaging her temples, then stops. "I'm not going to cry. I'm not," she repeats.

WE'VE SAT TOGETHER in silence for some time. I touch her hair. A loon calls from out in the cove. Muddy takes my hand. Unexpectedly, she spreads my fingers and places them over and against her moist cheeks and eyes and holds them there. Then she puts my palm to her lips. Then she lowers my hand, holding it in hers.

"I don't talk about this, you know. Not really. I haven't wanted to lose it by talking about it . . ."

"You won't lose it." I choose my words with care. "It's there. He's there. Always, a part of you. My father . . . he's still there for me too. I saw him when I was swimming . . ."

She wipes her cheek. "You saw your father?"

"Odd, what you see when you think your life is ending. I saw him, and my son, the way he looked before his mother took him away." I press her hand. "Don't be sorry to speak to me. People have to talk to each other . . ."

Muddy nods, seems more calm. "Course that's right," she says.

"Did the counselors you saw help at all?"

"I didn't want their help."

I'm trying to think of a reply when her fax machine begins to hum. She moves toward the desk. A page begins to print out. "I've talked on this machine . . . this computer for so long," she muses. "It's been a safe, careful way to speak. I type out my words. Go over 'em. Change 'em, if I want." She stops. "It scares me, some of the things I've told you." She pulls the page free, not reading it. "All I've ever heard about my father's death have been these meaningless words. Excuses. Apologies . . ."

15

"WHEN I FINISHED THE PART in your diary about Sarah Simmons, I had a question."

We've been eating the ducks Muddy roasted. I can't remember ever tasting anything so good. I'm helping her with the dishes. She's leaning against the counter, more than a little bit drunk. Her eyes are glassy. I've had some scotch myself.

"Would she have lost the case if she'd told the truth about being a prostitute? I mean she did it for just a short while? I don't get it."

"It's hard to get twelve people who'd all overlook that. Somebody'd want to punish her for it. At least, that's how I saw it then. Defense would've argued she caught the infection that way. That it was just dormant and slow to spread. They'd have pounded it hard. I don't know ..."

"How come that's the last entry in your diary?"

"I guess I got too busy to keep it. Or didn't want to anymore."

"So what happened after?"

As she says this, she starts to slide sideways off the wall, smiling as she does so. I catch her and help her toward her bedroom. I hold her elbow as she unlocks her door and whisper her good night.

Success and wealth are intoxicating drafts to those not used to them. They vindicate the actions that bring them about. They're society's measure of virtue. Sitting alone, leaning back against a wharf piling under the night sky, I repeat Muddy's question to myself—"So what happened after?"—and recall the exhilaration that Harry and I felt so many years ago having scored against Barings & Huckleby. How, after that, could I have doubted our methods? How could I not have been reinforced in my judgment?

Despite the confidential nature of the Sarah Simmons settlement, word has a way of getting out. And following that victory our phone started ringing. I tried a big auto negligence case and won. Our fee was over $150,000. Transferring my criminal experience to civil cases was natural. The juries were the same. The witness preparation, the strategies, the smoothing over of blemishes in a case was the same. Accentuate the positive, as one of my colleagues preached. Deemphasize the negative. I did. The juries sensed my passion for my clients, and I amassed a string of verdicts in our favor. Not that I won every trial. But I seemed to win most. I thrived on the cases, on taking on the causes of the injured, the crippled. And the money rolled in. I liked spending it. I bought my first house. I joined a country club. At certain parties I'd get high. At others, we'd have vertical wine tastings—samplings of Pichon Lalande or Lynch Bages from all the great years, '86, '82, '70, '61. I built a wine cellar. Dining out and heavy drinking became the norm. My social interests turned promiscuous. I liked the chase, the heavy breathing when I undressed a woman the first time, that first capitulation. I was less interested in the tedium of a relationship. There wasn't time. Or perhaps I was still gun-shy. I don't know. But it was the cases that I obsessed over. They came in flurries and drove me, and our firm prospered.

From IUD trials, I branched into other medical device cases, product liability cases, and eventually found a specialty litigating medical malpractice matters, all fascinating and so much more lucrative than criminal work. I'd usually take a contingency fee of one-third of what I recovered for the client. Sometimes more, when the risks were greater. Cases that settled quick were a windfall.

Initially, Harry enjoyed our success. We had celebratory lunches together at La Pavilion, at Lion d'Or, lunches that started early with martinis and went on all afternoon with wine. But gradually Harry got fretful, sullen. From the start, he'd been more tentative, more deliberate about which cases he'd take. After Sarah Simmons, he handled a number of legal malpractice trials, mostly for established firms, defending the powerful, paid well by their insurance companies. He worked several of these big cases but grew dissatisfied with his role as a defense lawyer, expected to discredit the hapless plaintiff through cross-examination, to make the victim look greedy, unworthy, when Harry knew very well that the contrary was true. He began working on some class actions but didn't seem much engaged by those either. Just after we marked our three-year anniversary, he was asked to join the faculty of one of our city's law schools, to build a clinical litigation program. He was courteous enough to inquire of me if I minded his taking a leave of absence. I didn't, though I knew he wouldn't be back. But I was winning cases. And revving up the good life. We parted friends, and I wished him well.

With Harry gone, I hired a second secretary, then a paralegal. I had my first seven-figure verdict. I traded in my Saab for a Mercedes. I sold my first house and bought an elegant townhouse uptown. I tried my hand at golf. I was asked to teach as an adjunct professor at the National Law College. I vacationed in St. Barths in the winter, skied in Aspen, summered in Nantucket. A decade of hard work and fast living that now seems a blur. I was raking it in—making more money in the civil area than I ever expected. I had mostly sworn off criminal work. So, when Joseph Williams walked into my office with his family in tow, his wife and four kids, his two brothers and their kids, his supervisor from work, and his dog, Jefferson, and wept as he told me how he had shot and killed his next-door neighbor, how he was charged with second-degree murder, and pleaded with me to take the case, I would have said no, indeed I started to say no. But for the intervention of Linda Morrison, I would have, surely.

After I'd first met Linda back at the agency when she was in nursing school, we'd run into each other periodically. I'd see her occasionally over the years at a party or a fund-raiser. I knew she worked as a registered nurse at the National Hospital for Children. While trying to evaluate a complicated medical case involving a child, I thought to call her one afternoon to see if she would help interpret the nursing chart. Over time we began seeing each other, though she kept me at a distance. She'd gotten married, and then separated and divorced, but still harbored feelings for her husband. It was six months before we first made love, the night we went to one of Bill Clinton's second inaugural balls. The gala was held at the Shoreham and the Dom Perignon flowed freely. The next afternoon, over brunch at the Old Ebbitt Grill, she told me not to expect it to be a regular occurrence. Friendship, she said, was her first priority. But when the mood struck her, she'd take me home with her or stay over at my place. She was Margaret's opposite, but of the many women I'd dated since Margaret, I was attracted to her the most. Linda defined herself through her profession. She often worked overtime, double shifts, complaining to me bitterly about the doctors, the administrative staff, claiming often to know better than the experts what her patients needed. Her apartment was full of pediatric and nursing journals. She really cared about her infant patients and talked about them incessantly. I didn't mind her obsession with her work so much, as I was certainly preoccupied with mine. Her insecurity about money didn't bother me either, even though she often carped about living on a nurse's salary. I was making plenty and enjoyed paying her way. More than anything, I think, I appreciated the friendship we were building.

Linda called me while Joseph Williams was in my office. He had been an orderly at her hospital for twenty years, she told me, and was a good man. She asked me to help him, as a favor to her.

His story went like this: One year before, after saving money his whole working life, Joseph Williams had accumulated enough to buy his first home for his family through a city-subsidized housing program. He had done so, even though it meant moving his family across town to a neighborhood in Northeast, where the subsidized homes were available. He began fixing up the two-story brick house, surrounded by a small yard, enclosed in a fence. Though they were strangers to the block, it was a dream come true. They had been in their new home for two months when on a warm afternoon in April a neighborhood boy had coaxed Joseph's fourteen-year-old daughter into a van where three other boys from the block were waiting. The boys took turns with her, holding her down, covering her mouth. When she got home Joseph took her to the police. The boys were arrested but claimed she consented. The police believed her.

From that moment on, none of Joseph's children could leave the house without being tormented or beaten by groups of neighborhood juveniles, male and female, all friends of the boys she had charged. His seventeen-year-old son, Joe Jr., was sent to the hospital with a broken rib. His youngest daughter had her clothes ripped off her and her face ground into the mud on the playground, her nose fractured. It got so bad that Joseph had to pull his kids out of school and order them not to leave the house. They'd been prisoners that way for a month when the shooting occurred.

Joe Jr. couldn't take being a virtual prisoner in his home anymore. Seeing that no one was on the street, he had left the house and walked to the mall. On his way home he had been spotted and surrounded. Fortunately, his mother was home. Hearing her son shouting, Flora Williams first called Joseph at work and then ran out to her son, trailing her other kids behind her. She pulled her surrounded family back inside their yard. Others from the neighborhood, hearing the commotion, joined the fray. Among these were the mothers of the juveniles arrested for rape. One of them, a large woman and one of the most vocal, carried at her side a baseball bat. When Joseph got home he saw his family inside their fenced yard. Pushing up against the fence were at least twenty people, adults and adolescents, screaming threats, hurling epithets, yelling accusations. Joe Jr., with tears streaming down his face, was yelling at the woman with the bat who was standing just across the waist high chain-link fence. The lady was ignoring him and chanting, "Whore! Your sister's a whore!" at a loud pitch. Joseph told his son to go into the house. Joe Jr. turned and ran. The chanting continued and the vehemence of the threats increased. Moments later Joe Jr. came running back out into the yard. He had Joseph's registered .38-caliber revolver in his hand, waving it wildly. Joseph turned and took the pistol from his son. As he turned back to the woman holding the baseball bat before him, he fired one time shooting her in the heart.

Because of his working record, his family history, and the fact that he had never before been arrested, Joseph was allowed out pretrial without bond. His coworkers from the hospital had all chipped in money for a defense fund. So had his relatives. He had raised five thousand dollars. Samantha, Joseph's nine-year-old girl, his youngest, offered me the envelope. After hearing his story and conferring again with Linda, I had decided to accept the case. As I reached for the money, Samantha pulled back. "Promise me you'll help my daddy," she pleaded. "Promise me?" I nodded to her as I accepted the fee.

My first step was to go up to the office of the U.S. attorney. Morgan Langrell was the senior deputy then, and I had made an appointment to see him. I'd hoped that enough time might have passed for the hatchet between us to be buried. In his office I argued for a clemency plea, one that would allow Joseph to remain in the community under a sentence of probation. The mitigating factors justified it, I entreated. I will find him another house, move him away. On that occasion, Morgan was very professional. At least at first. When I arrived at his office, he shook my hand, took my coat, treated me with courtesy. He waited until I had spoken my piece. Then he began his lecture. He explained to me, rather laboriously, the importance of building respect in the community for the law and the courts. He went on about the necessity of bringing killers to justice. His voice became increasingly condescending. When I asked him to consider the rape of Joseph's daughter, to put himself in Joseph's shoes, he turned cold as blue ice. "I have eleven uninvolved eye witnesses," he spelled out. "Eleven! It's an airtight case. The victim was standing with the bat down at her side. She never raised it. Each witness will so testify. Each one saw your client shoot the lady without hestitating. For no reason. Examples must be made. You can plead to the indictment. I'll agree to a reduced sentence. With good time credit he'll be out in nine years. If he goes to trial he'll get and serve fifteen to life. Now if you will excuse me . . ." He turned his back on me and picked up the telephone. A secretary materialized and offered me the door.

As one of the conditions of his bond, Joseph was not to venture back into the neighborhood. He and his family had moved in with one of his brothers. I helped him arrange with a real estate agent to put the place up for sale, but I retained a key. I went and lived in the house for two nights. During the second day I called Linda and she came over and stayed with me. I roamed the rooms, thinking of him, thinking of his ordeal. The second night, after Linda and I had eaten Chinese carryout, I sat on the back porch steps, staring at the fence, listening to the street sounds around me, the sirens in the distance, the rap music beating from car windows, the occasional gunshot. In the morning I walked the perimeter of the fence. I was there to become Joseph. It was a transforming moment for me. As if I were in a trance, events evolved in slow motion. I stood there with my family in danger, my children battered and accused, my son hysterical. I heard the screaming and the threats, and I felt my eyes, which were his eyes, watch his son come out that door with the gun waving in the air. I took it and turned to face those against us, all of them, including the mother with the baseball bat, anger and hatred in her eyes. I saw her and knew why I had come. I knew what he had done and what I had to do to save him.

I DON'T RECALL exactly how I planted the seed in the mind of Joseph Williams, but plant it I did—and nurture it—until it became his and he knew it for his truth and his salvation. And I remember his face as the idea first got through to him, as he saw what I had seen, and knew it for its rightness and power.

The law of self-defense includes an important subjective element. If a man believes that he or a family member is in imminent danger of grave bodily harm, that man is legally justified to use force, even deadly force, in self-defense. I bought myself a baseball bat. With Joseph watching I timed Linda Morrison in the yard outside the office, smashing a cantaloupe with it. It took her about a third of a second to bring the bat up from her side to destroy the melon, which I had placed on top of an upside down trash can. I explained the law to him, again and again. Every witness out there, I laid out for him, every witness outside that fence, was either to the side of or behind the woman he had shot. No one but him, and perhaps his son, had seen the woman's facial expression, her neck muscles tense up, her arms begin to tighten, her jaw begin to clench. No one but him saw what he saw. No one else but him was in harm's way. No one else was in jeopardy from the reach of that baseball bat once it started on its path.

At trial the government witnesses, in their eagerness to ingratiate themselves with the jury, fell into the trap one by one.

"Did you see that handgun come out the back door?" I would ask.

"Oh yeah!" they'd uniformly answer. "I saw it good!" one volunteered.

"Did you think it might be loaded?" I'd continue.

"Of course" was the common refrain. "I wasn't going to stand around to find out," another responded.

"So what did you do?" I'd urge them on.

Some said they ran. Others said they got scared, or careful. These I took further. "So, knowing there was a hysterical kid, waving a potentially loaded gun just in front of you, I suppose you kept your eyes glued on him, on the gun, to make sure it didn't get pointed at you?"

What could they say? One by one they admitted that they either turned and ran or fixed their eyes to that gun. "Not one," I pointed out in my closing argument, "not a one, by their own admission, was looking where Joseph Williams was looking or saw what Joseph Williams saw: the face, the eyes, the setting muscles of the decedent, her reaction to the gun, her tendons cinching up, the readying of her own body to swing that bat, which in its trajectory could have crushed his skull or his son's. Not one could have seen it. Not one was looking there. And so Mr. Williams's testimony stands uncontradicted, unimpeached, that he fired in self-defense, believing in his heart of hearts in that split-second he had in which to act, that his life and his son's life were at risk."

The jury had learned about the rape of his daughter. We also had called character witnesses for Joseph. The jurors knew he was a decent man and that he had lived forty years as a law-abiding citizen. And his testimony, after days of preparation, mesmerized the jury. He spoke softly, with regret, as he explained why it was that he believed—in that instant there was for him to act—that he and his son were in mortal danger. Why it was he shot in self-defense. That he saw the lady there, with her body language, her neck muscles clenching, her jaw tightening, her hands and arms flexing, readying, her eyes betraying herself, preparing, and he knew, in every way, with every instinct, that the lady had panicked and was about to swing.

We showed the jury a videotape we had made using the cantaloupe, demonstrating how quickly the bat could have arched from the victim's side to intercept the temple and crush the skull of Mr. Joseph Williams.

The jury acquitted him. Of course they did. As they should have.

Linda had taken off from work to watch the trial. The night of Joseph's acquittal, she told me that she wanted us to spend more time together. She wouldn't give up her own apartment but began staying over at my place more. She liked, she said, being a kept woman. But she was still oddly restless and very independent. She insisted on going to parties with her girl-friends and taking vacations without me. As I said, she was the first woman since Margaret that I wanted to be close to. It was time for me, perhaps, to build a real intimacy. I told her I was ready to be faithful and asked for a commitment in return. She'd agree, say she wanted the same, but then change her mind. She'd excuse herself by saying she was too burned from her first marriage to give herself fully. That she needed more time. We semilived together like this for two years. I began to press her. I could have been more patient. When our conversation turned into an argument one evening last year and she moved out, I should have gone after her. But I was too full of my own importance. I was waiting for her to return to me. And when she started seeing a younger doctor, I thought it was only a ruse. I still considered her the closest thing to family I had. I tried then to woo her back. But I suppose it was too late. I tried, though, right up to the end . . .

16

MUDDY WAKES ME UP at sunrise, sitting by the edge of my cot and shaking my arm. Her eyes are red, but she seems excited. Her hair's tightly bound and tucked under a green cap that advertises Murphy's Irish Stout on the front. She holds a cup of hot coffee for me and urges me to sip it. Once I'm really awake, she motions for me to follow her to the glass doors that look out over the river. When I'm slow to respond she pulls me by the arm.

"What do you see?" She points out toward the mouth of the cove. At first I squint against the light. A red sun, massive in the dawn, hovers above the trees across the river, firing the water with streaks of color. There's some commotion out past the point. Gulls are clustering in the sky, wheeling and diving toward the river. "Look through the telescope," she says. I work the knob to the lens as she guides the scope to the place she's pointed. Then I see. The water looks to be boiling under the circling gulls—splashes and froth over an acre of river, wavelets colliding, spray flying, the flash of an arcing fish completely out of the water. "They're blues breaking," she says. "A big school. They're in a feeding frenzy. It's gonna be a warm day, again. Put these on and come on." She hands me the canvas overalls and hunting jacket and kicks toward me the ragged tennis shoes she's found for me. I dress quickly and follow her out to the dock. She's already loaded the fishing gear onto the boat and is starting the engine. "You're certainly well enough," she says. "And this'll be a treat."

We ride over the flat surface. Steering the wheel with her knees she rigs a silver spoon with a yellow-feathered hook onto a steel leader, tying it to the line running through one of the casting rods. We can see the fish breaking and the gulls screeching above and diving for the pieces of bait fish the blues leave in their wake. About fifty yards away from the frothing water she cuts the engine and we glide forward. "Do you remember how?" she asks.

"I think so. What about a license?" I say sheepishly.

"I have a boat permit," she answers. "Covers anyone in the boat. And there's no limit on blues. Go ahead." I open the bale of the spinning reel, loop the line over my finger, bring the rod back and whip the spoon far out. Before I can even start to reel in the lure, the line tightens and begins to run, sizzling off the spool, spinning the drag. "Drag's too loose." She laughs. As I twist it, the fish rises out of the water, whipping the air with its tail, and falls back in the river with a loud slap. It runs crosswise to our coasting boat, and I begin to reel hard. The rod bends in half, and when the fish turns away I can hardly wind the handle of the reel.

"Jesus," I exclaim.

"It's a hoss," she adds. She pushes my shoulder. "But come on. You're stronger than it is!"

After several minutes I have it close and she nets it. It's longer than my arm. She brings it over, dislodges the hook, and puts the fish in the live-box, whistling at its size. Then, using a canvas bucket, she scoops water from the river and douses the fish. I can't take my eyes off it. It doesn't resemble any bluefish you'd see in the markets in Washington, even the ones supposedly fresh. Its stripes of green, deep azure, silver, are iridescent, vital, muscular. "It sure looks different from the fish in the store," I say.

"Out here we call 'em 'greenies.' They taste different too," she adds. "Look—"

The school of feeding blues has moved into us. It's as if we weren't there. Above us a hundred gulls, their white bodies luminous in the light, whirl and bank, yawping in the air, while others hurtle into the water. All around us pirouettes of silver reach into the ether and fall back, a fish-thick boil.

"Damn!" I say.

"Yeah," she whispers back. "When they jump, I like to think they're trying to cross over to heaven." We both wait, soaking up the moment. "Throw your line again," she says after a while. "We've got our supper, but I'll smoke as many more as we can get."

I throw the lure and it seems a fish takes the spoon before it hits the water. "You're flying solo this time." She laughs again, picking up a rod. "I hear my own greenie calling."

She casts and whistles when her fish hits. As fast as we can reel and cast, they strike. In no time we have fifteen fish in the live-box. Muddy disentangles a line that has wrapped around the gills of one she's caught and throws it in with the others. She sits back, wraps her leader neatly around her reel, and sets her rod down. Her face is wet from perspiration. "I'm late," she says, wiping her brow. "I promised Agnes I'd tend things for her today. She has to run to Baltimore to see her specialist about her diabetes." Muddy reaches over and rinses her hands in the river, then looks out over the water. The breaking fish are moving away, off toward the channel. We're all alone on the wide river, carried by the tide, drifting south into the Choptank, the sun rising warm in the east, the vast bay shimmering beyond in the distance. The only sound is the occasional slush of water against the boat's side and the distant cry of a gull. "But it's almost sacrilegious to work on a morning like this." She takes my rod and winds the line neat as well, then starts the engine. She puts it into gear and moves the throttle forward. The boat planes high and runs smooth. We travel quickly back to the dock. "I'm going to jump out 'cause I'm late," she says. "Would you tie the boat up? Scale and fillet the fish for me?" She smiles, tucking her hair up tighter under her cap. "Wash and dry four fillets, and douse them with the olive oil in the kitchen cabinet? Keep 'em all refrigerated. We'll have 'em fresh tonight. Maybe tomorrow we'll smoke some." She eases the boat up to the wharf piling and hops out. She wraps the forward line around a cleat. "Oh, and freeze a few fish heads for bait?" And then she's gone.

She's left me with a bigger chore than I realized. Even tying the boat takes me some time. I don't want to embarrass myself by tying it too tight and letting the ebbing tide stretch the lines or tying it too loose and letting it scrape against the dock. When I'm satisfied, I haul the fish onto the wharf, and then rinse the fiberglass floor of the boat clean with the canvas bucket. I find a sharp knife in the kitchen. Scaling and filleting the fish takes the rest of the morning. I sit on the dock and work methodically, occasionally looking up to watch the changing river. I want to avoid thinking. I want to stay in the present . . .

But I can't. The past sweeps uninvited through the mind. I promised Muddy I'd tell her the story tonight of what I did wrong. I'm not sure I'm ready. There's something I'm missing still.

I relive my mistakes. How the trained intellect failed to detect its own undoing, case after case, year after year, failed to notice its own backward slide as the compromises became commonplace and took their toll. An imperceptible erosion. Like the erosion of the shoreline by the tide. Undetectable on any given day, in any given month. But after ten or twenty years, a marked contrast. The landscape changes. Islands disappear.

After Joseph Williams, after that transforming experience in his backyard that morning, I stood in the shoes of and actually became so many other clients, took their places as I had taken his, relived the tremors that shook their lives. I became Barbara Anderson, whose health clinic told her there were no appointments available when she called with chest pains and that night had a heart attack. I became Rosa Marquez, who was split from breast to hip with a carving knife by an ex-boyfriend who chased her home and caught her in the lobby of her tenement apartment house because her landlord had refused to repair the lock on the front door of the building. I became Jimmy Mathers, dying at age twenty from the chewing tobacco he had become addicted to on his farm at age eleven, unable to speak, a cancerous hole the size of a golf ball eaten through his jaw, and who had written the tobacco companies requesting only that they pay for his medical bills and for his funeral. There were others too, I admit—clients who were not so sympathetic or clearly deserving, when the real Victim in the process was harder to identify, when just winning spurred me on. When the money was too good to pass up. All of the cases had problems. All of them had another side. But in becoming the clients, in seeing things through their eyes, solutions were found to the problems. Creative solutions. I won most of these cases for my clients. I won them also for myself. It became easy, almost second nature to manipulate the facts to my advantage. I had become a master of spin.

I think of how far I traveled from my beginnings as a public defender and of the transitions I've made along the way. When I began as a young novice, all I did was point out to Manny Owens a habit he had of sniffling so that he would look his best when he testified. With Joseph Williams, on the other hand, I had helped manufacture testimony. I had taught him exactly what he needed to say—the only thing he could say—to have a chance at an acquittal. There was nothing in the Code of Professional Responsibility to condone that. But, again, even with Manny Owens, back at the beginning, by changing his habit of sniffling, didn't I change the facts? I didn't want him to sniff like a cocaine user before the jury. He *did* have a sniffling habit. Probably he *was* a cocaine user. Didn't I alter the truth there as well? Yet no lawyer would fault me for my preparation of him. So wasn't it really just a question of degree? And if so, who is smart enough to know exactly where the blurred line between right and wrong lies?

THIS AFTERNOON I set out for the first time on my own beyond the confines of this yard, protected as it is by the ruddied oak canopy overhead and the now russet dogwood leaves along its border. Opposite the back lane is a cornfield. I hear the Canada geese from the house and go toward the clamor of their barking. They have filled the rows and furrows, and rummage through the husks for kernels of yellow corn, carping one to another.

Canada geese are an organized species. While they're feeding they post sentries every fifty yards or so around their perimeter. These guards are easy to spot. They stand with their long necks craning high, their heads swiveling from side to side, alert on their posts, watching for predators—fox, raccoon, man. Canada geese mate for life. When I was young, my father hunted them, studied them, and often talked about their habits. He would remember with awe and regret those times he wounded a bird from his blind in the creek, dropping it into the water so that it couldn't fly. Its unhurt mate would settle in the water to remain at its side. Sometimes, chasing them in his gunboat, his shotgun in his lap, he'd get within range and shoot the mate before finishing off its wounded companion. Other times, when he got close enough to shoot, the wounded bird would dive. This, my father had learned, was a signal to its mate to fly to freedom. The wounded bird, swimming to the bottom, clung with its beak to the rooted grass until it drowned. He marveled at the instinct that engendered this sacrifice. He believed that the glory of flying over the earth and water, transecting the continent itself, must have ennobled the species. He hated that the birds down by the ferry dock were fed crusts by the tourists from the wharf and had gradually given up their instinctual migration in order to become year-round beggars for bread. "You'll never see one of them sacrifice itself," he once mumbled to me. "They've lost their honor. They've lost their way."

WHEN I GET BACK to the house, Muddy is not yet home from work. I see that the door to Muddy's bedroom is unlocked and slightly ajar. I hesitate, debating with myself, but in the end I push it open. My eyes are still adjusting from the brightness outside, and while I can see that the wall opposite her bed is covered with photographs, it takes me a few moments to realize what they are.

Taped together is a montage of pictures of wreckage from an explosion, like wallpaper, all of the same car, a black Mercedes, its doors blown off, its windshield gone, its hood crumpled and hanging to the side, one bumper torn loose. Some of the photos are in faded newsprint, others are glossy stills. Close-ups of the undercarriage, cratered and ripped, of the interior seats, shredded, of the burnt ceiling—these all run together. There's an overhead shot of the street, with debris surrounding the car and two bodies covered in sheets on the sidewalk.

Tacked to the adjoining wall to my left are newspaper clippings and pages of computer generated text. There's an article strung together from the *London Sunday Telegraph* about the Nicaraguan Resistance—the contras. Next to it is a piece from the *New York Times.* There are cutouts from newspapers from Latin America—from *El Nuevo Diario, La Prensa, La Tribuna.* Some paragraphs are highlighted with a yellow marker. I glance more closely at the text of some of the articles in English. Some of them are accounts of so-called vengeance killings, after the cease-fire between the contras and Sandinistas. Some are stories of paramilitary killings. Of abductions and disappearances. There's a photograph in *El Nuevo Diario* of a middle-aged man in a military uniform. It's circled in pencil. The face looks familiar. Below the picture is an article written in Spanish. I can puzzle out enough to get that the man was a senior officer with the contras—Rafael Bustillo. As I read further, I see his name referenced in another article in Spanish. On the floor below are books, one about the Sandinista revolution, another about the contras, cocaine, and the CIA. Next to the books are stacks of computer printouts. I look at the report on top, an email in Spanish sent from someone in Managua. I decide to see what I can find on Muddy's computer. Leaving the bedroom, I pause at the table next to the bed and the photographs of Muddy with her father. There are several of the two of them together, hugging and smiling. In one she hangs off him, her arm around his neck. She's laughing and her eyes are bright, innocently happy.

On the computer, codes block several of her files. I try to think of different passwords, her full name, her name reversed, her nickname, but get nowhere. Frustrated, I go online instead and key in contras, Sandinistas, Nicaragua+revolution. The search engines find stories, propaganda sites, fact sheets—all harrowing depictions of another place, another time.

Nicaragua, I learn as I read, was ruled by the Somoza dictatorship from 1934 until the Sandinistas took power in the late 1970s. The Somozas had sucked the country dry, diverting what little wealth it had, confiscating a full quarter of the land. Reports claimed that following the 1972 Managua earthquake, which killed over six thousand people, the Somozas diverted the millions in foreign aid to Swiss bank accounts and sold to Europe the blood plasma that was flown in by the Red Cross. Poverty, illiteracy, and disease wracked the country. By most accounts, the Sandinistas, led by Daniel Ortega, made sweeping improvements. Collective farming was organized, schools and hospitals built, land distributed. But the Sandinistas were leftists, and when Ronald Reagan took office, he set out to undo them. I read and remember—the old knee jerk conservative cowboy—making the contras his tool to begin the covert war.

I flick to a different website and read about the free elections held in 1984 and how Ortega's government won nearly seventy percent of the vote. And how Reagan then stepped up his campaign. I remember now hearing vague reports back then of the contras, trained and financed by the CIA, trying to destabilize the country. Of the World Court's voting to condemn the United States. Of Reagan's ignoring the condemnation. I had not been aware, as I read further, of the contra attacks on the collective farms, the health centers, mining the harbors, crippling trade. The contras, I read, built base camps over the border in Honduras and in El Salvador from which to mount their operations. The Sandinistas, with Soviet weapons, fought back. Neighboring sympathizers for each side provided arms and aid. The country was thrown into turmoil.

I recall discussing the whole Central American crisis one

night after a human rights fund-raiser at the Shoreham Hotel. Harry's law clinic had received an award for its work assisting refugees who'd fled the Pinochet government in Chile. The topic turned to the contras. I remember hearing skepticism about a Nicaraguan cease-fire that had just been reached. Now I read how it was breached in late 1989, months before the election. The article on the computer screen claims the contras went on a killing spree—a preelection campaign of terror. I recall others blaming the numerous assassinations during that time on the Sandinistas. The 1990 election brought to power a coalition of political parties led by Violetta Chamorro and the contras. I surf to other websites to get a balance of views and read on. About how the cease-fire was reinstated. Honored, anyway, in the breach, for the vengeance killings continued thereafter with chilling frequency. Not just in Nicaragua but across the borders in El Salvador, Honduras, and Guatemala. "Government policies don't erase memory," one commentator wrote. "Children baptized in blood and trained in brutality are not easily redeemed . . ."

Car wheels crunch on the loose gravel driveway outside. I see the outline of Muddy's Jeep fill the window. Shutting down the computer, I move into the hallway just as she enters the kitchen.

17

MUDDY'S HOLDING A GROCERY BAG in one hand and two bottles of wine in the other. She sets everything down on a counter and opens the refrigerator, takes out the fish fillets, and inspects them. "Thank you, Jack," she says. "Not half bad." Reaching in a drawer, she locates a corkscrew. I take it from her and open a bottle. She holds out two glasses and I pour some wine into each. "I need to take a little ride," she says. "It's close to dark. No one's looking for you anymore anyway. Why don't you come?"

She wraps up some of the fillets in plastic baggies and brings them with us. She drives up Tilghman Island Road, through St. Michaels and then left over the Ferry Bridge spanning the

Miles River. "I spent a lot of time fishing and swimming in this river as a girl," she says. "The mouth of the Wye's just up there. There's the old chapel ruins," she points. I can just make out through the trees a rectangle of crumbling stone walls, tangled and choked with vines.

"When did you get the tattoo?" I ask. "I saw it in the shower."

"It's an osprey. A hunter," she replies. "When I turned twenty-one I moved away to Baltimore for a couple months. To try out the city. Hooked up with this guy who lived over a tattoo shop. Ran a charter boat. Turned out to be a real asshole. When he gave me a black eye one night, I was gone. City was getting on my nerves anyway."

Past Tunis Mills Muddy takes a left down a dirt road, where six or seven trailer homes are scattered on a hard-packed tree-less lot in no particular order, as if they've been randomly dropped there. She pulls up to one with rusty aluminum siding, and two dogs come running toward us. A child sits on a tire in the dirt playing with a plastic dump truck. A dark-skinned man walks around from the back just as Chula hollers, *"Hola!"* from the front door. The screen bangs behind her. Muddy takes the fillets out and gives them to Chula. They hug, chat for a few moments, disappear inside briefly, and then Muddy's back in the Jeep and we're heading again toward Tilghman Island.

Muddy flicks on the radio. The end of a country song plays out. The hourly news comes on. The newscaster begins report-ing on the latest polls predicting the primary election and on another surge in Internet stocks. There's mention of an upcoming trade conference. Muddy changes channels, then switches the radio off. She turns quiet, introspective, almost brooding. Driving back over the Ferry Bridge, the river to our left has filled with floating ducks and geese, thousands of shadowy silhouettes bleating softly in the dusk.

AS WE DRIVE HOME, I try to think about what's happening. I've gotten in deeper than I ever should have allowed. What I want is to hold a hand out to this woman. To be honest, more than a hand. But she lives a stable life. Her fixations are disturbing, but clearly she's maintained her equilibrium for years. If she chooses to hold her grief close, who am I to interfere? And with what?

There was a time, just months ago, when I was a force. Just my appearance in a case could shift the balance. People hired me because I had influence, clout; people paid to hear my advice and heeded it. I don't have much to offer now. Just a rag man, a person believed drowned, without an identity, a man stripped bare.

She wants me to tell her what I did. But it's not one day, one decision, one miscalculation that has done me in. It's a story. The last act is driven by the scene before, and that scene by the one before it. And even those last sad mistakes—how do I explain them and not convey what has been happening to me here, over the past days, here with this girl in this simple cottage on the river?

BACK AT DUN COVE, while Muddy's in the back room I take a quick hit of scotch. I then refill the wineglasses. Muddy chooses a Janis Joplin album and sets it playing. I peel potatoes while she prepares the fish fillets. After washing and drying them, she chops anchovies from a tin, and using butter, fresh minced garlic, and some olive oil, she makes an anchovy paste, which she slathers over them. Where did she learn all this? "I worked for a while in the kitchen at the Inn at Perry Cabin," she says, reading my thought. She sets the fish aside and puts the potatoes on to boil. She spreads out some hummus on a plate and dribbles olive oil and paprika on top and arranges pita bread alongside. I carry the plate out to the flagstone patio overlooking the water. The sun has dropped behind us. The swans float along the shore, barely moving. She starts the grill and sits with me, gazing out over the settling river.

We eat outside wearing sweatshirts, talking little, mostly watching the cove and darkening sky. After it gets too chilly we go back in, and she starts a fire from the cedar sticks by the grate but leaves the glass door open. I move her desk chair over by the cot, facing the fire. We pour more wine and slowly sip from our glasses. The room is warm. She pulls off her sweatshirt. She breaks the silence by telling me she's taking some time off from work, that these days are just too nice to be inside. "Each of these days," she says, "is a gift." I wonder where this is leading. I tell myself she's old enough to know what she wants. But I'm old enough to know not to further complicate her life. Not to lose my head, if I haven't already. Or is this just vanity on my part? Am I flattering myself? Reading in more than is here? That's when she asks me if I will begin. "Will you tell me, now, what you did?" is what she says.

I gulp down my wine.

"Jack?" she asks again.

SO HERE I AM, standing, resting one foot on the hearth watching the fire. A pose. I tell myself I want to be truthful. To offer Muddy a real picture. To give her some insight into my motivation. But instead I find myself talking about Margaret. About how unprepared I'd been when Margaret left me, how unaware I'd been of how unhappy she was. About not knowing, back then, what to do with Stephen—with Margaret's demand he be adopted. About how I wondered what he looked like, grown now to manhood. Muddy asks me if I know where Stephen lives. I don't. My guess is that Margaret is still in Jacksonville. The man she married is named Robert Traywick, I say. Jesus. I'm asking this girl for pity. And avoiding her question. She just nods and waits.

I try again to oblige but end up talking abstractly and in clichés about redemption, the reclamation of a life. How from the day she pulled me from the river the idea has wavered out there on the horizon just beyond my reach. Like an ephemeral dream.

She listens but pushes for facts.

"But what did you do, Jack, to get in so much trouble? Specifically. I want to know."

"There was a woman I had been seeing for some time," I finally manage.

I WADE IN, trying to describe Linda and our relationship, Linda's work at the children's hospital in the city, how I sometimes consulted with her on my medical cases, and how I would pay her. And occasionally, when she saw some child brought into the hospital who'd received negligent care and been hurt, how she'd try to refer me the case. In those instances I promised her a referral fee, and she sometimes made serious money.

"She sent me a case one day," I explain. "It involved a new-

Tim Junkin

born who was transferred to D.C. from a small hospital in southern Maryland. The doctor in charge of the labor and delivery had been negligent, blatantly negligent. His name was Hewitt. During the mother's labor he'd been called numerous times by the hospital nurse who was concerned at what the fetal heart monitor showed—that the baby was suffering from low oxygen and needed to be delivered quickly. The parents were from Belize and could speak little English. They brought a copy of the medical record to my office. Ramirez was their name. Each time the nurse called Dr. Hewitt, who was seeing paying patients in his clinic close by, he told her to run a different test. Every test was the same—nonreassuring. The doctor waited four hours from her first call—until all his private patients had been seen—before coming to the hospital to examine Maria Ramirez. Once there, of course, he ordered an emergency cesarean section, but it was too late. The baby—they named her Angelina—was born alive but severely brain damaged. The cord had been wrapped tightly around her neck, and she'd been deprived of oxygen for hours. Angelina was transferred to Linda's hospital, where, after a week of trying everything, the doctors advised the parents that the only humane course was to remove her from life support. They're Catholic. Were new in a foreign country. Initially refusing, they suffered for weeks over what to do. Their priest was asked to intervene. Eventually, of course, they agreed."

I pause here. Hesitant to continue. Such a grim story. There will be no happy ending. I look at Muddy for a reaction. She blocks me with a gentle stoicism. "Go on," she urges.

"Okay, then. In Maryland at the time there was a statute passed at the behest of the medical insurance lobby. It protected doctors from being sued for negligence in delivering newborns. The largest verdicts had often come down in these baby cases, as the victims can live a long time and need so much in medical and rehabilitative care. These costs, added up over an expected lifetime, can be huge. So the insurance lobby got this statute passed. The Newborn Medical Recovery Act. No other citizen lost the right to sue. Only infants injured during birth by negligent doctors."

"Sounds about typical," Muddy says stiffly. "But I thought there was a right to sue. Even if it's just there to placate people, at least I thought there was that right."

"In place of the right to sue the statute set up a no-fault compensation scheme. Like worker's comp. This, supposedly, provided protection to the infants without their having to prove negligence—as though the statute was passed to protect them. To my way of thinking, it was a farce. The compensation scheme paid only for medical expenses that the compensation board deemed, quote, reasonable and necessary, unquote, and then only if there was no other source to pay—no insurance or medical assistance. As for compensation to the child, it paid only if the child reached age eighteen and then only two-thirds the minimum wage in the state. In the case of Mr. and Mrs. Ramirez, since their medical bills were covered by Medicaid, and since their baby died before reaching working age, they would receive nothing at all. Not a cent. Not even reimbursement for the funeral expenses."

As I tell this, I remember meeting the parents, listening to their broken English, seeing the pain in their faces, and I am angry all over again. They'd given me photographs of them holding Angelina. She was full size. Seven pounds. She looked healthy, beautiful, except that her eyes were shut. I move from the hearth to sit on the cot, to finish telling all this to Muddy. I tell her how as I listened to them I believed they'd lost their child because of a bad law and a callous doctor—someone who, confident he was immune from suit, chose to remain in his clinic billing patients rather than hurry to the hospital to care for an immigrant woman and her suffering child. "The law was wrong," I told Muddy. "I decided to challenge it as fundamentally unfair, as unconstitutional."

I stand up again, fidgety. "You with me?" I ask. "So far so good, right?"

She remains nonjudgmental. "So far so good," she replies.

"My clients, after losing their baby girl, had left Maryland and moved into Washington to live with a relative. Nine months passed. They'd been to several lawyers who declined the case because of the statute."

My wineglass is on the mantel, and I retrieve it and take a swallow. "I knew it was financially risky," I continue, "as I would have to advance all expenses. And I knew it would be an uphill fight. But looking at that little child's photograph, I wanted to do it."

"You ever hear of Don Quixote? Tilting at windmills and all that?"

"You're too cynical for twenty-three." She is, I realize.

"Well?"

"I filed the case in federal court in Washington. I could do this based on diversity of citizenship jurisdiction, since the Ramirezes lived in D.C. and the doctor lived in Maryland. He had a second office in Washington also, which made it legal to sue him there. Since the negligence occurred in Maryland, though, Maryland law applied. His lawyers, hired by his insurance company, filed a motion to dismiss the case based on the statute. I opposed it. I spent weeks in the law library, researching constitutional law. I argued my side before the federal judge. To my surprise he agreed with me that the statute was unconstitutional and allowed the case to go forward. I hired medical experts ready to testify that the doctor's neglect caused the damage to the child's brain. With the momentum of the judge's ruling in my favor, if we could win before a jury, I felt we might even survive the Supreme Court.

"The night before the trial, while I was preparing, Linda Morrison came to my office. She was nervous, upset. She knew about the statute and she hated it too. She had sent me the case and stood to gain a lot if we won. Linda told me, though, that she had done something wrong. The baby's hospital chart, after weeks, was thick, several hundred pages. In her fervor to help the family, she had removed from the chart the results of a genetic test done while the child was at the hospital, which showed a genetic abnormality. In the hands of the defense, it would be used to blame the child's brain damage on a genetic defect as opposed to the doctor's negligence. If discovered, it could cause us to lose the trial. Linda had come to me asking what she should do."

Muddy whispers. "You jiggered it, and it unraveled . . ."

I THROW NEW CEDAR SPLITS on the fire and watch them ignite. The coals below glow red and hot. We can hear, along with the fire, the waves washing the shore. Muddy has pulled her scarab free and holds it in her fingers, turning it. "I can see us there," I answer her. "I can picture to this day Linda and me sitting there, both of us stunned by what she'd told me. But I hardly missed a beat. I remember pacing for only a minute or two before giving her my answer."

I pause at this and move to the cot. And then I really do try to explain myself to Muddy. "In some corner of my mind I must have sensed that going along with Linda's fraud was going farther than I had ever gone. Yet the case seemed important beyond even the clients—seemed more important, certainly, than this detail that jabbed at my conscience. I thought of the Ramirez child. I thought of the statute that I believed was so wrong and that I believed I could change with this case. Like Sarah Simmons, like other clients before and after her, I felt that in some way I had become the person I was representing. Not only Angelina Ramirez but also those children yet to be born who might suffer her same fate. I'm sure I told Linda all this. I know for certain I told her that with the trial judge's ruling and the compelling negligence of Dr. Hewitt, I had the best chance any lawyer would ever have to overturn this law. I offered her my solution, a way out, a justification—one that was slick—a lawyer's trick . . ."

"Like you'd never before used a lawyer's trick?" Muddy adds.

"Of course I had."

"So?"

"I told Linda that discovery in the case was closed. Discovery's the fact-finding phase. For each side it was over, and the defense had no knowledge of the genetic test. The chances of it surfacing were minimal. I told Linda that if she chose to consider her disclosure to me as an attorney-client communication —as her seeking legal advice from me on a legal matter within the privilege of an attorney-client relationship—then I would be duty bound to keep what she told me confidential. And I told her I would do so—that I would forget I ever heard what she said. The alternative, I told her, would be to come forth with what she'd done, whereupon she'd most certainly be fired, would probably lose her nursing license, might even get prosecuted herself. I'd lose the case, and the statute would remain unchallenged. She considered what I said. What choice was there? At least the way I presented it.

"She even paid me a dollar for the consultation—to make our attorney-client relationship official."

MUDDY HAS GOTTEN UP and stands looking out through the screen door. Opening it, she steps out on the patio. I hold back. I've told Muddy most of the truth. I can't bring myself to reveal the other part. About my trying to sleep with Linda that night and her refusing.

"Jack?" Muddy calls softly.

I go outside behind her. A harvest moon has risen over the river. The surface glows like a reflecting mirror across the way, a satin covering. The water in the cove, though, shimmers strangely. An eerie florescence wavers just under the surface. Muddy steps to the side, making room for me to stand next to her.

"It gets this way sometimes," she whispers. "Every now and then. It's rare to see, really. 'The wands of the river fairies,' my father used to say. It's the phosphorescence in the plankton. Like little tiny underwater lanterns strung everywhere. The water is just full of green light." Her arms are crossed, and she drops them to her side. She brushes the back of my hand with the back of hers. "It's something to wonder at, don't you think? Sometimes I'm surprised that this river here's not enough. Is not all I need. But it's not, is it? For any of us?" Before I can answer, she goes on. "What you did wasn't so different from what you'd done before, was it? I mean *you* didn't change that medical record. And you *did* have an obligation to give Linda her legal options, didn't you?"

WE STAND OUTSIDE watching for a good while, until I sense Muddy shiver. I put my arm around her and lead her back inside. She pours the last of the wine into my glass, then holds the empty bottle upside down. I go into the kitchen and open the second bottle and bring it out. I throw more splits on the fire and sit down on my cot, and she pulls her chair close in front of me. "The trial started the next day." I want to finish this. "It lasted two weeks. I won. The jury awarded the parents a large sum. Nine hundred thousand."

"Wow. Congratulations."

"Yes, well, thank you. But . . . The doctor, as expected, appealed. When a federal judge throws out a state statute, there's a right to appeal, all the way up to the Supreme Court."

"What happened there?"

I tell her how we first had to win at the circuit court, which we did. The case had made me prominent in D.C. and Maryland in the struggle for victim's rights. Several constitutional experts offered and provided me free help. With their assistance I prepared an even more extensive legal brief and filed it before the Supreme Court. I was well coached, articulate, and persuasive during the oral argument. And when the Court handed down its decision, it was in our favor. I had indeed truly won. Or so it seemed. The statute was thrown out as unfair and as a denial of equal protection.

"I got paid. I pocketed a third. I was written up in all the law journals. Linda got a nice piece. But then the case, as you say, unraveled. And my world got turned upside down ..."

Muddy takes the bellows down from off a hook under the mantel. She leans over, working air onto the coals. The fire backlights her slim figure. "So how did it happen?" she asks. "That you got caught?"

I tell her how. How shortly after the Supreme Court issued its ruling the defense lawyer attended a hospital fund-raiser— for Linda Morrison's hospital. How of all people, he ran into the geneticist who'd done the test on Angelina Ramirez. How they started talking. How the case came up. How one thing must have led to another. How the next day the lawyer called me. Unbeknownst to me, he had telephoned the U.S. attorney's office in Washington first. He got my old nemesis—Morgan Langrell. Muddy winces at his name.

"Langrell'd been appointed as *the* U.S. attorney for Washington," I tell her. "Top dog. He jumped on the case. When the lawyer called me, Langrell was taping the call."

"Oh, shit," she murmurs.

"Yeah."

I try to tell the rest straight. That when the defense lawyer told me what he'd discovered, I knew the verdict was lost. The ruling on the statute would still stand, but the lower court judge would have to grant a new trial. But I wanted to protect Linda. I lied on the phone, denying any knowledge of the genetic test. The lawyer acted like he believed me. Langrell subpoenaed me to testify before the grand jury. I should have hired my own counsel, but I was too full of myself, overconfident. Again, I told myself I was protecting Linda. Rather than advise the grand jury that I couldn't answer their questions because of the lawyer-client privilege of confidentiality, I claimed to have no knowledge of the matter. I could have thought it through better. They were never after Linda. They were after me.

"Well, with all that personal stuff between you and Langrell—"

"Of course. They had dusted the hospital medical chart of Angelina Ramirez for fingerprints and then matched them with those of hospital employees. Linda's prints were all over the chart. The prints of other nurses were on it too, but Linda was the only one not involved in the child's care. Before my grand jury testimony they had used their typical tactics on her, threatening her, frightening her. They had flipped her, cut a deal, and she had told them everything. When I phoned her the night before my grand jury appearance, she played dumb, just as they had instructed her. She sounded depressed, flat, denied having heard from anyone. I didn't catch on. I went into the grand jury, took an oath, and lied, still convinced I was protecting her. The next day, when I called her again, she told me what really was happening. Told me I was caught, guilty, about to be arrested. They had me, she said. She turned cold on the phone, hostile, blamed me for dragging her in, for convincing her to cover things up. Said she'd been fired, that she was going to lose her license and her career. That she never wanted to hear my voice again. Called me a crook, which I am. I defrauded the court in a case of national importance. I lied under oath to the grand jury. They froze my bank accounts to ensure they'd get the nine hundred thousand back. I panicked and stole a trust account check from my office. That's how I got this cash. Trust account money isn't mine. It's clients' money. I took it. I became a perjurer and a disgrace. Perhaps also a coward. And Linda . . . Well I didn't expect it . . . I couldn't face it. I ran. I had to run. I was preparing myself over there." I pointed out toward the river. "Over there at Boxmoor. I was steeling myself. Preparing myself for the end, preferring it to being dragged back to Washington for the humiliation I'd face. And so when they found me, I took to the river. At least I did that. I swam out. When I kept seeing my lost son's face, though— Stephen—I realized I wanted to live. But I did swim out there to die. Maybe you should have let me . . ."

Oh, Stanton, you weak bastard, I think to myself.

18

I HAD, SOME TIME BEFORE, turned my gaze to the floor. It takes me a while to look back up. Muddy's watching me. "You didn't mean that," she says uncertainly. "That last remark—about maybe I should've let you drown ..."

"Sorry," I stammer. "You're right. That last part wasn't true. Things have changed for me. And are changing still, faster than I can keep up. I don't know why I said that. But you're right. That last part I didn't mean."

She takes her wine and swirls the last sip before finishing it. Then pours herself a half glass. She glances at me, her expression unsure. She puts her glass on the floor and crosses her arms.

I know my face must betray my dismay—over the gloss I've put on the whole sordid affair, over my concern as to how Muddy would react, and now, superimposed on this, my regret for my insensitivity—that last self-pitying remark, made for dramatic effect, out of old rhetorical habit I suppose. I reach out and slip my fingers around her arm and then pull it toward me. She lets me take her hand.

"Yes," she whispers. "I see. But, no. You didn't mean that. You're alive now. And it's not so bad . . ."

She turns over my palm and begins examining the lines there. She traces the patterns with her finger. "You meant right, I know." She raises my hand to her lips and kisses my palm. Then she wraps my hand in hers. "With the Ramirez baby. With Sarah Simmons. Even with those young men back in the beginning. When you were a defender. It's not so simple, sometimes, to know what's best. Hard sometimes to figure . . ."

"I slid right into it," I say. "It seemed such an obvious answer. For the case, for Linda and me. Such a perfect solution . . . It all just got so easy . . ."

"It *is* hard, sometimes, isn't it, to know what to do? To be and act grown?"

"You talk yourself into things. At least, I do."

"In your world the truth was not so important. There was something else you were after." Her tone turns wistful. "In me, for some reason, there's a voice says it matters."

"That's not a bad thing."

"I hope not . . ."

"Of course it matters. Whether it matters most, over all else, I don't know. That's a harder question. But, yes, it matters."

She stretches apart my fingers, examining them. "Seems

you've always been there for your clients, though, haven't you? Strong for them . . ."

"Tried to be," I say.

She looks up. "Well, you shouldn't have swum out there like that." She presses my thumb.

"No," I answer. "I know. But it's never quite the same, is it? You know? For yourself. Dealing with yourself?"

"What?"

"Having that strength."

"You mean it's easier to do it for others . . ." Muddy nods to herself, and seems to appreciate this. She begins to gently knead my hand.

"Can you read it?" I ask. "My palm?"

She smiles sadly. "I wish," she says. "This line here, I think, means you've got a future. It's a nice long one."

"Thanks to you, again."

"To timing, huh?"

"Right."

"Only half bad, now."

"How so?"

She shrugs. "When I was a little girl, you know what I'd pretend to be?"

I shake my head.

"A yak." She smiles again, more shyly. "Daddy took pictures of me. I'd crawl around the house and howl like a yak. I think I'd seen a picture of a yak in a book or something. Pretty strange, huh? And then when I got older, I wanted to be Annie Oakley. She moved here, you know. Lived in Cambridge. Hunted and fished these same waters. There's a museum, there. She beat all the best shots in the country. Pretty amazing, really."

"Like *Annie Get Your Gun?*"

"Yeah, but she was real. A crack shot. Better than any man. Steady as they come."

Muddy lets go of my hand and rests back. She takes her amulet and puts it up to her lip.

"You always wear that don't you?"

"It's my charm. My good luck bug."

"Where'd you get it?"

"In a fishing village. In Honduras. A present from my father. It's a beetle shell. A scarab."

"It's Egyptian?"

"They have their own scarab beetles in Central America. For some people, they're still a charm. I learned about them. The females roll their dung into balls and lay their eggs inside. The hatched beetles are protected and nourished. They climb out. New life from shit." She crinkles her face. "Yuck, eh? Well maybe it's a good image for me. For you too. In Egypt they used to believe the scarab pushed the sun across the sky. Here, though, they've put the name on a nasty speedboat. One of those cigarette boats ... The Scarab ..."

I reach over and touch the shell. It's warm from the fire.

"Daddy found it in a market stall. A few days before he was killed."

Muddy's voice goes quiet as she says this. She shivers, involuntarily. She takes a moment. "If only we could learn from each other's mistakes," she says, seeming to complete a broken thought, her voice resigned. "But we don't do that. Do we?" She raises her eyes to mine. "I mean if we could only really help each other."

Muddy gets up and stirs the fire again, adding more of the

201

cedar to the flames. "I figure you do owe me," she says lightly. "And I've got a couple promises I want you to make."

"A couple?"

"Yeah." She laughs as though her request were a trifle. Sitting, she reaches for my fingers again. "You know, I haven't had anyone to share this house with, to share an evening meal with, in a while. I had a friend over in Neavitt who used to visit. He was studying landscaping at the college. He wanted me to be more normal, though. I think I scared him off."

"When was that?"

"Last time I saw him was spring. Before him, there were a few others. Most of the men here, though, the ones I meet anyway, they're a little on the wild side. Need some smoothing out. My Aunt Ruthy claimed they grow up late around here. Slow to develop. Something in the water, she used to say."

"She looked after you, after your father . . ."

"She moved in and lived with me until graduation. Till I got settled and in a routine. Here and at the store. And even after, she'd come by often. Before she got sick."

"When did you graduate?"

" '95."

"You don't mind being alone?"

"Sometimes I mind it. Chula visits. I have a few friends. Raptite, my ganja and bee man, he's a hoot. He plays guitar in a band, and sometimes I'll go listen. But I'm settled in. Like an old maid. I've gotten fixed in my ways. Me and the river. Least until you decided to swim over." She takes off her Murphy's Irish Stout cap and shakes her hair free. It falls, catching the firelight. She brushes her bangs back with her fingers. "It never really bothered me. I mean I wanted it at first. Then I tried not to notice it. Being alone. Maybe I did. But I pretended not to."

"I've upset things," I say.

"No. Maybe. I mean I was ready for some company. Must have been or the river wouldn't have handed you over so easy. I've been thinking about it. People . . . at least people like me . . . Well, like maybe wanting someone's not so bad. If only . . . if only I could afford it."

"You can afford it."

She tilts her head coquettishly. "You're not even staying . . ."

"Right," I answer quickly. "I didn't mean me. It's just that . . . Well, you've been more than good to me, Muddy. I wouldn't know how to thank you."

"You've been okay for me too, Jack."

"What promises do you want me to make?"

I watch her then, as she drops my hand. She gets up off her chair and kneels in front of me on the braided rug. She smoothes out her long hair, her eyes lowered. Is this really happening? She raises up and kisses me lightly, quickly, just brushing her lips over mine.

That's all it takes. A taste, a rush of blood. I know that any restraint that's left is slipping away. I let out a long breath.

She blushes slightly but seems amused. "You told me you'd be truthful," she says. "That's one of the promises I want you to make. That you'll tell the truth. Will you promise?"

"Muddy, I've been in your bedroom," I blurt out. "I've seen what's there."

She settles back, startled, unsure.

"Your bedroom door was open. I went in for just a minute.

I apologize. But I was curious. Wanting to know you better. I saw what you have there, on the walls."

She stares, taking this in. She looks away, uncertain. She begins arranging her hair, twisting it back with her two hands, winding it tight.

"The second promise you must make is that whatever happens, you won't try to interfere with my life." Her voice is flatter, directed away. "I'm grown. I'll choose my way. I know things don't usually work out in this world. Whatever you do. But I'll pick my own way. Will you promise?"

"What about your bedroom? What you have on the walls? You need to move on. We're the same in this. We both do."

She interrupts me. "The future's unsure for everyone. A big fat question mark. And you've got to leave here soon anyway. In a couple of days. You need to promise that too. I'm asking you to promise all this. In return for what I've done." Her voice drops off with these last words.

I hold my tongue. I won't commit. "You told me you'd talk to me as well. All of this . . ." I motion toward the newspapers stacked on the floor, and then toward her room.

Her eyes seem to quicken, to dart like a bird's.

I take a moment to let her calm down. She does, but then seems to drift away, to retreat behind a mask. "Help me to understand," I ask. "Share some of this?"

"You're pushing me, Jack," she says quietly. "Anyway, it's not shareable."

"Who is this Bustillo?"

She glares at me. "Just in there for a minute, Jack? Right!"

"I don't know anything. That's why I'm asking."

She watches me, looking for something. I stay silent, waiting. She lets her hair go and exhales slowly.

"Promise first?"

I nod and say, "Okay. I promise."

Shifting her position, she draws her feet up tight against the inside of her thighs. She says "Okay" back, but her voice is still flat. She puts her hands together under her chin, as though in prayer. She remains that way for a time. Then she begins to speak, softly. I have to strain to hear.

"When I first came home I couldn't do anything." She closes her eyes. "For six months or so. I could barely eat. Then I drew the face of the man who placed the bomb. The face of the man I saw back away from the car. It was one of the first things I could do ..."

She pauses and blinks her eyes open, her face controlled. "He was the one. I'm sure of it. I know it on my life. I've never forgotten it. I sketched his face from every angle. With a beard, without. With a mustache, clean shaven. Even as I imagined it aging. Daddy left me some money, so I hired a lawyer—we took the sketches to Washington. We went to all the Justice Department people. To the State Department. To everyone. They all acted sympathetic, sincere. So concerned. Everyone promised to help identify him. We never heard back.

"A year or so ago, after I had met Chula and gotten to know her, when she was here one day, she recognized the man. From my drawings. Just a coincidence. She says he was a National Guardsman and a contra terrorist. Now he's a wealthy land-owner in Nicaragua. Very rich, with the aid of our government. Chula knew his face from the newspapers. With her help I learned his name. It's Rafael Bustillo.

"So we took *this* information back to Washington. Same shit as before but worse. They said I must be confused. That he was a big-deal coffee farmer. Important, respected. And that there wasn't enough evidence anyway. That is what they said. That there was nothing to be done."

Muddy stops like she is finished. I try not to move. I can see the tears welling up in her eyes. She rubs them with her thumbs. Then puts her hands on her knees, dropping her head.

"A second before the explosion," she says softly, "I heard sounds. The wind . . . a crumpled paper rustling down the street . . . It drew my eyes and I saw it. And then an airplane's hum. Like on and on. Like time had stopped. And then I was knocked back against the door. I fell hard on the cement landing. I lay there and already knew. I already knew, Jack . . . There was a ringing in my head. I couldn't hear anything else. But I knew. There was smoke everywhere. The car was rocking. My father was on the sidewalk. He looked like he was kneeling, tilted, but one leg had been blown away. He was swaying from side to side. There was blood all over the pavement. He was just swaying there, but when I got to him he reached for me. Blood came out of his mouth. A lot of it. His face was badly burned. I held on to him until they pried me loose." She lifts her shoulders up, defiant. "So there . . ." she whispers.

I drop down off the cot, onto the floor, inching as close to her as I can. She stifles a sob. She stays still at first, but as I reach she helps me put my arms around her. She rocks toward me and rests her cheek on my shoulder. I just sit still as she cries silently.

After she stops, I use my fingers and then my shirt to wipe her face. I touch the corners of her lids and dab at her chin. She kisses my arm. "Give me a minute," she says. She gets up and goes into the bathroom. I hear water running. I try to clear my head, to think my way through all this, and then she's back, drying her face with a towel. She lifts both our wineglasses off the floor and hands me mine.

"Like you said, I *will* be moving on with this." She speaks deliberately, quietly. "The time is coming for me to do that. I know. It just has to take its own pace. So here's to getting past it. And surviving . . . Here's to both of us making it . . ."

We drink, and she leans up and kisses me on the cheek, lightly again. "Come with me?" she asks. She takes my arm and walks me to the bedroom. She opens it with her key. She goes in, but I hesitate, standing in the doorway. "Okay, here's a start," she says, smiling. "Will you help?" She begins taking down the photographs and articles taped to the wall, peeling off the tape, letting each paper fall to the floor. I watch and then join her. We clear one wall and begin on a second. She leans sideways, into me, and then kisses me, awkwardly, brushing my cheek, but I turn and catch her lips. Gently at first, a light touching, which leads to another, feathery, a delicate parting. And then more, mouths opening, tasting, and then full and slow and part rough. I drop the paper I've taken down. She presses hard then, avid and eager, and I squeeze her tightly back. I pin her to the wall, kissing her neck, her face, her still damp eyes. She hooks one leg around me, drawing me closer, bringing my lips back to her mouth. I fumble at a button. She helps me. Her blouse comes open, her breasts are in my hands.

She runs her fingers through my hair, then gently pushes my head back. There are tears still in her eyes. "God," she says, and laughs. I laugh too. We kiss again, slowly. And again. She turns me and moves us both to the bed. There she pulls me against her with a frantic strength, which I return. I breathe and taste her hair. Reaching down, I unsnap her jeans. She raises up her hips and wiggles to help me pull them free. She watches my face. Hers is colored with a deep flush, her eyes glistening, expectant. With her fingers, she takes my zipper. I bury my head in her breasts, tasting her nipples, then in her belly, hot and soft. She makes a deep guttural sound, and looking up I watch her lift her hands over her head and take the headboard and press back against it. She brings my head back up, strokes me, kisses my face, my mouth. Slipping a hand into my trousers, she touches my erection. Then pushing my waistband down, she guides me to her. She arches to meet me as I enter her. I try to lead, to go slow, but her need is unlike anything I have known. We roll each other over and she straddles me, her lips apart, her face hungry, feral, as she moves on me, slow then faster, urgent, determined. My hands on her inner thighs feel the flex of her tendons. We roll over again. I pull my head up to watch her face and to see her body move. She puts her palm against my forehead, as though in a blessing as she arches again, and then again, tightening me against her with her other arm. There's a straining and a shudder and a gasp as I pull out and then clutch her close. And all I know for certain is that being there with her is beyond anything I ever expected.

PART THREE

Allenwood

19

THE LATE AUTUMN DAYS, one after another, always rough me up. Maybe it's the shortening reach of the sun. Or the warmth receding. Whatever the reason—the coming of the winter solstice, of early, encroaching darkness—it takes me down. All my life. And it's true here too, where I now live.

I'VE KNOWN OTHERWISE. A year ago, during that short spell with Muddy, it was different. It was as if the seasons reversed themselves, as though summer returned to warm us with streaming yellowish light, thick with dust and falling leaves. The river turning purple at dusk. It was both a renewal and a long good-bye. I gave myself over, taking what was offered, giving back what I had. The nights together were never long enough. They seemed to rush by. We'd go fast, slow, hardly sleep, and then the dawn gulls were crying out over the cove.

THE FIRST MORNING, Muddy brought me coffee and cinnamon toast and kissed me. "Your beard is growing in handsomely," she said. "I'll be out on the dock."

After showering and dressing I went outside. The day was a replication of the one before and the one to come, sharp and clear, the river running blue out beyond the cove, the trees rustling along the shore, the mud flats exposed, fetid, glistening from the receding tide. Muddy's smoker was venting off to the side of the cottage, emitting the smell of smoldering apple chips, Worcestershire sauce, and fish in the air. She had pulled her Mako up into the reeds. Emptied it of its gear, which lay strewn about the wharf. She was painting the hull with a large brush, covering the white fiberglass with a drab olive color. I watched her work, intent on her task. She had her hair tight up under her green cap again.

"I'm camouflaging the boat," she volunteered. "There's a late season for sea ducks this year. You can shoot from the boat." She looked up. "Want to paint?"

We finished the boat by noon and, after cleaning up, lunched on smoked fish, cheddar cheese, white grapes, and beer. After we ate she put on a record, Louis Armstrong singing "In My Solitude."

I JUST WENT WITH the holy flow, without hesitation or remorse. After all, the need was shared, as keen in her as it was in me. I took it for what I thought it was. A blessing. A gift of grace. Something you're willing to stake your life on. Even for someone as lost as me.

Still, at odd moments during that time, I recognized an unease on Muddy's part. There was an occasional skittishness, a pulling back, something withheld. Maybe she was just more realistic.

"We have to talk about this," Muddy finally said. "I think it's best to just get it out."

"Yes," I answered. "I've been meaning to—"

"It's okay," she interrupted.

We had made love and, afterward, wrapped in blankets, gone out to the patio. We lay down together on the chaise and watched the geese migrating over the river. Muddy propped herself up on her arm and was pulling at the graying hairs on my chest, teasing me, but then turned quiet, more sullen, studying me.

"I've been thinking of a plan," I lied.

"Right," she said sadly. "I mean everything's changed, but nothing's changed, has it, about you having to leave."

"I'm ready. I know it's time."

"I suppose." She sighed, burrowing in next to me.

"For sure."

"Okay, what? A plan, huh?"

"Yeah."

"God, Jack. Things never happen when they should."

"Sometimes, no."

"The honest truth you already know. I wish you didn't have to go. But it doesn't matter."

"It matters, but I still have to."

"Wishing doesn't make it so."

"It's all right, Muddy."

"It's not all right. But—"

"But I *do* have to."

She looked out toward the cove. "Yes."

"Of course. For my own sake."

I followed her gaze. The river was still. A cat's-paw tripped along the surface near the shore, causing a tremor in the watery reflection of the trees. An osprey glided over the shallows.

"I don't want to leave you either. But I know I'd be discovered here. I know too many people. From here, from D.C. who come here."

Muddy shuddered. She looked back. "Have you thought about just turning yourself in? Getting it over with?"

"I don't want that." With a finger I played with her hair. "I want to live now."

She tucked in even closer.

"And hell, I'm nearly fifty. Six or seven years in prison at this point is just too much. I'd rather take my chances. Find some simple, honest work. The law won't be looking for Jack Stanton, except to wash up bloated on some beach. If I go far away from here, if I'm careful and a little lucky I may never get caught."

"They shouldn't send you to prison."

"Oh, but they would. I'm the kind of example they like. But they've already seized my savings. Probably taken my townhouse. There's enough there to square the trust money I took and to reimburse the insurance company for Ramirez. Having me won't help anybody. I think I'll pass if I can. Just try and live quiet, live decent."

"I'd like to lend you some of my money. I could give you a few thousand."

I touched her face.

"I'd like to."

"I have enough to get started. With what you brought me from Boxmoor. Enough to buy a used car. Pay rent and live for a while. Until I find a job. If you wouldn't mind taking me to Washington. I can get what I need there."

"That's your plan?"

"Uh huh."

"I see."

"Well, it's a start."

"I could take you tomorrow," she said slowly. "But the truth is, I was hoping you'd stay a bit longer. Maybe another week? How about till Tuesday?"

"I'd like that," I answered. "If you think it's okay."

"A week is nice and neat. And I have some things you could help with. And some things I'd like to show you."

I nodded.

She bit her lip, then nodded back. "A week is good. But you'll leave next Tuesday? Before I get up? Okay? Because I don't want to have to talk about this again?"

WE TOOK THE JEEP the following morning and drove down the highway and over the bridge and the bay, stretching blue toward Baltimore. Entering Washington we drove down New York Avenue. The traffic was congested and we crept along for miles. Near Bladensburg Road, I had Muddy park and wait in a motel lot. Up the block was a pawnshop that had been owned by Bird Fletcher, a client of mine from years before who'd beaten a forgery rap. I gambled that he was still there. The glass door to the store was cracked and so dirty you couldn't see inside. A young Hispanic man stood behind the banged up wooden counter decorated in spray-painted graffiti. He wore an earring and a silver stud in his upper lip, and on his biceps, just below his rolled-up T-shirt sleeve, was a tattoo of a Mayan sun. Behind him, an array of junk lay on a table and against the wall—a guitar and several wind instruments, a mounted deer's head, a collection of baseball cards, some brass platters, some trophies. I asked if Bird Fletcher was around. He folded his arms in silence. I waited. The curtain over the door rustled behind him. Walking bent over with a cane, the old, wiry black man came through from the back. He looked up, squinted, and recognized me. He gave me a toothless grin and offered me his hand to shake.

For five hundred Bird told me he'd have me a driver's license and social security card. "Professional discount," he croaked. I asked him if he had an old wallet around to throw in, and he nodded. He showed me a list of people recently deceased and asked me to choose a name. I decided on Frank James. I'll find a brother named Jesse and rob banks, I mumbled.

In the back he took my picture with a handheld camera he kept in a drawer. "Lose yourself for two hours," he said. "You can pick 'em up at noon." He never asked me why I wanted this stuff.

I took Muddy out for a long breakfast and then walked back, paid Bird, and tucked the new identification in my wallet. Muddy then drove me over to Benning Road where a string of used car lots, all fenced in with galvanized razor wire, littered the neighborhood. She dropped me off and went looking for a drugstore nearby. At the car lot, a puffy-faced man with red eyes and a Jersey accent showed me a Ford Escort, six years old, seventy thousand miles, with decent tires. I took it for a test drive with him seated alongside and agreed to buy it for twenty-nine hundred. I told him my new name, gave him my new social security number, and showed him my driver's license. I told him I was moving south and would telephone him as to where to send my permanent tags when they arrived. I slipped him an extra hundred for his trouble.

As planned, I met Muddy on the way out of the city at a McDonald's parking lot and followed her back across the bridge, down Route 50, out St. Michaels Road and down past Tilghman to her cottage. Inside, she showed me what she had bought at the drugstore—black hair dye, liquid hair straightener, and tinted reading glasses. "This is almost fun," she said, "creating a new life." She sighed. "If only we could."

EARLY FRIDAY, MUDDY ASKED me to help her over on the Wye River where she hunted. "I might as well enjoy your strong back *in every way* while I got it." She smiled.

Before we left she had me help load the back of her Jeep with lumber from her shed and with cornstalks she had hacked up from the field with a machete. She brought twine and an aerosol can of spray adhesive. We drove through St. Michaels to the bypass and for a short way on the highway before turning off on a small side road. We traveled through miles of thick woods under an archway of shadowy trees until we reached the open fields adjacent to the Wye River. Muddy pointed down a long dirt lane. We followed it awhile and turned out into a cornfield. The ground was soft in some places, but she revved the

Jeep through, out into the middle of the field. We stopped and got out. Bits of broken stalks and husks littered the fallow rows. Southerly, under the sun, the deep but narrow Wye meandered snakelike toward the Miles River and Eastern Bay. She pointed to our right and away from the water. Across the farm there was another clearing and farther on a white paddock fence bordering a wide landscaped lawn. There were gardens, behind which stood a huge, brick, colonial-style mansion, surrounded by a series of what appeared to be white clapboard outbuildings and red barns. "That's Wye Plantation," she said. "I've been coming here since I was little. I used to run through the gardens over there and play in the barns."

Muddy brushed away some dusty stalks with her foot uncovering a weathered plywood board that I had failed to notice. Stooping down she lifted it. It was hinged on one side to an underground plank, the backbone of a pit that had been dug into the ground about five feet deep. Inside was a wooden bench large enough for several people to sit. The dirt floor was littered with shotgun shells. "There's been many a duck and goose taken out of this field," she muttered. "The pit needs some tidying, though."

Following her instructions I helped her arrange and tie the cut cornstalks to the plywood top, causing it to blend even more into the field. We hammered in some additional supports to the siding of the pit. Muddy then sprayed the aerosol adhesive all over the outside of the plywood top and kicked dirt and more corn straw onto the adhesive until the wood was completely concealed.

"How do you even find this?" I asked.

"Oh I just know where it is. First, I hunted it with my daddy. Then after. It's a prime spot. Real prime."

"When's the season start?"

Muddy considered. "Well, the duck season goes in and out. And this year, for the fifth year in a row, there's no season on Canada geese. But we do get some snow geese in here sometimes. They've come back nice from a few years back." She kicked her foot one more time, scattering the dust. "It'll all start soon, Jack. Soon enough anyway."

20

NOW, MORE THAN A YEAR since that last week with Muddy, I still often look back, trying to isolate specific moments that I can cling to, count on my fingers, see in my mind's eye. From here it all seems too dreamlike, surreal. Still, I ask myself, how did I fail to recognize the mounting evidence, the warning signs?

The afternoon we returned from our trip to the Wye River, Muddy asked me to help her take the front seats out of her Jeep. She used a screwdriver and a wrench, and after they were out she hosed out the inside of the car and rinsed the dirt off the wheels and frame.

"Nice to be able to just wash the insides clean," she said, "isn't it?"

Just as she was finishing, I heard the hum of her fax from inside the house. She handed me the hose and asked me to wrap it and went through the kitchen door. When I came in she was standing, blocking the computer, which was on. Her voice was hoarse and she spoke haltingly. "Something from Chesapeake College," she said. "Nothing important. Just a project I'm working on for my class. A research paper that's late, is all. I'll get an extension."

I nodded. "What's it on?"

She shut off the computer. "Fish farming," she answered distractedly.

As I moved toward her, she folded up the paper in her hand and put it in her back pocket. "Can I ask you something?" she said. "I mean it's kind of off the subject."

"What?"

"How did you get the courage to swim out like that?" She moved from the desk. "I mean to swim out so far? It's just that I've been wondering. I mean you know I think it was wrong. And stupid. But it must have taken a certain amount of courage."

I assumed Muddy was referring to our coming separation.

"Well, we all need it, don't we?" she added. "Sometimes?"

"I don't think it was courage so much," I answered. "More desperation. Maybe the opposite of courage."

She nodded halfheartedly.

"What is it, Muddy?"

She shook her head.

I stepped close and put my arms around her.

"Thank you," she murmured. She hugged me back, took a breath, then pushed away, "How's the Jeep look?" She coughed. "Let's finish, okay, and get the seats back in."

As we tightened the last bolt, a steamy mist rolled in off the river, surrounding us, veiling the landscape, ethereal, accompanied by a light but steady rain. This seemed to relax Muddy. She went around to the patio and sat down to watch the change. Then she went to the shed and returned with gloves and her hand spade. "I love to garden in the rain," she said. With an outstretched hand, she coaxed me outside. We worked together until we were both drenched, weeding and pruning, moving bulbs with her spade, our knees on the softening earth, the rain's quiet hush soaking the ground around us. We came in shivering. She ran a deep, hot bath, which we took together, and then we sat on the patio under the canopy roof and watched the rain on the river and the mist swirling out over the cove in the waning light.

The next morning was clear, and the air had turned cooler. By afternoon, though, the sun of the late Indian summer was warm. We took another drive in the Jeep, this time down past Cambridge. Muddy turned off Route 50 and we went through the town of Church Creek and on past a sign to Taylors Island.

"This is the narrowest part of the bay," Muddy explained. "Directly over there, on the western shore, is Cove Point. This is the place the Indians crossed. And camped. For a thousand years. It's one of my favorite spots." Due west, across the water, we could see the high cliffs of Calvert County and the white rotundas of the nuclear plant.

We got out and sat on the grass watching the ships move south toward Norfolk and the open sea. A sailboat tacked northwest toward Annapolis. The tide was low and still falling.

We walked along the pebbly beach. Out in the channel a tug pulled a barge north. Muddy kicked over a rock and picked up a small triangular black stone. "Here," she said, giving it to me. "Shark's tooth. Good luck." She reached up and kissed me. "There are arrowheads here dating back to forever. Gives you a sense of perspective."

We hunted for relics but didn't find any. She challenged me to a stone-skimming contest and won easily. We sat on a bench and talked about our childhoods, growing up around the river.

"Did you miss terribly not having a mother?" she asked.

"I don't really know," I said. "I don't know what it would be like. How 'bout you?"

"Yes. I mean I had my aunts, Agnes and Ruth. But they didn't live with us. It wasn't the same, I could tell. Kids need the real thing. My father always told me that Mama was up in heaven throwing stars. I always liked to picture her that way."

We drove through Cambridge on the way back, and Muddy pointed out the Annie Oakley House. "That's where she lived," Muddy said. "She beat all the men marksmen, the best there were, in Cincinnati in like 1875 or something. Twenty-five bull's eyes out of twenty-five shots. Became friends with Chief Sitting Bull. Can you imagine? A woman? Toured the world with William Cody. She had a dog named Dave. She'd shoot an apple off its head. Not bad for a girl, huh?"

"Not bad," I agreed.

We stopped in the town of Trappe and had an early supper at a café. The place was about half full, and in spite of my nervousness no one seemed particularly interested in us.

"I think you can make it," Muddy said. "Once you're out on your own. No one's going to know you."

"Maybe I can," I answered.

"You don't look anything like that drowned lawyer I pulled from the river . . ."

THAT LAST WEEKEND, Muddy asked me to pose for her. In two hours she had sketched my features in charcoal. The portrait was complimentary. My beard strengthened my chin, and my face looked strong and youthful. "It's just a start," she mused. "I want you to have it," she said, rolling it up for me to pack. "I have others. In here"—she tapped her temple—"and here," she said, touching her chest. I thanked her but chided her again that she should move on to color and to tackling the rich beauty of Dun Cove and the river she knew so well.

WE TOOK TURNS cooking for each other. We stayed up late and watched the moon set and looked at the stars through her telescope. She knew the constellations by name and pointed them out, Orion, Cepheus, Cassiopeia. She even attached an infrared device to her binoculars and showed me the river at night through these special lenses, the water lit with the tinged filter, eerie but clear. We watched the beacons blinking red or green and followed the boats that ran out the creek in the dark. Sunday morning, we tied string lines to the fish heads she had instructed me to freeze and crabbed off the end of the dock. With the first bite, the string, slack in the clear water went suddenly taught. "Pull it easy," she said, and I brought the bait up steadily toward the surface until the big blue crab was visible, yanking back on his prize, and Muddy dipped it out with the crab net. We had five lines out, and crabs began to fill a small basket. We kept the big males but let the small ones and the females go. When one large male climbed out, I pinned it with my foot against the dock board. It was scrapping mad and tried to pinch my shoe. "Have you ever seen a crab hypnotized?" I asked Muddy, thinking of an old trick of my father's. "Watch. I hope this works." I held it by its back-fin joint, where it couldn't reach me with its big snapping claws. I turned it belly up and began to stroke its fat, yellow underside with my finger, talking to it. I tickled it and gradually it folded in its two pinchers and stopped moving. Turning it up on its head and balancing it there, I held it to her in the palm of my hand and she took it laughing.

"You *are* the clever one, now aren't you, Jack Stanton? No wonder your juries did what you asked." She dropped it back into the river. "An offering," she said.

We steamed the crabs in beer and Old Bay seasoning and picked and ate all afternoon. Afterward, she helped me dye my hair and beard black and apply the straightener. With the glasses she claimed I looked just like a poet she had seen in a magazine.

She opened her lacquered box and told me she had just enough pot left for one small joint. I even took a hit myself, out on the dock, watching the moon rise and the night fall and the lights on the river grow in their brightness.

ON MONDAY, WE SPREAD a blanket at the river's edge. Muddy pointed out the signs for the changing tide, showed me the drift of the sea grass, the lapping of the waves against the dock piles, the slack and the ebb. We went for a walk and she found a doubler in the shallows, two crabs joined, the female in molt, its shell half off its back; I spotted a great blue heron at attention on a mossy stump. Muddy took my arm; the swans swam back and forth in the cove.

After dinner, I found her in the kitchen shaking and in tears. She quickly bucked herself up, scrubbing her face roughly with a dishtowel. But she stayed upset. We both were. Even as we clung to each other in her bed. I held on to her late into the night.

In the morning I got up to leave, as I had promised, while it was still dark. I had put my few things in the car the night before. Somehow I managed to get out of the bedroom, make it through the kitchen, and out the front door.

21

RIDING AWAY INTO THE BLACKNESS of the predawn, all I
knew was to drive. Drive steady and far. Forcing the miles between us.

I hadn't given much thought to exactly where or why—
certainly not enough—though in my fog of loss and self-pity
I headed south, toward the warmer climates, pretty much in-
different to my destination. Atlanta, maybe, or southern
Florida where a person could easily disappear into a city.
With the new identity I had procured I wasn't worried too
much about starving. I had enough to get settled, and I could
always bartend or sell cars or work as a clerk for H&R Block
giving tax advice. I even had a vague notion of trying to lo-

cate my son, not that I would let on who I was. I just wanted to watch him from a distance, see if he had married, had a family. But none of these plans had yet clarified. My thoughts, despite my best efforts to will them elsewhere, were not on the future but back in Dun Cove.

I drove hell-bent to honor my pledge to her, but more, to follow the only decent course—to leave her—to allow her an open chance for a future with someone who had a future. I drove across the twin gangling spars of the Bay Bridge and bypassed Washington on the beltway heading south. I turned down 95 and drove until my gas tank needed filling. I drank coffee and ate doughnuts and pushed on, past Richmond and down through North Carolina. I drove and tried to think of anything but her.

When I hit the Georgia line and neared Savannah, I started to feel faint. I pulled into a drive-through lane at a Burger King, bought food, and pushed on. By Jacksonville I had to stop. I found a motel with a bar attached and rented a room, paying for it in cash.

It was late when I ordered dinner. I sat at the bar, exhausted, eaten through with hurt at what I had cost myself. A television was on overhead. Throughout dinner and afterward, I ordered a stream of Jameson's on the rocks trying to drink myself to where I could sleep. I hadn't seen a television since before Boxmoor. "Swimming out to drown." What grotesque and pathetic behavior, I remember thinking. The eleven o'clock news reported on a U.S.–Central American trade conference that had begun that morning near St. Michaels, Maryland. Footage was played of some of the delegations landing on the grounds of Wye Plantation by helicopter. The rear of the buildings and wide lawn, now busy with people, were similar to what I had seen from a distance a few days before. I couldn't hear too well as the volume was down. But exiting a chopper and standing in the grassy background like an attendant or minor player in one of the delegations was a face on the TV screen I faintly recognized. I tried to place it. He backed away into the shadows and was out of the picture. It bothered me. Where would I have seen that face before? And then with terrible clarity it came to me. I had seen that face in Muddy's bedroom. In a photograph. And in her sketches. It was the face of Bustillo. The man she believed killed her father.

I laid two twentys on the counter and pitched out to the car. I pulled out of the parking lot and headed back north.

FOR THE FIRST HOUR or so I drove on sheer adrenaline, my mind racing, my eyes popping from my head, the night highway only a savage link between one frightening scenario and another. Repeatedly, I slammed my hands on the dash at my own blindness. Phrases of Muddy's came back to haunt me. Cryptic remarks that I had passed over at the time as vague in their intent, unimportant. I recall her chastising me early on, while she was still tending to my burns. She was a patient nurse, and her touch was delicate as she'd swab and bandage me. "There are ideas worth dying for, mister," she once mused as she pressed the cool cloth to my forehead. "Causes. Sacrifices that change lives and history. But, God. Just to give up your precious life for nothing. If you want to lose it, at least trade it. If you still want to die, do it for a reason ..."

Another time, while she was sitting with me, she started rambling about the writer, Salman Rushdie. Something she had seen in the newspaper had gotten her started. The more she talked the more incensed she became. "He's a British citizen," she said. "The country of Iran declared war on him. Why hasn't Britain declared war on Iran? What's the point of being a citizen of a country that doesn't stand up for its citizens? A country's just a big village. Isn't that what Hillary Clinton said? To declare war on any one person should be looked at as declaring war on the entire village."

At the time I made little of those ramblings. I was still dehydrated and sick from all the salt water I had swallowed and was not focusing on what she said. Driving north, though, these previous conversations cascaded through my mind. What was she going to try to do? Could I get back in time to stop her? To help her?

I took coffee and gas at an all-night convenience store outside of Charleston, but I was fading and I had to struggle to stay awake. I began trying to count the yellow lane dividers racing under the car. They came too fast, bleeding into one continual neon directional. I drove, almost without knowing it, barely aware of my surroundings, slapping my cheeks to rouse myself, shouting into the night air rushing through the open window. Projections of my worst fears appeared and disappeared like the lights from the approaching cars, like splices of film on a movie screen—Muddy, running through gunfire, men chasing her, crying out, hurt, her face draining of color, her young body on the ground . . . I slapped myself to bring my attention back to my driving.

I caught myself nodding off several times. Once for too long. I had swerved onto the shoulder. Finally I pulled into a truck stop somewhere in North Carolina. Inside, I ordered coffee at the counter alongside a few other red-eyed drivers, haggard and unshaven. One seemed more fidgety than the rest. He was eating quickly and his eyes were dilated. I chose him as a likely candidate. I waited outside and collared him as he was heading for his tractor-trailer. Making up a story about having to drive all night, about an emergency medical situation with my daughter, I took out a fifty and offered it to him. He looked me over carefully, then took it, handing me a dark capsule in return. "Black beauty," he stated. "Dexedrine. It oughta do the trick."

It didn't take long to kick in. After it took effect, the miles rushed by with the night and my flying thoughts, all jamming together in a mix of fear and hope, the drumming of the asphalt, my own rampaging stream of memory and intention, my efforts to formulate a plan, the false clarity brought by the drug, my certainty of purpose, creeping doubt, all merging and coalescing in the hours of the predawn dark.

As the sun rose over the Virginia landscape I continued to race north. The thought had occurred to me that I could be wrong, that Muddy could be sleeping safely, could be going to the store to work with Agnes. It was possible, but not likely. I drove on, watching the speed limit, careful not to get stopped, pushing forward.

I hit the proverbial wall around ten. It happened quickly. The drug's effect had run out. My whole body felt slammed. I was light-headed. Just sitting upright was an effort. Crossing the Bay Bridge I remember little except for the refrain I had started repeating in my mind. "Just get to Muddy . . . Just get to her . . ."

I turned off Route 50 to take the shortcut into Wye Mills. Traffic was heavy in the small town. The road to Wye Plantation was blocked. Police cars lined the curb. When I reached the checkpoint, they wouldn't let me pass. I turned out and took the back roads toward St. Michaels. I sped through town and turned down Bozman Road. Agnes was in the store when I wobbled in. Asking her about Muddy, I must have been a sight. At first she didn't recognize me and asked me who I was and why I wanted to know. I told her never mind but that it was important, that I was afraid Muddy might be in trouble and I quickly explained why.

Her initial skepticism turned to fear as she recognized me. "Muddy is off this week," she answered. "But don't you go bother her again. No. You better leave here, mister." She picked up the phone with a hand that had started to tremble. "Go on," she said. "Leave, now. I'm going to call the police."

I stumbled to the car and turned out the parking lot and drove back out Bozman Road turning left toward Tilghman Island. Driving down toward the cottage I prayed that Muddy would be there. As I approached I saw her car in her driveway and drew a breath of relief. I drove a half block past so as not to alert her to my presence. I stopped, my motor running, and felt the sag of exhaustion acutely. I parked and walked back tentatively, crouching down to watch the cottage for a few minutes. I saw no movement and crept up to the window. There was no one inside. I straightened up and walked down to the dock. Her boat was gone. Looking back toward the house, I saw that the patio door was open so I went into the living room. Strewn about the floor were the papers she and I had taken off the bedroom wall and later stacked in the garage to be thrown out. Her computer was on. I moved her keyboard mouse slightly and her screen saver vanished. A document appeared titled "Proof of Guilt—Rafael Bustillo." I was starting to read, when I saw through the window a green sedan pull into the driveway, a red light flashing on its dashboard. Another car pulled up behind it. Then another. I was too tired to move. In an instant there were a half-dozen cars surrounding the cottage. Men burst through the door, guns drawn, and told me to freeze. I guessed they were federal law enforcement types, though they didn't identify themselves. They yanked me up against the wall, patted me down, and cuffed me. Several of the men had begun gathering up the documents on the floor, plowing through drawers, overturning furniture, ransacking the cottage. As they pushed me outside and to the cars I saw Muddy in the back of one of the sedans. Her face was defiant, her eyes pumped and hard like those of an athlete having exceeded all physical ability, set, intense, inward-looking. She was in handcuffs but seemed uninjured. I cried out her name and she turned, focused, and saw me. "Don't say anything to anyone, Muddy," I shouted as they pulled me toward another car.

"Shut up," I was told.

"Not a word until you hear from me!" I strained to look and saw an almost imperceptible nod as they shoved me down and into one of the cars. My head struck the door frame and then all went dark.

22

A WINTRY SKY HAD SETTLED over Washington when I arrived, a damp, chilly, low cloud cover pressed against the earth, presaging the cold and barren season. I had briefly lost consciousness in the police car and came to only to doze off again. From the journey I remember muted sounds of highway, of traffic, nausea, a throbbing pain inside my skull. I was driven first to the federal building in Greenbelt, Maryland, just outside the D.C. line. There they confiscated my false identification. Although they hadn't found or searched my Ford Escort, once they fingerprinted me it wouldn't take long for the computer to match the prints with the ones taken of me when I was first hired as a public defender. My prints were on file like those of all federal government workers. Whether the fake identification would have fooled them for a while, I don't know. But when they booked me, I told them the truth about who I was. After a short wait, I was transported to police headquarters on D Street in downtown Washington, a building next to the courthouse and just across the street from where our offices had been when I was at the agency. A detective interrogated me for maybe forty minutes. I admitted that I had been staying in the cottage. I denied that Muddy knew my true identity or that I had any knowledge of her plans concerning the conference. I asked him what she had done, but he wouldn't respond.

Later that evening, a young man dressed in a three-piece gray suit, upright, and smelling of aftershave, was admitted to my cell. He didn't offer to shake my hand. He introduced himself as Randolph and described himself as an assistant U.S. attorney, a representative from Morgan Langrell and from the U.S. government. Morgan wanted to see me the next day, he said. Morgan's request was that I hold off hiring counsel until after the meeting. Morgan might have a proposition for me. One that I would find appealing. If after the meeting I wanted counsel, of course, I could hire whomever I pleased. "Morgan figures it won't be necessary," the assistant added disdainfully. "He said you can take care of yourself." The tone of Morgan's messenger, Randolph, suggested he thought otherwise.

Shortly after he left, a guard brought me a plate of cheese sandwiches and applesauce. I was too tired to eat and went to sleep on the cot in the corner of the cell.

The next morning I was served a bowl of cold eggs, slid in through the bars. Even the smell was revolting. Sometime in the afternoon I was transported in a van the block and a half to the building that housed the office of the U.S. attorney. The lobby was circular, sweeping around a stone statue of the Lady of Justice—a blind woman holding out a pair of balancing scales. The guards had shackled not only my hands but my feet as well, so I had to shuffle along. Two marshals led me past the metal detector and into an elevator that we took to the top floor. They escorted me down a long, plush-carpeted corridor to Morgan's office. The corner suite was paneled in shiny mahogany with ceiling-high windows that looked out over the city. To the southeast, the Capitol dome rose above the surrounding hotels and office buildings. Westerly, through the opposite window, the Washington Monument vaulted skyward, still trapped inside its millenium web of grillwork and tubing, the scaffolding erected for its restoration. I watched as the sky behind the obelisk flashed with lightning. Seething clouds irradiated, then went dark, flickered on and then dark again, like lampshades shorting off an electrical charge.

In his spacious office, seated on a wide burgundy calfskin couch was Morgan, his jacket off, his yellow suspenders running neatly up his Oxford blue shirt, his manner stolid, stony. Behind him, draped with an American flag, the round seal of the Department of Justice adorned the wall. Seated to his left in a matching leather chair, seemingly relaxed and at home was my old colleague, Everett Wheeler. At a corner desk sat the alert young Randolph. A sweetish perfume wafted from his side of the room. As I was brought in, Everett rose, a scowl creeping over his face. He repeated my name several times, patting my shoulder, and then turned to Morgan. He asked somberly whether something couldn't be done.

"Sure." Morgan answered. He nodded at the marshals and both the handcuffs and leg irons were removed. I bent and rubbed my ankles to restore the circulation.

"Sit down," Morgan offered. "Coffee?"

I declined with a mumble.

Morgan waved his hand and the marshals withdrew, shutting the door, leaving just the four of us in the room.

"Christ, Jack, we thought you'd drowned. Glad you're okay." Everett reached over and shook my hand. "That was slick." He winked. "And nice disguise there. But you *have* landed yourself in the shitheap now, haven't you? I tell you I'm sorry. Sorry as can be. What the hell prompted you to start monkeying with evidence? Christ, Jack. And lying to the grand jury? You know better, friend. Damn. You can't just take the law into your own hands. Things happen, I guess. They do have you by the short hairs, though, don't they?" Everett managed to sustain a grimace of sorrow. "I'm sorry, Jack. Really. But you know what? There's an irony here. 'Cause you've lucked out. I mean I'm here to help you. You just stumbled your way into good fortune." He relaxed his features and smiled. "But you've always been lucky, Jack. Always. You got a lucky streak across your back."

I made a slight movement, tilting my head forward.

Everett looked at Morgan, who indicated he should continue. "It's the girl, Jack. See? This business with the woman. It's bad, Jack. Costly. Lots at stake. For my clients. Coffee. Corporate landowners. Good people. Important people. That's why I'm here. I'm going to help you and them." Everett shook his head like it was all he could do.

Morgan then rose, straightening his tie, taking his time before speaking. "You want a break here, Stanton? You don't deserve one. Certainly not from me. But I'm sure you'd like one, wouldn't you?" He walked to the credenza where there was a plate of finger sandwiches next to the coffeepot. He freshened his cup and dabbed at the corner of his mouth with a napkin. "Circumstances have necessitated a reevaluation of your situation. Issues have arisen that dwarf yours in importance. And I have marching orders here. You're going to be given a deal. We need to bargain."

Leaning back, Everett took a silver cigar case from his suit coat pocket. He removed from it a gold toothpick. "You lived with that girl, in her cottage, for nearly a month. Isn't that right, Jack?" He squinted at me as he worked the toothpick between two incisors. "Isn't that right?"

"Where are we going here?" I asked.

"She has upset some delicate and very lucrative arrangements," Everett continued. "Arrangements involving Central American trade. Long-term commodity agreements. She has impugned the reputations of important people. Embarrassed our trade partners. Our allies. They're angry and want an immediate and decisive resolution." Everett raised his eyebrows. "They don't exactly understand the nuances of our judicial system. This lady has tried to resurrect skeletons long ago put to rest. Her accusations are harmful, frivolous, and need to be squelched. This is larger than me or you, Jack." Everett raised the toothpick like a miniature scepter. "It is for the good of . . . well, the many, not just the few. It's for the greater good . . ."

"You want to play dumb, Stanton?" Morgan queried, his voice low, directed away, toward the wall.

"I'm not playing anything."

"She disrupted an international conference. This is an important issue to the administration."

"Where is the girl?" I asked.

Morgan turned. "She's detained for the moment at FBI headquarters. We're going to hold her at St. Elizabeth's Hospital. Even though her acts occurred in Maryland, I've been asked to step in. I've agreed to be specially assigned to handle this. Partly because of you, Stanton. Because of what we need from you."

I listened, still unclear on what had occurred.

"If she had committed any serious crimes, I'd just prosecute her and put her away for a long time," Langrell continued. "The woman acted in the role of a terrorist. She disrupted an important trade summit. Though it was supposedly a private-sector conference, it was on land the federal government had temporarily leased, and agreements were at stake that affect our national security. Central America is our underbelly and gateway. Fighting terrorism is a priority. Then this happens in our front yard. We need to make an example of her. Like Everett said. For the greater good, Stanton. And that's why you're here."

"What did she do?" I asked.

"I just told you," Morgan snapped. He snorted and stepped toward the couch. "Except she didn't break any law that'll really put her away. That's the problem we're faced with." He stirred his fresh coffee with a spoon, then sat back down.

"I'm lost," I said.

"We could charge her with trespassing. But that's nothing. She had a gun, but it was unloaded. We checked and it was registered to her. We've considered a concealed weapon charge, but no one remembers seeing her. And that's not enough here. She deserves a long sentence. Like I said, she's a terrorist of sorts herself. But she didn't threaten anyone. There's no kidnapping or assault. We're holding her on an extortion charge, but it'd never stick. She didn't extort anything. We don't have squat."

Randolph was sitting upright, observing, his arms folded across his chest.

"The government wants more than just to convict her on some minor gun charge," Everett added. "It needs to deter this kind of behavior in the future. And my clients don't relish the spectacle of a jury trial over some minor offense, with all its publicity. Probably just what she's hoping for. No, they want an example set. And they want her discredited. That's the key, Jack. Discredited. Her allegations cause trouble for everyone."

"We could, I suppose, charge her with harboring a fugitive." Langrell watched me, trying to gauge my response. "Of course, we'd need to prove she knew you were one. A fugitive, that is. We'd probably need your testimony for that anyway."

I shrugged, trying to keep my face a blank.

He frowned. "But that's not enough either." He settled back. "No. She upset an international summit. She's disrupted trade. Made accusations against important, stabilizing allies. Might as well have thrown a bomb in there. No. We need more. Your cooperation, Stanton. You know the game. We're offering a deal."

"She's a crazy little bitch, Jack," Everett expanded. "You know it. You lived with her. We just need to prove it and things'll settle down."

"My people want this handled fast and handled right," Langrell added. "I would never give you this on my own. But like they say, necessity is the mother of invention. In this case, of cooperation and compromise."

They had both stopped talking at once. A roll of thunder curled in from across the river. It started to rain against the windows. I asked if I could have that coffee now. Langrell motioned toward the credenza. I rose and went to it. Suddenly I felt hungry and took two of the little sandwiches with my coffee. Everett nodded his encouragement for me to eat.

"The strategy is unusual, Stanton. Something *you* might think up." Langrell hooked his thumbs under his suspenders. He glanced at Randolph. "We got our smart Turks too ..."

"We're going to charge her with extortion." Randolph took up his cue. "On federal land. Maybe with carrying a concealed weapon. In federal court, in Greenbelt. But these are just charges. Cover. We spent all night and morning working this out. We're going to raise the issue of her competency. Under Title 18, section 4241. We're going to prove that she's incompetent to stand trial. Legally insane. A danger to herself and others. We'll avoid a jury. We might even get a closed hearing."

Randolph was obviously pleased with the plan. He went on. "If we prove there's reasonable cause to believe she's incompetent, the judge has to keep her locked up for a sixty-day study."

"We'll get an automatic extension for another sixty days after that," Langrell interposed. "Maybe more extensions to follow. She'll be held at the John Howard Pavilion at St. E's. Given what she's done, and with the right encouragement, they'll find her incompetent, probably for a long while."

"If it's done right, it'll be a coon's age before she ever sees daylight," Everett interjected. "Her claims will lose credibility."

He finished with his toothpick and returned it to his case. "An example will be set. Our friends south of the border will be placated. We will be amply appreciated. And you, Jack"—he placed his hands out, palms up in a satisfied supplication—"you will go free."

Both Langrell and Everett waited.

I swallowed my food and a sip of coffee. "How are you going to prove she's crazy?" I said. "When she's not."

"Jack, Jack," Everett gently admonished. "You know better than that. Of course she is. She was fixated on this thing. It was all over her little house. We've got her writings. Her clippings. Those obsessive drawings. She's got a history. Medication. An arrest record for crazy shit. Dumped rotten crab bait all over a courthouse. Did you know that? Put a gun to her own head here. She's obsessed, Jack. Jack, you're the spin king. We've seen you. Interpret the facts. That was always your forte. The facts are easy here. Just turn them the right way."

"We've got one of her prior therapists," Randolph offered.

"He's got some tax troubles, Jack."

Randolph frowned.

"That's enough, Everett," Langrell cut in.

"Jack knows the game, Morgan. You think you're going to fool him?"

Langrell eyed me. "You going to help yourself here, Stanton?"

I met his stare. "I'm listening hard, aren't I?"

His lips retracted, showing his teeth. Not exactly a grin. "Her shrink'll testify. Some type of bipolar disorder." He spoke slowly, deliberately. "She can sound normal at times. But lurking there are these delusions, masked by her conscious attempt to sound rational, delusions that she's fighting some conspiracy, that she's some kind of angel of vengeance or something. He's got a theory all worked out. She's incompetent. He'll sell it. Crazy and dangerous. She refused the medication he prescribed. He'll leverage that too. Problem is, Stanton, he hasn't seen her in a few years. That's why we need you. You were with her for weeks. The good doctor needs evidence of recent conduct. Your testimony will clinch it."

"Any decent lawyer will challenge this."

"It's arranged, Jack," Everett answered. "The federal public defender is conflicted out. Mr. Langrell here already let them know you might be a witness. You worked a case over there, remember? On loan. During your agency days? When they needed an outside lawyer for a codefendant?" Everett chortled to himself. "So they're out. The panel administrator over there happens to be someone I knew on the Hill. When the public defender's unavailable, she makes the appointment of counsel from a list they have. I happened to talk to her this morning. Conveniently, an old fifth-streeter type will be appointed today. You might have run into him up in Baltimore. Charlie Sanders?"

The term *fifth-streeter* was a derogatory nickname ascribed to the lawyers who used to hang around the old D.C. courthouse on Fifth Street, many without offices, hoping for appointments to indigent cases. Of course, I knew Charlie Sanders from past days. All too well. Charlie had to be near seventy now. By reputation, he'd been an alcoholic for years. Word was, he often slept though portions of his trials. Used the Baltimore courthouse cafeteria as his office and the lawyer's lounge as his home.

"Charlie's *semi*retired," Everett snickered. "He lives now in Lanham, out near Greenbelt. Somehow he got himself on the panel list."

"She might hire her own lawyer," I countered. "She's not indigent."

"So far she won't even speak to anyone," Randolph volunteered. "And she's got no immediate family. No one close. We move fast enough, she'll never have the chance. Once it's done, it'll be hell to undo. We can delay it. Take years."

The thunder boomed again from just overhead. Rain beat against the glass.

"Maybe Mr. Stanton doesn't want to play ball," Randolph remarked.

"Nonsense," Everett countered, drumming on the table.

"What's Mr. Stanton looking at, son?" Langrell gave the floor back to Randolph, delegating his assistant to dangle the carrot and the stick.

"Well, there's the Ramirez trial. Knowingly using materially altered evidence in a federal court. That's criminal contempt with a wide-open sentence. And conspiracy to obstruct justice. Then perjury in the grand jury. Grand larceny. The trust account, Mr. Stanton," he added as if I needed the explanation. He averted his eyes. "Burglary."

"Burglary?"

"You did break into my bay house, Jack," Everett said grimly. "And misused it, and our friendship I could add."

"You showed me the key. Told me I could stay there any time."

"Jack . . . Not as a fugitive. But hell, let's forget the burglary. I can't press charges against an old friend."

"Cut the crap, Everett. We got plenty. Tell 'em, Randolph."

"Forgery. The false ID," Randolph explained again. "All together, under the federal guidelines, I don't know." He picked up a pad on the desk, pretending to engage in a quick calculation. "Some of these would merge, but you'd serve a good five to seven years. Maybe more."

"Randolph's a wiz at this shit. That's why I keep him close. All gotten too complicated for me." Langrell acted amused at his own joke. "But we're prepared to go the distance on this, Stanton." He sniffed at the air. Then he spat something off the tip of his tongue, evincing distaste in his expression. "We don't want to fuck around. You cooperate, we'll let you cop to false statements. We'll recommend probation. It's a lock."

"They'll revoke your license, Jack." Everett had put his hands behind his head. He turned from side to side like he was stretching his neck. "Can't do anything about that. But you'll be a free man. In five years you can reapply. The government will support your request. Won't it, Morgan?

Langrell flicked his hand.

"I'll get you work in the meantime." Everett rose and walked to the center of the room and began twisting his torso. "Lobbying work. You won't be on the front line of course. But you'd be a good backroom strategist. The pay will suffice."

"Well?" It was Randolph.

I swallowed. "You want me to lie and convince the court she is delusional?"

"Goddammit, Jack!"

"We want you to testify truthfully that she is delusional. Incompetent. Insane. And, yes. Convince the court."

Randolph stood up. "I'm not sure Mr. Stanton can be trusted."

"Sit down, Randolph." It was Everett. He glanced briefly at the assistant, who obliged. Everett then took the stance of a golfer. Taking his time, adjusting his feet, equalizing his weight and balance, he imitated a golf swing. He held his finishing pose for several seconds. His face had turned red.

"How's your handicap, Jack?" He ignored his own question. "Jack has always known where his self-interest lies. Haven't you, Jack? He's an old dog. Old dogs aren't interested in new tricks. Are they, Jack? There's a golden rule for lawyers. Jack knows it well. Look out for number one. Get paid up front. Protect your ass. Jack mastered it. Didn't you, Jack?"

"Maybe he's confused about the truth, sir," Randolph quipped.

"You lied to the grand jury, Stanton," Morgan mused. His inflection was deliberative, curious. "I thought you were smarter than that."

"Linda," I answered. "To protect her . . ."

Morgan came off the couch and sat on the table's edge in front of and slightly above me. His tone turned cruel. "You're bullshitting us, Stanton. You're pathetic. I know for real, from her, that you two were no longer lovers. That she had called it quits on you. Dumped you. Hell, she had another boyfriend. You two had a business relationship only, to share fees from the cases she sent you. She didn't give two shits for you. You were the same about her, not that you didn't try again to slip it to her, you sorry fuck. But you lied for Stanton, not for Linda. You lied for the great Stanton's reputation. For self-interest."

With this change of tactics, I felt my will buckling. Giving way. A frightening recognition that there were aspects of truth to what he said. Not that I didn't care for Linda, because I cared a great deal. I still flinched at the thought of her turning on me. Langrell detected this, that his remarks had hurt.

"You got caught," he pressed. "You thought you could go on manipulating the system forever, for your own ego, for the great glory of Stanton. Then you lied to cover your fraud. You're a chameleon. Always have been." He paused, then continued, tempering his voice. "This is serious, Stanton. I am serious. It needs to happen. I'm not letting her go, with or without you. So you might as well benefit. And it's going to be easy for you. You just do what you've always done. What comes natural. We're going to keep it easy and simple. Here, all you got to do is take what you know about this female flake and interpret it to fit our theory. Just like you did so often and so well for those *clients* you represented for all those years. This time it's for yourself. To save your own sorry ass. You can do it. And you will do it." He exuded arrogance and power. Cold certainty. He held my gaze until he was through with it. Then he got up as though disgusted.

"What else is it you want, Jack?" Everett asked. He and Langrell exchanged glances. "He's just bargaining, Morgan. He's an old pro, remember?"

Langrell waited.

"You want to be free on bail, Jack? Is that it? We can arrange that, can't we, Morgan? I'm sure there's an accommodation that can be reached."

Langrell turned to Randolph. "What'll fly?"

"Fifty," the younger man answered.

"I'll ask for a fifty-thousand-dollar bond. Put up ten percent, he'll be released," Langrell told Everett.

"If I put up five thousand, Jack, promise me you'll stay here and testify." Everett resorted to his country-friendly routine. "Promise me that? I don't want to lose my bond money now."

"I wouldn't let you lose your money, Everett. You should know that."

"It isn't often that a man who has lost his life is given a chance to reclaim it. You do want your life back, Jack?"

I took a deep slow breath before answering Everett. With conviction in my voice I said, "Yes, Everett. I do."

"I knew you'd see how the bread gets buttered, Jack."

"Give us some facts then, Stanton." It was Morgan. He signaled for Randolph to write down what I said.

I hesitated. "I'll have to think back," I said.

"I want facts. Incidents you observed. Not opinions."

"She spoke of fairies that lived in the river," I said quietly. "With wands of fire. She called bluefish "greenies" and spoke of them going to heaven. Something about throwing stars. She heard voices. Voices telling her what mattered. She was obsessed with contras and Sandinistas and all of Central America. She would sit out in the rain, trancelike, until she was soaked. I can speak to her drawings, to what she had on her walls, to her obsessive behavior. She'd get excitable, almost manic. Give me more time. I'll have plenty to tell."

Langrell's phone rang. He picked it up and whispered for a moment. "I've got to go," he said. "Everyone's in a flurry about this shit. Have Stanton initial the notes," he added. "Fairies and lanterns in the river and voices is a good start. We'll nail everything down when I prep you. And make sure you shave and wash that ridiculous shit out of your hair."

"When's the hearing going to occur?" I asked.

"Soon. A week at the most," Langrell answered, putting on

his jacket. "We don't expect much of a fight from Charlie Sanders. Should go smoothly."

"Who's going to be the judge?"

Langrell turned toward Randolph, who answered. "If we file our motion today, our sources tell us we'll probably get Asa Cole. He'd be good."

Asa Cole, I thought. Jesus. After Asa got his appointment to the city bench he had changed, undergone a metamorphosis. I'd seen him only rarely over the years, but I'd heard comments about him from time to time. He'd become as tough on criminal defendants as any judge on the bench. Become a prosecutor's judge. Never believed the defense. Suffered defense lawyers with incredulity and impatience. His iron fist endeared him to the Republicans. George Bush, in his last days, had elevated him to a federal seat on the United States District Court in Maryland. Asa had introduced me at that bar luncheon last summer at the Army Navy Club. He'd seemed friendly but preoccupied, aloof. He congratulated me heartily but then worked the room like a politician. Later he complained to me about the chronic pain he had borne for years from the arthritis caused by his prosthesis and injury. He still wore spectacles, but they were thicker. Behind them his eyes were sunken with black, hollowed-out bruises underneath. "My head incessantly rings," he also had told me. "With the clamor of excuses, empty rhetoric, whining apologies, the cacophony of an overburdened system. I have little patience with the drivel of unprepared lawyers. There's too much to do. Never enough time. And too, this is an isolating job . . ." I thought at the time how his speech sounded canned, like he'd given it one too many times. I thought also how sorry I was to have lost touch with Asa, but what a different person he'd become and how relieved I was not to have to appear before him.

"I know Asa Cole," I said.

"Of course you do," Everett echoed.

"Somebody should tell Charlie Sanders. He might want a different judge. Since Asa knows me. That is, if I'm going to be a witness . . ."

This time, after they digested what I said, all three men laughed, even Randolph. "Charlie Sanders would have to file a motion," Everett chuckled. "He doesn't even have a typewriter. And I doubt he'll even interview your little friend before the hearing. I'm not sure he could find his way to St. E's if he tried . . ."

23

EARLY THE NEXT MORNING, Friday, I was taken before a magistrate for a bond hearing. As promised, Wheeler put up the ten percent and I was released. He would get it back so long as I showed up for my own court appearance, the date to be set in the future.

Everett told me that Muddy's hearing, at the request of the government, had been expedited and set for the following Thursday. He offered to drive me up Connecticut Avenue to my townhouse, but I declined, thanking him. Randolph had returned my real identification and wallet I'd left on the dock. I had money for cab fare, I told him. But I wanted to walk for a while first. To get some fresh air and relish my newfound freedom.

Everett was not pleased that I wanted to be alone. "I promised Morgan I'd keep my eye on you," he said. "So don't get lost. Saturday night's Fight Night. I got a table for eight and you're coming. I'll introduce you to some of your future friends. Tuesday, you report to Morgan to go over your testimony."

I agreed to all of this. He cocked his head and looked at me coolly. I thanked him again and walked out into the morning.

The day was clear, washed by the rain of the night before. Puddles filled the potholes on the roadway, and streams of dirty water still filtered down the curb and trickled out from the alleyways. The streets smelled of asphalt and wet garbage, of roasting coffee and bread, of the soaked burlap and drenched bodies of the homeless pushing their carts past me on the sidewalks.

I caught the metro subway to Dupont Circle and then a bus to Georgetown. I walked along the quay. The ash-colored river was high from the rain and carried in its current tree stems, branches, and debris. I walked along where Margaret, Stephen, and I used to stroll, back when our lives were before us, when the future was open and there for the dreaming as well as the taking.

I walked back up toward Wisconsin Avenue. Several times I ducked into alleys, rousing rats from the trash bins, sliding between buildings, wondering if I was being followed. When I was certain that I wasn't, I used a pay phone near the university and called Harry Bonifant. He answered from his law school office. The news of my arrest hadn't reached him.

"It is really you, Jack, isn't it," he said quietly. "You know I never really bought that shit about you drowning. Something about it never sat right. I was just waiting." He suggested we meet at a new Cajun place on Seventeenth Street. "I've had a hankering to smell boiled crayfish lately," he said. It was almost as if we saw each other all the time and there was nothing surprising about my call.

Harry listened as I told him much of the story of my escape from the city, my days at Boxmoor, my rescue by Muddy, and my time with her at Dun Cove. I told him what little I knew about the trade conference. He added some information that he'd heard around the law school. I then briefed him on my meeting with Langrell and on what the government intended. "I'm going to need help with this, Harry. A lawyer with backbone," I said as I finished. "Someone who won't falter under the pressure. I've got a little money. I can raise more. Do you know anyone I can trust with this?"

Harry, as was his way, was reluctant to judge me. He told me, though, that he had read all the press reports about what I had done, before I fled the city, and that the picture wasn't pretty. "I thought you might have called sooner," he said.

"I didn't want to mire you down in my drudge," I responded.

"You're looking for someone you say you can trust. To run with a plan you're concocting. To take on the government. This may be an indelicate question, my old friend, but it begs to be asked. Why would a lawyer in good standing agree to trust you?" Embarrassed for both of us, he glanced away.

We had ordered two plates of jambalaya and coffee, which the waitress set down. As Harry ate, I began to describe my involvement with Linda and the Ramirez case. Just as I had to Muddy. When I got to the part about the grand jury, though, about why I went there and lied, I faltered. Morgan Langrell's accusation had been hovering in my thoughts like a fear I couldn't shake.

"What are you leaving out, Jack? It's there in your face. Tell me. They say confession is good for the soul, you know."

In the distance we could hear the ringing of the bells from St. Matthew's Cathedral, faint, like tinkling chimes, tolling the hour. The noise of sirens grew and drowned out the bells. A motorcade came by, horns blaring, a series of wailing police cars, lights flashing outside the windows, leading a group of limousines followed by more police.

"Al Gore," Harry indicated, pointing at the limo.

The noise receded. "It's Langrell," I said. And then I told Harry about Langrell's condemnation of me. "It was like he could see into me. And the worst part," I added, "was that it struck me as true. Mostly true anyway."

I had lied about it to Muddy. This I regretted. I had told Muddy that my perjury was to protect Linda. The fact was I thought I could get away with it. Because to tell the truth there, in the grand jury, would have undone me as a lawyer, would have destroyed the career by which I had come to define my life, by which I attributed to my life any value it had. And because it had gotten so easy for me to slide around the truth, to fix it up. I wiped my face with my napkin and looked at my friend. "I just got too caught up in it . . . I just lost it somewhere, Harry . . ."

He had been quietly assessing what I told him. He withdrew into his own contemplation. I waited for several minutes. "I suppose you got some strategy," he then drawled, "percolating in that brain of yours?"

He saw that I did.

"I said to you once," he then went on, "that I wasn't sure I had the stomach for private practice, for litigation. It wasn't, though, that I shied from a good catfight."

"No," I replied.

"But I've built a clinic here that has been a strong teacher, that has offered a dose of decent thinking to my students. In the profession we chose, that's what's worked for me. I'd hope any of them would take this case. But like Asa used to say, I shouldn't expect them to do something I won't do myself." Harry pushed his plate away and wiped his mouth with his napkin. "I haven't been in a courtroom in years, you know. I wouldn't want to have to start learning how to dance all over."

Listening, I sensed that my instincts were right, that Harry was ready to help. "Muddy's good to the bone," I said. "Eccentric. Badly hurt. But she brought me back. Helped me find a way to start liking myself again. I wouldn't want to start back on any slippery slope either."

We eyed each other over our coffee cups.

"I've got a few thousand in cash," I said. "Stashed in this old Ford I bought, down on the shore. More, if I can access my brokerage accounts."

"That ID of hers of the Nicaraguan is suspect, though. It was how many years ago? It's stale. You of all people should know that."

"She drew his picture before she ever saw a photograph. She drew it over and over, year after year. Personally, I think she's got the right guy. But that's not the issue here. She's the issue."

"Yeah. Well, the world's gotten spooked over terrorism, Jack. For good reason. Our notions of the right to protest, civil disobedience, all of this is falling victim to that fear. What she did—could be hard to save her."

I watched him weighing the situation. I let him work his way to a decision. He wouldn't take any money, he finally said. Wouldn't even consider it. "What is it you have in mind?"

I briefly outlined my plan. He told me he wasn't sure it was wise. Or that I could help anyone, particularly myself. He wasn't at all sure I was thinking straight.

I asked him to wait until the following week to see Muddy. Until the last minute. To keep them off guard. "See her in the morning, if you can," I asked. "And give her a sign from me. Tell her she called my first bluefish a 'hoss,'" I said. "And that I've been listening to Satchmo. Can you remember?"

Harry took a small pad and pencil from his jacket and began taking notes. "Since the Satch was from New Orleans, okay. I like her already. And how big was this hoss?" he asked smiling.

"Big. But no match for those Mississippi River catfish you used to brag about." I patted him on the arm. "If it goes well, come pick me up. I'll be at Union Station, waiting outside. I still have my bar membership card at home, so I can pass through with you on a legal visit. Take me back with you to see her. I just need to see her once."

"Asa won't go easy 'cause it's us, you know. Probably be harder. He's gotten mean as a polecat. If we don't lock it up, he won't flinch in sending her away. But he is still independent. And iron tough." Harry paused. "Things have changed since we were at the agency. We meant to improve things. But the truth is the streets are a lot meaner. Asa's a prosecutor's judge because he knows all the tricks and he's sick of crime. But at least he's not owned by anybody."

"If we played it straight, played their game, we might win the competency hearing," I offered. "But it would be a long haul. They'd probably get their sixty-day study. We'd need experts. It would be expensive. And the outcome would still be uncertain. And then, even if we won that part, they'd prosecute her for the trespassing and a weapons charge, and she has no defense there. My plan, if it works, might set her free altogether."

"Yeah. But your way's a dead end for you. They'll hate you even more. For you it'll be ground zero."

"Maybe." I leaned back and watched the ceiling fan slowly revolve. I brought my gaze down to meet Harry's. "Everett asked me, there in Langrell's office, whether I wanted my life back. I told him yes, that I did."

Harry paused, before nodding. "Your call there, partner," was all he responded.

Our waitress appeared and started to remove our plates. Harry asked for the check and paid it, waving away my protestations.

I thanked him. "You'll need to do some research, Harry," I said. "Asa always demanded lawyer preparation. Be nice to have a memo ready."

"I do remember a few steps," he quietly replied.

"Be like old times."

"You going to keep your disguise?" He allowed himself another faint, appreciative smile. Then he repeated the cliché we had learned at the agency, that any lawyer who represents himself has a fool for a client. But he had agreed to see Muddy. And to take me in to see her after he had. Knowing Harry, he would follow through with the rest of what I had devised as well.

I DIDN'T WANT HARRY to drive me home, in case my house was being watched, so I took a cab. The townhouse, three stories high, had been searched from top to bottom and was a mess. Drawers were out, and papers and clothes were strewn everywhere. The mattress was half off the bed. An old search warrant, from when I had run, was thumbtacked to the wall. I tried to straighten up some.

In the kitchen a dusty film had settled on the counters, and black ants crossed the floor. I swept them with a broom until they disappeared into the cracks under the baseboard. I shaved and tried to wash the dye out of my hair. In the liquor cabinet I found a bottle of single-malt scotch. I drank with the television on, watching every news show I could find. I ordered Chinese delivered from the Yenching Palace and ate and finally slept. The next morning I went to the library and read news reports of the conference, and of Muddy. There had been a mix of responses. A few reporters had taken seriously a plea she had apparently made for an investigation of Bustillo. Others dismissed her claims as ravings. An old Ronald Reagan quote, referring to the contras, was dredged up: "One man's terrorist is another man's freedom fighter." The writer of that article dismissed Muddy's claims as old news and argued that disruptive protestors like her should be imprisoned.

Everett had left several messages on my answering machine. I called him back. "I assume you're thinking of a way to present your testimony," he said. "Of the many examples you will tell the judge of her luny behavior. Morgan will want to hear them on Tuesday."

I assured him that I was.

AROUND NOON, I TOOK a Greyhound bus out Route 50, past Annapolis, across the bridge, and into Easton. Then I hired a cab to take me out toward Tilghman and to my Ford Escort. It was still parked there, a dozen houses down from Muddy's cottage. The cash I had stashed under the seat was where I had left it. The car started right up. Before leaving, I pulled into Muddy's driveway. The cottage door was blocked with yellow police tape. I tried the knob, but the door was locked. I walked around back. The wind was blowing the tide out, and the exposed dock piles looked like long, dark, knobby legs. Whitecaps filled the river. I couldn't find the swans at first. Then I saw them, out of the wind, bunched together in a crook of the cove.

ON SATURDAY EVENING, I put on the tuxedo from my closet. It felt odd after all that had gone on. A white limousine pulled up outside. Everett introduced me to two of his cronies, a commodities trader from Chicago named Philpot and a tall gangly Floridian named Jones who wore a string tie and cowboy boots with his silver tuxedo. Jones patted me on the back like he knew I was his friend. They were having a discussion in the limo about the O. J. Simpson trial. Everett had the last word. "Justice was done," he pronounced. "Absolutely. The government failed to prove its case. In front of the jury it got. Tough shit if it was racial. Good lawyers use that to their advantage. Don't they, Jack? It's beside the point whether the fucker did it or not. The proof fell short. That means not guilty. That's the right result. That's justice. I applaud the verdict. Pure and simple."

Fight Night is a celebrated institution for the male Washington elite. Designed and disguised as a charity dinner to raise money for battered and abused children, it had grown into the ultimate boys' night out. Only men were invited. The cheap tickets went for five hundred dollars per plate. Ringside seats were twice that. The evening began in the ballroom at the Washington Hilton at seven with an open bar and cigars stacked on silver trays. Precisely at seven-thirty, velvet-draped double doors were opened to a corridor and about two hundred female models, ages eighteen to twenty-five, all dressed in revealing evening wear, paraded in for the men to view and meet. Several models were assigned to each table as hostesses, to run for drinks, cigars, whatever. The models were encouraged to enjoy the drinks with the men. No other women were on the premises, at least not within sight.

Everett had bought one of the ringside tables. Bottles of Louis XIII cognac and iced bowls of beluga caviar were there for his guests. One of the models, Patty, a previous Miss Delaware runner-up, alternated between his lap and Jones's. Everett kept slipping the girl twenty-dollar bills. I smoked coronas and concentrated on the cognac, hardly tasting the dinner of beef Wellington, white asparagus, and boiled potatoes carved into tiny pugilists.

In past years boxing greats such as Joe Frazier, Sonny Liston, and Sugar Ray Leonard had attended as celebrity guests. Muhammad Ali had even been there once. This year a rock group was in the ring as prefight entertainment instead. The first bout, a welterweight fight, led a card of seven contests beginning at nine. Toward the middle of the card, a black man from Trinidad was boxing an Irish mick. The black was in his early twenties and bands of sinew rippled along his back and torso like corded whips. The mick was older, thirty maybe, and was taking a bad beating. He had been down once. His left eyebrow had been split and patched with a butterfly bandage, and the eye was swollen closed. His cheek was plum colored and vitreous. I asked someone about the match. "That's Jugo Rambard," the man said, pointing to the black. "He's an up-and-comer. The mick's just a journeyman. He's paid to take a beating."

As they fought, not twenty feet from our table, the model, Patty, was giggling on Everett's lap while he nuzzled her cleavage. Philpot had found a girl too, a slender reed in peach satin. Jones was loudly telling a joke about Panama poontang. I heard a swipe and a grunt. A rain of sweat and blood sprayed the table. The mick was caught in the near corner, was being pummeled, and then was down, bleeding from his mouth on the canvas. Everett had taken a napkin and eagerly blotted the front of Patty's dress as she playfully pushed his hand away, laughing. The mick tried to rise. The black boxer let him, then began to hit him again. I was on my third cigar. I felt the room start to turn and told Everett I needed to go. He yelled after me to take the limo, but I shuffled out and hailed the first cab that was in the waiting line outside.

24

DURING MY FIRST MEETING with Everett and Morgan Langrell, I got a sense of what Muddy had done. And I'd read the newspaper accounts and listened to the television reporters give their slants to it. But it wasn't until that next Monday, when I got to speak with Muddy, that I was able to put the final pieces together.

When Harry took me with him to St. Elizabeth's Hospital to see her, Muddy and I talked on telephones, from opposite sides of a thick, blurry, Plexiglas partition. Not being able to touch her made it easier. She told me what happened.

The day I left Dun Cove, Muddy had finalized a written compilation of proof linking Bustillo to six different contra vengeance killings in Nicaragua and Honduras, including the car bombing that killed Gutierrez and her father. With some help from Chula, and through skillful use of the Internet, she'd been amassing her facts for over two years. She'd learned to access declassified documents from the State Department and the National Security Council. She'd downloaded the results of Freedom of Information Act requests on the activities of CIA operatives. She'd corresponded electronically with Chula's contacts in Honduras. She'd even gone to Washington and researched the microfiche files of the National Security Archive, a nongovernment public interest database of international terrorism. Initially, she'd intended to take her findings to the press, though she didn't expect much. When Chula's contacts let her know that Bustillo was coming to the trade conference—coming, for all intents and purposes, *to her*—her plans changed. She prepared a written confession for him to sign. She meant to exploit his well-known affinity for girls, to get him alone, and then to force him at gunpoint to confess and reveal the details of his crime against her father. She had readied herself, she told me, to shoot him if she had to.

Using her fax machine as a copier, she had made several duplicates of the compilation of proof against him. She had put these, along with her sketches of Bustillo, in a soft satchel folded into her backpack. She hoped to distribute all this to the press as evidence of his guilt. She had also folded in a set of evening clothes. In the outer pocket of her pack, she had stored the flat snub-nose Colt. She wore the binoculars, with their infrared attachment, around her neck.

Waiting until almost dark, she took her camouflaged boat out through the narrows and up the Chesapeake into Eastern

Bay, and then north and, hugging the shore, east to the Wye River. The trip by water at night, a serpentine journey around two peninsulas, must have taken several hours. Once within hearing distance of Wye Plantation, she cut her outboard and paddled. She pulled the boat up onto the shore and hid it in some cattails near her hunting field. Her plan was to use the goose pit as a base. She was dressed in hunting clothes and nearly invisible in the darkness.

The trade conference, it turned out, was the culmination of months of preparation and negotiation by the various interests involved. In attendance were representative delegations from every Central American country, Mexico, and the United States. Important new trade agreements and corporate partnership agreements concerning agricultural products, primarily coffee and soybeans, and oil, minerals, and technology had been agreed upon and were to be announced to the world. The conference would be carried live on certain preselected international networks. Groundbreaking agreements were to be presented, executed, and applauded through carefully staged events for the invited media. Security was tight. Only the delegations, certain dignitaries and invited guests, and those with press clearance were permitted on the Wye Plantation grounds.

Muddy, aware only of some of this, lay hidden in the hedges and trees that bordered the plantation, watching through her infrared binoculars. Security guards roamed the lawn, and behind them the guests attended the evening's functions. A large tent had been set up behind the main structure, where cocktails were being served. Over the evening hours, she had studied every male that moved between the buildings. It hadn't been difficult to pinpoint where security was lax on the fenced perimeter and later to locate Bustillo. She first spotted him outside on the grass, with a group of men who were smoking cigars. Like the rest he wore a tuxedo. Leading the others, he had disappeared into the main plantation mansion, where a formal dinner was under way. Muddy changed clothes in the dark. She put on her black silk dress, pearls, and high heels. Using a pocket mirror she had combed her hair and applied lipstick as well. When Bustillo came back outside and walked by himself past the greenhouse toward his lodging, she was there, not far from his path, prepared to play the part of a young reporter awed by the money and power about her, open to the night, ready to meet him. But before he reached her, before the confrontation ever occurred, something changed her mind, made her turn and walk away.

ST. ELIZABETH'S HOSPITAL is D.C.'s public mental institution. City operated, its reddish brick buildings take up several blocks off Martin Luther King Avenue in the southeast quadrant of town. The hospital has had many famous residents. Ezra Pound was housed there after World War II. John Hinckley, the man who shot President Reagan, is interned somewhere in there now. It's a dreary, forbidding place. Endless corridors seem to lead to nowhere. I followed Harry that day, winding through them, past a security check, through locked steel doors, to visit Muddy.

They brought her into the interview room wearing a blue hospital smock. She shuffled along in torn paper house slippers. Her face was tear stained and streaked. Her hair was matted. Harry spoke to her first. She answered his questions, but her eyes had fastened on mine. He was angry as he handed me the phone. Despite his protestations of earlier that morning, they had continued to refuse her a shower.

As I took the phone, Muddy shook her head. "I thought we had made promises to each other," she said. "You weren't supposed to come back. Why did you? Why are you here? Did they let you go?"

I had been given only fifteen minutes to talk to her. Harry was nervous even about that. This was supposed to have been a legal meeting, as she was not allowed visitors. He had smuggled me in as his assistant and was pacing as she and I talked. I told her I was fine. That there was nothing at all to worry about concerning me. I told her I would have Harry explain everything when there was more time. But that right now I needed to know exactly what happened. That she needed, now, to let me help her. To talk to me. To follow the advice Harry would give her. Muddy laid her forehead against the glass. Then sat back, reaching out, touching the partition with just her fingertips. I put my fingers there too. She was clearly frightened. Disoriented.

"Okay," she said through the phone. She squeezed her eyes shut, then opened them. "But you should know this, Jack. I had planned it for so long. To force him to admit what he did. To force him to sign the confession. I even had on the perfume I found out he liked. But then I thought of all that had happened with you. With us . . . And I left him alone."

I sat there with this filthy black phone in my hand, with the ceiling lights buzzing overhead like an electric insect, pulling out of Muddy what she had done. I knew that my welling emotions were only a hindrance. "You did right, Muddy," I answered, after she explained that she had walked away from

Bustillo. "And thank God." I tried to smile. "Though from what I understand, you didn't exactly leave him alone."

She was crying. "I know it won't come to anything," she said. She swiped at her eyes. I didn't expect it would. So now what's going to happen? Tell me, Jack. I'm scared, Jack. I don't even know where I am . . ."

WHAT MUDDY HAD DONE instead of trying to kidnap an international thug and force him at gunpoint to a confession, instead of trying to match her capacity for brutality against his was what filled the television reports and newspapers.

After Muddy walked away from Bustillo that night, she had worked her way through the crowd toward one of the red barns adjacent to the main hall and outdoor tent. Dressed as she was for the evening, she had blended in among the guests. She waited and watched and then managed to take her satchel into one of the barns. She had spent the long night there, huddled in a horse blanket, alone with her thoughts, with her fears and with her courage. In the morning, she had waited for the conference to begin. Press tables, cameras, rows of chairs, a stage and podium were set up under the tent. During the first intermission and coffee break, Muddy had put copies of her compiled evidence against Bustillo on some press tables, along with her sketches. When the conference reconvened she had walked out on the stage to the rostrum and microphone with her unloaded snub-nose pistol in her hand, raised and pointed at her own temple. The conferees were stunned into silence. With the television cameras rolling, she had warned the crowd not to approach or she would kill herself, and promised to speak for only a minute. In a shaking voice she began reciting the evidence against Bustillo, pointing her finger at him as she spoke. She ordered him to stand. For some amazing reason Bustillo obliged, and Muddy continued while he stood nervously looking around for help. She asked the reporters to refer for supporting proof to the documents she had left at each of their tables. Holding up one of the sketches, she steadily told the story of her father's death and enumerated the evidence she had compiled that pointed to Bustillo's guilt. Finally, the spectators began to react. Someone shouted to turn off the cameras. Few of the cameramen complied. Bustillo then called out something in Spanish, turned and was suddenly surrounded with security. As the din grew louder, Muddy called out the names of those she believed Bustillo had murdered. The group surrounding Bustillo rushed out of the tent. And many others began leaving hurriedly as well. Security guards arranged themselves between Muddy and the cameras. When she could no longer be heard over the noise and was blocked from the view of the cameras, she dropped the pistol to the ground and sank to her knees. The pistol was kicked away as they swarmed over her.

Federal officers took her to a back room of the plantation house, but the damage to the conference was irreparable. Bustillo had left. His and several other delegations had called for transport, and limousines immediately departed the grounds, carrying people back to Andrews Air Force Base where emergency meetings were being scheduled with trade officials and corporate representatives, all offering excuses, apologies, damage control. The grounds of Wye Plantation became a mass of confusion. Officials of the conference were trying to salvage the day, though already there was talk of a suspension of meetings and announcements. Within an hour a government spokesman had declared to the press that Muddy was mentally ill and described her accusations as the ramblings of an insane girl. They had kept her in a back room, trying to interrogate her. Apparently, from what Harry had picked up from his sources, she had been strangely composed. She had given them her name and address and answered their biographical inquiries. As for the rest of their questions and demands she had just pointed at the documents she had prepared. "I have said what I came to say" was all she would tell them.

They got a search warrant, and in their rush to get evidence to support their claims of her madness and ameliorate the damage she had done, they had taken her with them. It was just coincidence that I showed up at Dun Cove minutes before they all did. An unexpected stroke of luck, I would say now. Timing.

25

WITH HARRY TUGGING AT MY ARM and whispering that we had to leave, I finished by telling Muddy that when this was all over I'd keep my promises. I said I'd stay away from her after I got us both through this. Muddy started crying again. I wanted to kick down the glass between us.

Drawn away by Harry through that maze of labyrinthine tunnels, I lost it too. He stepped ahead and let me follow behind.

Once outside, the light was bright and we had to shield our eyes. We walked across the street and bought coffee from a vendor truck. Children on tricycles were wheeling by on the sidewalk.

Standing there, I told Harry my plan for the following day. He was uneasy at first, but as he thought it through he agreed. "Just use one of your clinic cases as an excuse," I said, my voice still tremulous. "You often go over there on clinic cases, don't you? We're doing nothing wrong. We're violating no rules or laws. We're just being careful."

"I'll be there," he said.

I noticed, across the street, a stout female figure struggling up the steps to the administration office of the hospital and realized it was Muddy's Agnes. I pointed her out to Harry and explained who she was. After we finished our coffee, he set off to find her, to explain to her that Muddy wasn't allowed visitors but that she was well represented, to tell her what was going on, and to try to ease her confusion and fear.

My DOORBELL RANG at ten the next morning. Randolph was pacing on the building's stoop outside wearing an expensive tweed trench coat. A driver was waiting in a black Lincoln. Randolph escorted me into the car and we headed downtown for my pretrial briefing.

In the car Randolph was courteous but spoke only to answer my few questions. Morgan was anxious to hear from me, he offered. Judge Cole had decided to permit an open hearing but had promised to brook no nonsense. There would be no political speeches and no cameras near the courtroom. Morgan was going to give the opening statement himself. I would testify as the third government witness, after two of the case agents. Muddy's writings, sketches, and other property, all of which bolstered the government's position, would be admitted into evidence early, through the case agents. Her prior psychiatrist would take the stand after hearing my testimony. Another expert, a government psychologist, would follow him.

At the corner of Fourth and D Streets, the driver let us out. We went inside and walked around the stone sculpture of the Lady of Justice. Although lawyers with bar cards and other government officials with proper identification were not required to pass through the metal detector, Randolph indicated for me to go through. I emptied my pockets. My loose change clattered and rolled on the table. The alarm was silent as I stepped into the vestibule. Approaching the elevators, I heard someone hail me from behind. Harry had seen us enter and had followed us into the building. He flashed his identification at the marshal and sidestepped the metal detector, introducing himself to Randolph. "I have heard of you," Randolph replied shaking his hand. "We deal sometimes with your students."

"Right. Well I've got a matter to take up with one of my students' supervisors," Harry said indicating a file under his arm. "Upstairs. But I recognized Jack here. He and I were colleagues in the old days. Years ago. Public defenders together. Hello, Jack. God, I read about you. Paper said you drowned. How are you? Are you holding up? Could I have a moment?" he said glancing at Randolph. "Just a moment with Jack?" Harry had put his hand around my shoulder and was already leading me a few paces off. He turned me so that my back was to Randolph. We spoke for hardly a minute when Randolph interrupted.

"We need to go up, Mr. Stanton," he said in a loud voice from over by the elevators. "Mr. Langrell's waiting."

Harry signaled that he'd heard, then offered me his hand to shake. Concealed in his palm was a small tape recorder with, I knew, a miniature cassette inside. I took it as we clasped hands and slipped it into my jacket pocket. Then I turned to rejoin Randolph.

Upstairs Morgan was pacing, looking at his watch impatiently. "I've got an early lunch at Justice," he barked. "You're late, Randolph. Let's get to it, Stanton. What you got?"

"Where's Everett?" I inquired. I switched on the recorder in my pocket as I spoke.

"Tied up. He's out of this now anyway. You do your job, he'll take care of things."

I asked if I could make myself a cup of coffee. Langrell impatiently buzzed his secretary and ordered a pot. "Now talk to me, Stanton."

"I have a question for you, Morgan. I'm curious. I've been reading the papers. Who is this character, Bustillo, anyway?"

Langrell looked at me like I was an annoying child who was pestering him to play a game. "You're not going to rile me, Stanton. And Bustillo is not any of your concern. Like I could give a shit who he is. He's the obsession of this Susannah Blair who's caused me a big pain in the ass, that's who."

"Morgan, you must know something. Really. Who is he?"

Langrell flashed me an impatient look, then flicked his head at Randolph. His assistant chimed in, "The man's past is obscure. No one says he's a saint. It's all very murky. Apparently, though, he was a great asset to the contras during their war against the communist-backed Sandinistas. Served as an intelligence officer. Had ties with the CIA. Amassed great wealth during the struggle and afterward. In land holdings. Coffee plantations. Mineral rights. He fought on *our* side. On the side of the contras. Now he's a civilian but very important and influential with the government. That's all we know."

"Satisfied, Stanton?" Langrell walked to the couch and sat down. "We're waiting," he said. "And I'm running late."

"Could he be a terrorist? I mean hypothetically?"

"He's obviously not a terrorist. He's an ally. He was a soldier. A guerilla freedom fighter. It was a war. Not that I care. Iran-contra and all that shit's long over. No one cares, Stanton." Langrell was agitated. "What I care about is showing the world now that we don't coddle terrorists. We don't tolerate disruption. She had a gun, goddamn it. It's lucky the security people didn't start firing. People could have been killed. She deserves to be locked up and she's going to be. We need to make an example here. Now, stop wasting my time."

I waited for him to stop. I sat across from him and spoke slowly, distinctly. "This woman, Muddy, or as you know her, Susannah Blair, isn't insane, Morgan. Or incompetent. But as you requested I've thought of instances, certain conduct, that I could testify to, that might raise some eyebrows . . ."

He leaned over close, his raised hand interrupting, his face growing angry. "Listen, you lowlife. You better do more than that if you want your plea. You understand? Have I failed to make my meaning plain? She better seem a damn lunatic when you're done. Am I getting the message across, Stanton?"

"Easy," I said. "I make her crazy, I get my plea. That's the deal? I just want to be clear."

Morgan's self-satisfied look was all the response he made. He sat back.

"You thought I twisted the facts in the Sherman Allen case, didn't you?" I smiled, baiting him. "Or maybe with Joseph Williams?"

Langrell pointed his finger at me, turning his head quizzically, but I went on.

"I had mentioned fairies. How about this? Susannah told me not just once but on several occasions that there were fairies under the water with wands of fire. Holding green lanterns. Of course, she was just referring to something her father had told her, a way he had explained phosphorescence to her when she was a child."

"You're fucking around with me, aren't you, Stanton? Well, my patience is ended." He wrapped his knuckles on the table. "You know, Stanton, you *always* twisted the truth. Bent it. Turned it inside out to suit your purposes. I marveled at how good you got at it." His eyes turned predatory in that way he had. "So either do it here for my purposes, to put this girl away and get your life back, or don't and go to prison. Do it now. Do it or leave. Now!" He fixed me with that prosecutor's stare. I didn't move. He took my silence as acquiescence.

"So," he wheedled, "fairies is good. Wands of fire are good. I already told you. What else?"

I rose and went to the window. A funeral procession was slowly moving along New Jersey Avenue. A small group of walkers behind the hearse were singing and strains of gospel drifted up from the traffic below. Listening to the mournful ululation I felt a vague sympathy for Langrell. "I draw the picture the way you want it, I walk, Morgan. I walk." I spoke as though musing to myself.

He watched me.

"Where's my guarantee? My agreement?"

Morgan motioned toward Randolph. "He's written it up. You can read it. Truthful testimony as to her strange behavior, as to your concerns that she was mentally deranged, as to the insane conduct you witnessed, and you get the plea and the recommendation for probation."

"Give me a copy."

Randolph laid one on the table.

"What else you got?" Langrell pressed.

I stepped to the table, scanning the document. Then folded it and put it in my pocket. I switched off the tape in my pocket masking the sound with the crumpling of the paper. "She was obsessed with the bombing that killed her father. With all acts of violence in Central America. Her bedroom was wallpapered with photographs of the bombing scene. Wallpapered from ceiling to floor. Gruesome photographs. I can go over each one on the stand, if you want. I urged her to take them down. Press photos from newspapers were plastered on the walls too." While I spoke Morgan again indicated for Randolph to take notes. "From the papers in Central America. All of terrorists acts. Kidnappings. Killings. Disappearances. She trained as a huntress. She trained and readied herself for her day of reckoning. As I said, she called bluefish 'greenies.' She'd remark about fish going to heaven. She claimed she heard a voice telling her things. Believed once she was an animal—a yak, for Christsakes. She wouldn't have a telephone or television in the house. Wouldn't use them. She lived a solitary existence. Had some notion that the river was alive and had handed me over to her. She liked to sit outside in the rain for hours getting soaked. She's an artist but couldn't bring herself to draw anything but this face she was fixated on. The one she believed was Bustillo. She got the notion he killed her father from some immigrant she met protesting for chicken workers. As I said, she was obsessed with it. Got drunk on gin at night. How much more do you need, Morgan?"

Langrell rose and started putting on his topcoat. "That

sounds good, Stanton. Sign off again on Randolph's notes. Then go home and organize it. Embellish. Think of more. You're on the right track. Make it sound convincing. Like you always did against me. Don't fuck it up. Remember. She's delusional. Give me delusions. What you do in that courtroom tomorrow will define your future, your life . . ." He started whistling as he walked out the door. His secretary passed him with the fresh pot of coffee she had made.

26

MY COLLEAGUES IN MY NEW HOME here like to watch Court TV. They can't get enough of it. Shorn of my legal idealism and still recovering from an overdose of legal machinations, I myself avoid all exposure to courtroom drama. The allergy I have developed to legal dissimulation appears chronic.

It's interesting how our society has, in recent decades, grown so enamored with the spectacle of legal combat. It's become another national pastime, a sport, a form of amusement. The men housed here are no different from those outside. Their choice of entertainment reflects the predilections of our larger society. A trial can present high drama, with big stakes, with actors who will suffer the consequences of a poor performance, when a miscue can be catastrophic. In a trial, though, the search should be for what is real, for what is true. The judge and the jury, we hope, will strive to peer through the mystery, to discover what remains after all the trappings are stripped away.

I tried to avoid passing any final judgment on Morgan Langrell. He had obviously arrived at some level of comfort, had justified what he was doing. Perhaps without giving it much thought he truly believed, as I had once, that such dissembling *was* for the greater good. I don't know. I just know I was laid low by my own regret and loss as I shaved and dressed the morning of Muddy's hearing.

I HADN'T FULLY APPRECIATED the groundswell of media and community interest that had been building since Muddy's intrepid act. The federal courthouse was packed. Camera crews were stationed up and down the sidewalk. Reporters bustled around me, thrusting microphones in my face, shouting questions. My escorts had to clear a path to the door. Inside, Morgan Langrell, surrounded by a retinue of aides and assistants, paraded back and forth in the hallway outside the judges' chambers. I had been delivered by two agents from the FBI and, after receiving my last-minute instructions from Randolph, taken to an anteroom in the prosecution suite to wait. Because I was a witness, I would not be permitted to view any of the hearing until called to the stand.

At the morning break, Langrell strode into the suite followed by Randolph and others. He strutted around like a gamecock. It was the universal consensus that his opening remarks had been impeccably delivered and well received by

Judge Asa Cole. Langrell himself admitted that it went quite well. The only surprise in the proceedings had been the last-minute appearance of Harry Bonifant, as hired counsel for Susannah.

"A distant relative showed up," Randolph mentioned. "From down there where she lives. The bar referral service probably sent her to the clinic, and Bonifant, still a bleeding heart, agreed to step in."

"He's a has-been," Langrell muttered. "Though I held my breath when Judge Cole asked him if he wanted a continuance or a different judge. He might have kicked this over if Bonifant had asked."

"Why didn't he want more time?" It was a woman carrying a notepad who spoke. She was a special assistant from Justice.

"For what? They don't have the funds to handle this. I'm surprised he took it." Langrell turned to me. "When's the last time you saw Bonifant, Stanton? He was a partner of yours, wasn't he?"

"Years ago. I just ran into him over in the lobby of your building. On Tuesday. On my way to prep."

"How long did you speak with him?"

"Thirty seconds." I looked at Randolph.

"That's right, sir. I was there. Bonifant was over there on some clinic case."

"What's he got up his sleeve?" The question came from the woman again.

"You heard his opening," Randolph answered. "Whining about a trumped-up charge. About it being unheard of for the government to advocate pretrial commitment. The usual prosecutorial misconduct crap."

"Cole wasn't even listening," Langrell added.

There was a rap on the door. The bailiff stuck his head in. "Ten minutes, Mr. Langrell. Judge Cole wants to start promptly."

"Who's the first witness? Get him ready, Randolph. Bring him to me. I need a sandwich and a coffee. You, Johnson"—he pointed at an aide—"run down and get me something to eat. Turkey and cheese. Mayo. Have it ready at next break. Where's the doctor? The shrink? Have you scheduled a press briefing for later? Get me a makeup girl. Have her here. Where are my next exhibits? Keep an eye on the time, Janet."

Once the hearing had started again I was left alone in the side room. Alone to organize my thoughts as Morgan Langrell had ordered.

I was called to the stand after lunch. Two marshals escorted me through the double doors into the stately ceremonial courtroom used to accommodate a large gallery. Judge Cole motioned me forward. "Good afternoon, Mr. Stanton." I returned his salutation. The bailiff had me raise my right hand and administered the oath. I swore to tell the truth. I sat down. Muddy was there at the table next to Harry. Her hair was combed and her face clean, though they had kept her in hospital garb. I saw Agnes and Chula seated in the gallery, holding hands, their expressions anxious. Langrell asked me my name and occupation. I answered carefully. My testimony began.

27

TIME HERE IS MARKED by the daily prison count. Bells ring every morning at ten and every afternoon at two. We all then assemble to be noted. A gentler percussion, one resembling muted cymbals, signals the end of the process. Once it is over, we are all permitted to move around freely again.

The word *freely,* of course, is used here as a relative term. But I have begun to adapt, to settle into this new way of living. I try to see my situation as no more confining, really, than what I had before. In Washington I'd become caged by my own ambition, by my relish for competition and winning. I'd ingeniously created and then succumbed to the rationalizations I needed in order to prevail.

Here there are restrictions of physical movement. But there's a corresponding liberation of thought—the benefit of so much downtime. Building on the new beginning that Muddy gave me, I try to spend as many of these hours as I can in contemplation of what matters in a life. Just having this luxury, this chance to reflect—it's some solace.

I am a useful inmate. This is a minimum-security institution, a prison camp, and I'm just one of many prisoners with professional skills. The warden and a lot of my colleagues here have recognized my legal talent and solicited my help. I've made clear to everyone the ground rules. I work with facts that I can verify. Regarding predicaments that meet my criteria, I am willing to lend the skills and flair of an experienced legal writer. But that is the extent of my willingness to contribute.

There is one window in my dormitory cell. It looks southeast, and I can see fallow fields running toward the mountains, stippled with haystacks from last season's harvest. Beyond the fields, the Appalachians rise up. They're the oldest mountains in America. According to the warden, some of the oldest in the world. When I lived in Washington I used to occasionally visit the more southerly ranges in Virginia—the Blue Ridge, named for the haze over the summits, tinted by the sunlight. Here in Pennsylvania, the peaks seem grander, more precipitous. There is more exposed rock. I watched these Appalachians change over the winter. Crowns of snow capped the higher peaks. Ice fields hung in the crevices. It's spring now. On clear days I can make out the cataracts rushing down from the cliffs of red feldspar.

The pace here is slow. I could be a monk isolated from the world in meditation in a hermitage. Harry has sent me more

books than I could ever finish. He favors the historical and scientific classics and has sent volumes of Gibbon, Dana, Darwin,
and Freud. I've enjoyed Gibbon, I will confess. Fortunately, he
has sent lighter material too. One book I like a lot is on landscape gardening. I wrote him and asked for more on the topic.
In return for some tax work, the warden has agreed to let me
start a prison garden. "Vegetables only," he cautioned. I've laid
out the project on paper and requested the compost and seeds
I will need. Once the danger of frost is over, I plan to com-
mence the digging. Several of my colleagues have agreed to
help. From the yard, where we will start, the sky is large and
blue. Yesterday I was out there surveying the plot when it
started to rain. I didn't want to come in. I thought of Muddy . . .

As I BEGAN MY RECITATION to Judge Cole about Muddy,
seated on the witness stand in that crowded courtroom,
Morgan Langrell was standing at the podium. I had asked him
if I could describe the days I spent with her chronologically,
along with her bizarre fixations and eccentricities. With a fling
of his arm Morgan told me to go ahead, to take my time, to tell
the judge everything I could recall.

Once I had started, and Morgan picked up on the tone and
purpose of my testimony, he tried to interrupt and stop me. He
struggled to cut me off. His complexion turned purplish. That's
when Harry rose and objected, asking the judge to permit me
to complete my answer.

Judge Cole brought everyone up to the bench. He pushed his
octagonal glasses down on his nose and looked at me sorrow-
fully. "You appear to be digging a grave for yourself, Jack," he
said. "And I'm not sure even you can help this girl. Are you cer-

tain you wish to continue in this vein?" I indicated that I did. "Then the witness may finish his answer." He ruled with a sigh.

I retook the stand and began again. It wasn't that I left out any of the facts I had promised Morgan that I would recite and embellish upon. It's just that I put them in context and explained them as I told the story of Muddy, of a young girl who lost her father to terrorism, of a young woman who believed in a justice system that failed her, of a grown woman who wanted only that the truth about a murder be revealed. I told the story of how she saved my life but was willing to sacrifice her own to bear witness. I looked over toward Muddy whose head was in her hands.

By the time I completed my answer, Morgan had regained his self-control and was casting about for a strategy to undercut my testimony. He drenched his next questions in sarcasm and disgust.

"You told us different in our briefing sessions, didn't you?" he dryly asked.

I answered, "No."

He had me identify my initials on Randolph's notes. "You're lying now, Stanton. You're trying to help this deranged girl. Why? Because you seduced her, you sorry pervert? Because you feel guilty now?"

Muddy rose abruptly. "That is false," she answered him. Her cry was strong and clear.

Harry wrapped her in his arm pulling her down. Asa hesitated before hammering on the gavel.

With order restored I was about to explain my initials on the notes and to give my answer to Morgan's last question, but he denied me the opportunity. "That's all for this ... this excuse for a witness," he stammered. He turned to one of his agents. "Take this perjurer into custody. Charge him with another count of making false statements, with another count of lying under oath."

"Just a minute there, Your Honor," Harry said, rising. "If you please, I do have a couple of questions on cross-examination."

Judge Cole signaled for Harry to proceed. That was when Harry asked me whether any government officials had sought to procure false testimony from me to aid them in their fabrication of evidence against Muddy. The courtroom erupted, as did Morgan. He boomed out an objection. It took minutes for Asa to regain control of the raucous gallery. Pounding his gavel he finally silenced the crowd. Asa ordered a recess and ordered the lawyers and me back to his chambers.

We all filed through the side door, following the uneven sweep of his black robe as Asa limped ahead. The chamber was dark, barely lit. A silver carpet cushioned our steps. The furniture was all black, creased leather. The spines of well-worn law books, packed tightly into recessed shelving, covered the walls. Langrell was ranting about the allegations being outrageous, being an affront to the United States, about their having been levied without a factual basis. He threatened Harry with an ethical complaint before the bar.

The judge looked at Harry for an explanation. Harry took a handkerchief from his breast pocket and dabbed his brow. Then he reached down and wiped off his lizard-skin boots. Raising up he answered that I would testify. That I would provide the evidence and the basis.

Langrell condescendingly scoffed. He called me a known liar and perjurer. He went on that I had purposefully deceived the government about my testimony. That I was going to prison. And that any statements from my mouth were unworthy of consideration.

"Even so, Judge," Harry persisted, "I would like you to hear a brief proffer from Mr. Stanton."

Judge Cole nodded his assent.

I then tried to outline what had transpired in Langrell's office and described the government's strategy to improperly discredit and incarcerate Muddy.

"Hogwash," Langrell interrupted. "Pure crap."

Harry stepped up then and placed his briefcase on the judge's desk. Opening it, he took the tape player out. He had it cued. "I'll do this here, Morgan," he said. "To spare you whatever embarrassment I can." Harry turned it on, and the tape began to play back. The first voice we heard was mine:

"This woman, Muddy, or as you know her, Susannah Blair, isn't insane, Morgan. Or incompetent. But as you requested I've thought of instances, certain conduct, that I could testify to that might raise some eyebrows . . ."

On the tape, Morgan's voice interrupted: *"Listen, you lowlife. You better do more than that if you want your plea. You understand? Have I failed to make my meaning plain? She better seem a damn lunatic when you're done . . ."*

Harry recued the tape and pressed the button to play once more. It was Morgan Langrell's voice again:

"You know, Stanton, you always twisted the truth. Bent it. Turned it inside out to suit your purposes. I marveled at how good you got at it. So either do it here for my purposes, to put this girl away and get your life back, or don't and go to prison . . ."

Harry shut it off. "Do you need to hear more, Judge?"

Judge Asa Cole fixed the U.S. attorney with a stiletto stare. "Is that your voice, Morgan? Is that what you said? We can get the tape analyzed . . ."

Morgan couldn't speak.

Harry then took from his briefcase the compilation of proof Muddy had prepared about Bustillo with three of her sketches. "If you care to review this, Judge, you'll see it is not an insane rambling. Quite the contrary, it is coherent, well researched, and compelling. Whether the conclusions are true, I cannot say. But it could never have been prepared by an incompetent person. Also important, I have a motion here"—Harry held up his pleading—"with a written memorandum of authorities, requesting that all charges against this young woman be dismissed because of government misconduct. It is well supported with case law." He placed it before the judge. "I ask that you consider it."

Judge Cole was silent. He took off his glasses and cleaned them with a cloth in his drawer. He fingered the written motion and picked up the cassette player holding the tape of Morgan Langrell's words to me. "If you all will excuse me. I want to listen to the tape and review this pleading. Please wait in the courtroom," he ordered.

An hour later Judge Cole came out and took the bench. With a solemn voice and shaking his head, he announced his decision. He did not condone what Susannah Blair had done, he made clear. But he granted Harry's motion. The case against Muddy was dismissed with prejudice due to government misconduct. She was free to return home. The judge told Harry he wanted to keep the tape. He intended to refer the matter to the Department of Justice. Bedlam broke out. The media swarmed

over benches and surrounded Harry and Muddy. Morgan re-
treated to the side door. Glancing toward me with a jaundiced
face, he feebly crooked a finger. Randolph and the two federal
agents came over and took me into custody. "You spun us,"
Randolph choked out. "We're adding another false statement
count to the charges. You're under arrest. You've ruined yourself. You can kiss your life good-bye." I held out my wrists as
they fastened the handcuffs. Peripherally, from my left, I saw
Muddy trying to free herself from the mob around her. Harry
took hold of her. "Jack!" I heard her voice through the tumult.
Her hand was up. Raised high and steady. The agents pushed
me to the exit.

A MONTH, MAYBE five weeks ago, Harry drove up to visit
me. He brought me a good cigar, a tapered Monte Cristo. I forget now the names of all the differently shaped cigars. I used to
know them all. My friend the warden lets me smoke outside
the portico. I took Harry out there and showed him the garden.
Harry had reports of Muddy. He keeps in touch with her.
She is healthy and setting spring pound nets, he tells me. She is
working in a partnership with another young waterman. When
I first came here, I had made Harry deliver a request to her.
That she was not to come. That if she tried, I would refuse to
see her. It was the only way I knew to make sure she let this go.
He assures me, though, that she is fine. He mentioned that
while our government apparently has made no effort to for-
mally investigate Bustillo, it's been under increasing pressure
from the media to do so. A debate has ensued. Some argue that
Bustillo was a guerilla fighter and his tactics acceptable during
war. Others counter that murder and assassination, whether on

a small scale or large scale, are never acceptable. Bustillo, supposedly, is back in Nicaragua somewhere. The consensus, Harry reported, is that Bustillo would never do anything to harm Muddy, as it would only tip the balance against him.

Harry brings me other news. Morgan Langrell quietly resigned. He's been hired by a New York firm but only as an affiliate counsel. Because the investigation of his tactics is still pending, the firm wouldn't offer him a partnership interest. Linda Morrison's claim against me is nearly resolved. At my request, Harry demanded of my malpractice insurance carrier that it settle with her quickly and fairly. The final papers should be signed soon. Harry's also helped me liquidate my stocks and bonds and pay back the trust account and square up with the insurance carrier in Ramirez.

The appeal of my five-year sentence is under way. The briefing schedule has been set. Harry knows that I know it has little chance of success, as the sentencing judge, if anything, was lenient. Randolph had succinctly set forth the government's position at the time that I plead guilty. "Even though his testimony may have been truthful," Randolph pointed out, "he misled the government as to what he had to offer. He tricked the government into offering him a deal. If he hadn't deceived us, we never would have compromised so much. The deal, consequently, has been withdrawn."

ON MY WALL hangs a painting. A watercolor I received in the mail. The colors are brilliant and blend and change with the change of light in my cell. The scene is Dun Cove. The trees are in their new spring green. Gulls are working out on the horizon. The sun is early and rising in the east. Within the cooler, shadowed cove, fourteen swans are on the water, swimming in single file.

YESTERDAY I RECEIVED a letter, postmarked from Florida. The sender was named Stephen Traywick. The letter began with a description of how a young woman about his age and with the strange nickname of Muddy had tracked him down in a Jacksonville suburb and told him a story. Once she got started, he wrote, she talked to him for hours. Listening to what she told him had made him want to see me. He asked if he could visit in two weeks' time. He ended the letter by referring to himself as my son.

IN THE EVENINGS NOW, I sometimes wander out to the garden. We keep it freshly spaded and free of weeds. It smells like compost and earth and is alive with young shoots. Tonight there is no moon. The darkness of the distant trees blends into the darkness of the mountains, and only the stars offer light. I sit on the stone seat we made for the garden and study the wide universe overhead, grateful for the open space and land and quiet. I finger the shark's tooth I carry in my pocket. I close my eyes and hear the wind rustling the hayricks in the fields and, very far away, the nightwash of a river lapping the shore. I hear the river sometimes at night just before I go to sleep. I listen to the sound and try to picture that place. That rift between the water and the sky . . .

ACKNOWLEDGMENTS

I would like to thank my editor, Shannon Ravenel, for all her help. Thanks also to Duncan Murrell at Algonquin Books and to my agents, Robbie Anna Hare and Ron Goldfarb, for their insightful readings and comments. I am grateful as well to Laura Anderson, Elizabeth Burton, Hank Asbill, Lisa Howorth, and Blair Morris for their support. I especially thank my wife, Kristin Junkin, for her patient assistance.